JOHNNY SWANSON

ELEANOR UPDALE

David Fickling Books

OXFORD · NEW YORK

31 Beaumont Street
Oxford OX1 2NP, UK

JOHNNY SWANSON
A DAVID FICKLING BOOK 978 1 849 92068 1

Published in Great Britain by David Fickling Books,
a division of Random House Children's Books
A Random House Group Company

Hardback edition published 2010
This edition published 2011

1 3 5 7 9 10 8 6 4 2

Copyright © Eleanor Updale 2010

The right of Eleanor Updale to be identified as the author
of this work has been asserted in accordance with the
Copyright, Designs and Patents Act 1988.

All rights reserved. No part of this publication may be reproduced,
stored in a retrieval system, or transmitted in any form or by any means,
electronic, mechanical, photocopying, recording or otherwise,
without the prior permission of the publishers.

The Random House Group Limited supports the Forest Stewardship
Council (FSC), the leading international forest certification organization.
All our titles that are printed on Greenpeace-approved FSC-certified
paper carry the FSC logo. Our paper procurement policy can be
found at www.randomhouse.co.uk/environment.

Mixed Sources
Product group from well-managed
forests and other controlled sources
www.fsc.org Cert no. TT-COC-002139
© 1996 Forest Stewardship Council

DAVID FICKLING BOOKS
31 Beaumont Street, Oxford, OX1 2NP

www.kidsatrandomhouse.co.uk
www.totallyrandombooks.co.uk
www.randomhouse.co.uk

Addresses for companies within The Random House Group Limited
can be found at: www.randomhouse.co.uk/offices.htm

THE RANDOM HOUSE GROUP Limited Reg. No. 954009

A CIP catalogue record for this book is available from the British Library.

Printed and bound in Great Britain by
CPI Bookmarque, Croydon CR0 4TD

Author's Note

Some things in this book really existed, even if they sound made up.

For example:

Bacille Calmette-Guérin (the BCG vaccine) was approved by the League of Nations in 1928. It was not widely used in Britain until well after the Second World War.

Craig-y-Nos Castle is still there, though it ceased to be a sanatorium in 1959, and is now a hotel.

Vivatone Radio Active Hair Restorer was on sale in the shops.

And 'Maud Dawson's Love Answers', 'For the Chicks', and the advertisement for Umckaloabo really did appear in *Reynolds's Illustrated News* in 1929.

But nevertheless, this is a work of fiction.

Chapter 1

ATHLETICS, AUTUMN 1929

The teacher was smiling, but he wasn't smiling at Johnny. He was looking over Johnny's head at the other boys, lined up behind him to take their turn at the High Jump. And it wasn't a nice smile. It couldn't be. The scar running from Mr Murray's eye to his chin pulled the skin of his lips to one side and gave him a permanent sneer, even when he was in a good mood. But now he really was sniggering – inviting the rest of the class to laugh at the smallest, thinnest boy as he struggled with the run-up and brought down the pole.

Johnny could feel his second-hand shorts flapping against his spindly legs. He knew he looked ridiculous, and that his only hope was to pretend that he thought it was funny too. Of course he would fail. He breathed in, clenched his fists and started his run.

Mr Murray called out to him, catching the moment to put Johnny off his stride. 'Right then, Squirt,' he shouted. 'Show us what you're made of!'

The boys gave a mock cheer. Johnny forced a smile and clattered into the bar.

After the fall he brushed the mud from his knees and swaggered to the back of the line, grinning, even though he wanted to cry. Mr Murray blew his whistle and put a stop to the laughter, swiping at Johnny's head as he passed. 'It's nothing to smirk about, Swanson. This country needs men, not insects like you. You wouldn't have got far in the war.'

The boys groaned. They were expecting another tale about Mr Murray's bravery in France, where his face had been torn apart at the Battle of the Somme in 1916 – two years before any of them were born. But the teacher blew his whistle again and turned to the next boy in line: the muscular captain of the football team. 'Now then, Taylor. Show Swanson how it's done.'

Everyone cheered as Albert Taylor cleared the bar with room to spare; and at the end of the afternoon Albert was the winner and the class hero. No one wanted to know Johnny, however much he tried to turn his humiliation into a joke.

Mr Murray put Taylor in charge of clearing the hurdles from the games field and set off for the warmth of the staff room.

Taylor delegated the job straight away. 'You need building up, Quacky,' he said, using the nickname he knew Johnny hated. 'The extra exercise might make you grow a bit.' He threw Johnny the key to the shed and turned to the others. 'Who's coming for a game of marbles?'

The rest of the boys were happy to leave Johnny to lug the equipment away while they ran off to celebrate Albert's triumph, and to laugh about Johnny's shame.

Johnny had almost finished tidying the hut when he was startled by a snuffling noise outside. Had the boys come back to taunt him? Were they waiting to jump on him as he left the shed? He couldn't make out any voices, but he thought he could hear sticks of wood bashing against each other. Maybe they were going to barricade the door so he couldn't get out. They all knew he'd just started a job after school. They'd love to get him into trouble by making him late for his paper round. He pushed hard at the door, hoping to knock away whatever barrier they had already built.

The door swung open easily. There was no one there – just a big wooden hoop rolling away across the field. Then he heard a whimper and looked round. A girl was lying on her back on the grass behind the door. She had half a dozen hoops around her neck, and more looped over each outstretched arm. Like a beetle flipped upside-down, she was wriggling but couldn't get up.

'You knocked me over,' she sniffled.

'I'm sorry,' said Johnny. 'I didn't know you were there.' Although the girl was wearing glasses, he could see that she was crying, and had been weeping even before the door hit her. He lifted the hoops off her and helped her to her feet.

'They made me carry everything,' she said, brushing the earth off her gymslip. 'It's just because I'm new.' Her voice had an unfamiliar sing-song lilt.

'I thought I hadn't seen you before,' said Johnny.

'I only started here on Monday. I'm in Mrs Palmer's class. They all hate me already. It's because of my accent.'

'Accent?' said Johnny, pretending he hadn't noticed it.

'I'm Welsh,' said the girl. 'And I've got a Welsh name: Olwen. For some reason, all the other girls seem to think that's funny. And they call me "The Owl" because of my glasses. My specs kept falling off when we were exercising with the hoops. They all laughed at me.'

'Everyone gets picked on for something,' said Johnny, acutely aware that Olwen was taller than him, even though she was in the year below. 'They get at me for being so small. That's how I ended up having to put away all our gear. I'll help you stack those hoops in the shed. My name's Johnny, by the way. Johnny Swanson.'

As Olwen passed him the hoops, she told him about her new home. 'We had to move here from Wales,' she said. 'My dad lost his job in Swansea, and we had no money at all. So he wrote to an old army friend from the war to see if he could help us out. Lucky for us, he said yes. I don't know what would have happened to us without him. Anyway, now we're living at Newgate Farm.'

'Where's that?'

'It's just outside town. Dad's supposed to be working there, but he and Mum are both ill. They were sick even before we moved, and the journey just seems to have done them in.'

'Have you got any brothers and sisters? Are they at this school too? If you've got a brother he should defend you against those horrible girls.'

'Just a sister. She's a baby. She's too young for school. And she's ill too, now. Mum was worried about her this morning. It's her breathing, see. Maybe the country air doesn't agree with her. I really should go home and see if she's any better. It's a long walk.'

Johnny remembered his job at the shop. 'I must be getting along too,' he said.

They ran to the school gate together. 'Don't worry about those other girls,' said Johnny, as they split up. 'They'll soon get used to you. But if you have any more trouble with them, just come and see me.' He wasn't really sure what he was offering to do on her behalf, but Olwen seemed pleased to have found a friend at last.

'Thank you, Johnny,' she said. 'I'll see you tomorrow then.'

'Yes. I'll look out for you in the playground before school.'

The boys were still playing marbles in the street. Albert Taylor made a kissing noise on the back of his hand and nudged one of the others. 'Little Quacky's got a pet owl,' he said in a voice just loud enough for Johnny and Olwen to hear.

Johnny made his way towards Hutchinson's General Store and Post Office, just down the road from school. Joseph 'Hutch' Hutchinson limped out. He wasn't an old man, not yet thirty-five, and he still had a full head of chestnut hair; but his injured leg slowed him down, and he was getting plump through lack of exercise. His brown overall strained over his belly as he busied himself rearranging a display of apples. Before Johnny even reached the shop, he could tell that Hutch was angry.

'You're late,' said Hutch. 'I had the papers ready ten minutes ago.'

'It was PE day. We were up at the sports field.'

'And I suppose you broke all the records?' Hutch scoffed, lifting the strap of a large canvas bag across Johnny's shoulders. He squeezed Johnny's skinny arm. 'There's nothing to you. If it wasn't for your hair, I wouldn't believe you were Harry Swanson's son at all. He was a fine strong man, your dad.'

'I know,' said Johnny. 'I've seen a picture of him in his uniform.'

'Yes, but that would have been taken after the army cut off his golden curls.' Hutch ran his fingers roughly through Johnny's springy hair. 'You're his boy, all right, even if you are a bit of a shrimp. Now be off with you. There's folk out there waiting for the racing results.'

Johnny preferred the evening paper round. Not many people took two papers a day, and the bag was lighter than in the morning, when he visited almost all the houses nearby. He ran from one to another, trying to get his job done as quickly as he could. At the last house, Miss Dangerfield's, he pushed the paper through the letter box, and in his haste he let it clang shut.

'Can't you do anything quietly?' Miss Dangerfield shouted.

Johnny stood on tiptoe and opened the letter box to apologize. A musty, 'old lady' smell wafted from inside. He could see Miss Dangerfield advancing along the hallway to pick up the paper: muttering, dressed all in black as ever, and leaning on her walking stick. As she approached the door, Johnny could see how her hair had thinned almost to baldness on the top of her head. She straightened up and caught him looking at her. She was furious.

'Get out of it,' she yelled. 'You've no business spying on me!'

'I'm sorry,' said Johnny, meekly.

Miss Dangerfield lifted her stick and shook it at the letter box.

Johnny pulled away, and let the flap snap shut

again. 'Sorry,' he cried once more. 'It's just that your letter box is so high up . . .'

But his voice was drowned out by her shouts. 'Blooming children. Nothing but a menace. And I suppose you'll leave the gate open as usual.'

He shut it carefully behind him, just as he always did, and ran down the hill.

Back at the shop, Hutch was closing up. 'I'm chucking out these old biscuits,' he mumbled, without looking up. 'They're stale.' He scooped a handful of soggy custard creams onto a piece of old newspaper. 'Interested?'

Johnny sensed from his awkward manner that Hutch felt bad about teasing him earlier. 'Yes please,' he said. 'I really am sorry I was late.'

Hutch waved Johnny off without another word.

Johnny took his time going home. He would have to go past Miss Dangerfield's, and he wanted to give her a chance to calm down. He stopped and sat on the low wall of the graveyard to eat the biscuits. He couldn't help reading the paper they'd been wrapped in. It was last Wednesday's *Stambleton Echo*; a boring page, full of advertisements. People were selling old gardening tools, baby clothes, prams and books. Then one advert caught his eye. It was set apart from the others, in a little frame, and said:

> # TOO SHORT?
> ## Do you wish you were taller?
> ### *For the*
> # SECRET OF INSTANT HEIGHT
>
> SEND A POSTAL ORDER FOR 2/6
> AND A STAMPED ADDRESSED ENVELOPE
> TO BOX 23, THE STAMBLETON ECHO,
> 6 CANAL STREET, STAMBLETON, WARWICKSHIRE

Johnny read and re-read the advertisement. The Secret of Instant Height. It was just what he needed. But where would he find two shillings and sixpence? He didn't even have enough money for the stamped addressed envelope. Still, he tore the advert out of the paper and put it in his pocket. By the time he got home he had made up his mind to do anything to get the money, and to send away to Box 23 for the answer to all his problems.

Chapter 2

THE PEACE MUG

Johnny's mother, Winnie, was already at home. The front door led straight into the kitchen – the only downstairs room – and as soon as Johnny opened it he could see that she was ironing. She was pressing sheets: crisp white sheets quite unlike the ones they had on their own beds.

'They're Dr Langford's,' Winnie explained apologetically. 'They weren't dry enough to iron while I was there cleaning. Mrs Langford let me bring them home to finish them off. I'd hoped to get them all done before you got here. Tea will be a bit late, I'm afraid.'

'I thought the Langfords sent all their stuff to the laundry,' said Johnny. 'I've seen the van outside their house.'

'If you ask me, they're having to cut down on that sort of thing since Dr Langford retired,' said Winnie. 'Mrs Langford asked me if I would do the bed-linen, and I couldn't really say no. We don't want them getting rid of me too. There's plenty of people looking for cleaning jobs these days. They wouldn't have any trouble finding a replacement.'

Johnny took one end of a sheet and helped his mother stretch it out, ready for folding. They had to kick the furniture to the edges of their tiny kitchen to make enough space to pull it tight. 'Are they paying you extra for this?' asked Johnny, walking forward to hand over his end and pick up the fold at the bottom.

'Well, I tried hinting,' said Winnie, 'but Mrs Langford didn't seem to want to get the point. I didn't want to embarrass her – or myself. It must be hard for her. She's used to better things. She's from a posh French family, you know.'

They passed the sheet to and fro between them, giggling as one or the other dropped a corner, or wrongly guessed which way to turn next. Johnny thought his mother worked quite hard enough cleaning the Langfords' house every day without doing their ironing, too. But he liked the smell of the clean linen hanging to air in front of the hearth. And it was good to have an excuse for the fire to be lit.

'How was your day?' asked Winnie, patting the neat rectangle of folded cloth. 'It must have been nice to be out of the classroom and up on the field for a change?'

Johnny didn't tell her about how he had been laughed at, nor about Olwen, Miss Dangerfield, or the biscuits; nor about the advertisement for the Secret of Instant Height – which was really all that was on his mind now. 'Yes,' he said. 'It was good to be outside. But it was a bit cold.'

'Well, come and sit in the warm,' said his mother, shifting the clothes horse to make room by the fire. She caught her arm on the hot face of the iron, and stifled a curse. 'Oh, how stupid of me to have left that there,' she snapped, licking at a red mark on her skin. 'Get me down the ointment. It's on the top shelf.'

Johnny climbed on the arm of a chair and reached up to where his mother had kept all the dangerous and delicate things since he was a toddler. There were a couple of dusty jars of pills; a fine china mug decorated with flags and the word PEACE, which had been given out at the end of the war; and a flat round tin with elaborate writing on the top: *Dr Sampson's Patent Ointment for Cuts, Burns and Stings. A Soothing Solution in All Situations*. The lid was going a bit rusty at the edges, but he managed to prise it off, revealing a block of pungent brown cream, with a trace of the last finger that had scooped out a little, months before. His mother dipped in again, and started rubbing the oily mixture onto her burn.

'You'd better put it back straight away,' she said, 'so that we know where it is next time. Make sure you put the lid on tight or it will dry up.'

So Johnny climbed on the chair again. And while he was up there, and Winnie had her back to him, sorting out the ironing things, he took a look inside the china mug. He'd always known that his mother kept money in it: special secret bits of change that she felt she could spare to save up for Christmas – and he'd always known that he mustn't touch it. But he could see that there were coins inside – most of them coppers, but some of them silver.

He knew he shouldn't even think of taking the money, but for the rest of the evening he planned what he would do when his mother was asleep. So in the middle of the night he crept downstairs in the chilly dark, and tipped the money out of the mug and onto the table. Although it was cold, his hands were slippery with sweat. He dropped a penny. The coin rolled and then spun on the stone floor. It seemed ages before it came to a stop. Johnny froze, certain that his mother must have heard it; worried that she might even be able to hear his breathing, which sounded appallingly loud to him. He had no idea how he would explain what he was doing if she came in, but he wanted the Secret of Instant Height so much that he had to take the risk. There was no sound from her room. He counted the money. It came to nine shillings and sevenpence. He only needed two-and-six, with a few pence more for the envelopes and stamps.

He gathered up three shillings, and carefully put the rest back in the mug. The level of money had obviously dropped. Never mind: tomorrow he would get some stones to put under the cash, so that the theft didn't show. But surely it wasn't theft? It was borrowing. He promised himself that he would replace the coins, little by little, with the money Hutch paid him for delivering the papers. He wouldn't spend it on sweets or comics. By Christmas there would be nine shillings and sevenpence in the mug again. His mother would never know that any had been missing. And in the meantime, Johnny would have the Secret of Instant Height. That was all he cared about now.

Chapter 3

SENDING OFF

The next morning, Johnny left the house earlier than usual to help his mother carry the basket of sheets back to the Langfords'. On the way Winnie stopped off to check on their neighbour, Mrs Slack. She was an elderly widow who looked pretty healthy to Johnny, but always complained that she was ill. Winnie had mentioned once that she had 'trouble with her nerves'.

'Shall I do this washing-up for you, Mrs Slack?' asked Winnie, rolling up her sleeves and putting the kettle on to boil.

Mrs Slack waved her arm weakly in the direction of the sink. 'I just couldn't face it last night,' she said. 'I don't know what's come over me. It's all I can do to raise a teacup to my lips. Heaven knows how the floor will ever get cleaned.'

Winnie took the hint and asked Johnny to find her a bucket; then, while Winnie mopped, Mrs Slack listed her symptoms. Johnny tried not to listen. There were a lot of references to 'down below'. Mrs Slack kept pointing at Johnny and then mouthing words silently. 'I'd see the doctor,' she said, at full volume, 'but I don't like to trouble him with my little problems.'

Johnny's mother knew that she meant she couldn't, or wouldn't, pay. 'Dr Langford's retired now,' she explained. Johnny could tell from her voice that she had said this many times. 'But I could have a quiet word with him if you would like me to. It would save you going to that new man across town.'

'No. No need to put yourself out,' said Mrs Slack, in a tone that even Johnny recognized as meaning the exact opposite.

'Well, we'll be off then,' said Winnie. And they left Mrs Slack tucking in to a boiled egg and moaning about how she would be on her own all day.

'Poor soul,' sighed Winnie as they started off up the hill, each of them holding one handle of the washing basket.

'Do you think she really is ill?' asked Johnny.

'Maybe. Maybe not. But she doesn't have much of a life, and someone's got to take care of her. If my mother was still alive, I wouldn't want her to be all alone like that. I'd hope someone would drop in and make sure she was all right. It's the least I can do.'

Dr Langford's house was up on the hill, directly opposite Miss Dangerfield's. The doctor was leaving as Winnie and Johnny arrived. He was much older than Johnny's mother, tall and spry, with wisps of grey hair at the back of a big bald patch. Johnny was fascinated by the way the structure of the doctor's skull showed through the thin skin on his head. There was a prominent vein to one side that looked like a river on an ancient parchment map. You could see it throbbing when he was excited. Sometimes it seemed almost ready to pop. Today, Dr Langford hadn't shaved properly, and there were clumps of stubble under his chin. His smart trousers were gathered into bicycle clips at his ankles.

'My goodness, Doctor,' said Johnny's mother. 'You're up early.'

'Yes, Winnie,' said Dr Langford. 'I had a call from the sanatorium at Emberley last night. I'm helping them with an emergency case. A little baby and her parents.'

'Oh dear, the poor people,' said Winnie.

'It's a shame,' said the doctor, 'but I have to admit

to a certain excitement. It's good to feel wanted even when you've retired.' He bent down and pinched Johnny's cheek in the way that adults think is playful, but actually hurts a lot. 'And where are you off to so early, my boy? Surely it isn't time for school yet?'

'He has his paper round,' said Johnny's mother. 'It gives him a bit of pocket money, you know.'

'Of course,' said Dr Langford. 'I've seen you pushing the newspaper through the letter box. I'm sorry ours is so high up. It must be quite hard to reach.' There was another painful pinch of the cheek. 'You must eat up all your food, son. You're a growing lad . . . or should be. How old are you now? Nine? Ten?'

'Eleven,' said Johnny, embarrassed, and all the more determined to get the Secret of Instant Height.

'Well, I must be off,' said the doctor, climbing onto his bike and adding, with a wink to Johnny, 'I'll give you a ride to the shop, if you like.'

He lifted Johnny up and helped him balance on the crossbar, then swung himself onto the saddle and started to pedal. The bike rocked unnervingly, and Johnny wished for a moment that he had turned down the offer. Winnie waved, but Johnny didn't dare take his hands off the handlebars to wave back. The bike looped in a circle, but then steadied and picked up speed as the doctor's bony knees pumped harder. Seconds later, they were zooming down the hill. Johnny loved the rush of the wind against his face, and whooped with delight as they sped past the church and pulled up, wobbling again, outside Hutchinson's General Store and Post Office. Dr Langford helped Johnny down and rode away.

Inside the shop, Hutch was standing behind the counter, sorting out the morning papers.

'Early today, I see,' he grunted, parking his pencil behind his ear. 'Makes up for last night, I suppose.'

Buoyed up by the joy of the bike ride, Johnny found the courage to ask a favour. He needed Hutch's help if he was to reply to the advert for the Secret of Instant Height. 'Hutch,' he said, 'I want to buy a postal order and some stamps. Would you mind opening the post office so I can get them now?'

'That would be most irregular,' said Hutch, severely. 'The post office mustn't open till nine o'clock.'

'But I'll be at school then,' said Johnny. He didn't mean to sound desperate, but it did the trick. For once Hutch contemplated bending the rules.

'What's so special about this postal order?' he asked. 'What's the rush?'

Johnny thought quickly, and his words tumbled out. 'It's for my mother,' he said, making up a story as he spoke. 'She needs to send it to my auntie, who's ill. It's to buy her a train ticket so she can visit us. Mum wants me to catch the first post. She told me to get an envelope too. And an extra envelope and stamp so Auntie Ada can write back.'

He realized that he was getting himself into trouble. In a few seconds he had invented a sick aunt and invited her to Stambleton. He could already see that this deception was going to be quite hard to manage, and he also thought that it didn't sound very believable. But Hutch seemed convinced.

'Well,' he said, fishing for the keys in his pocket, 'since it's a medical matter, I think I can bend the rules just this once.' Hutch took off his brown overall, rolled down his shirt sleeves, put on his black jacket and straightened his tie, as he always did when working in the 'post office' part of the shop. He unlocked the safe and got out a large book, a cash box, his official rubber stamps and a big ink pad. 'Very well, Johnny,' he said, peering through the grille that separated the post office from the rest of the shop. 'How much is this postal order for?'

*

27

And so Johnny left for his paper round with everything he needed to send off for the Secret of Instant Height. He stopped at the cemetery and laid it all out along the top of the wall. He took the newspaper cutting from his pocket and copied out the address of Box 23 onto one of the envelopes. Then he addressed the other to himself, stuck on a stamp and folded it so that it would fit inside the first. He wondered whether he should have written a letter to go with the postal order, but decided that the newspaper cutting would tell the people at Box 23 why he was contacting them, so he tucked that inside as well. He checked twice to make sure that everything was correct. Then he licked the glue on the outer envelope and stuck it down hard.

The church clock chimed the half-hour. He was running late. He decided to reverse the usual order of his deliveries, so that Miss Dangerfield would get her paper first. He didn't want to be in trouble with her again. There were too many other things to worry about. Suppose his mother discovered that the money was missing? Suppose Hutch found out that he didn't really have an aunt? He wanted to tell someone all about it: someone who wouldn't tell on him; who would sympathize, and reassure him that he had done the right thing. He sensed that Olwen would understand. If he really hurried he might find her in the playground before lessons began. He posted the letter and started to run.

Chapter 4

THE MEDICAL

Johnny delivered all the papers before the school bell rang, but he couldn't find Olwen in the playground then, or at morning break, or at lunch time.

The last lesson of the day was Religious Knowledge. Johnny had been dreading it, because he hadn't learned Genesis, Chapter 46, verses 8 to 24: a long list of names which the teacher, old Mr Wilson, had set as a punishment for the whole class after a mass fit of the giggles the week before. Johnny had tried. He'd got as far as Reuben, Jacob's first born, and the sons of Reuben: Hanoch, and Phallu, and Hezron, and Carmi. But the sight of about thirty weird names looming ahead had driven him outside to kick an empty can around, and then he'd forgotten all about it. Now he was preparing himself for the thwack of a ruler against his leg, or a belt across his backside as a punishment.

Suddenly he believed in miracles. A big boy came into the classroom with a message for the teacher.

The lesson was cancelled. Everyone was to go to the school hall at once for a special assembly. There was a great scraping of chairs as the children jumped up, full of boisterous relief. It seemed that quite a few hadn't learned that fearsome list.

'No talking!' shouted Mr Wilson, who looked as surprised by the change of plan as the rest of them. 'Line up in alphabetical order and follow me.'

All the other classes were filing into the hall. The headmaster was on the edge of the stage, telling everyone to hurry up and to sit cross-legged on the floor so that the whole school could get in. It was only after Johnny had taken his place, crammed in between Albert Taylor and Ernest Roberts, that he noticed two people sitting on chairs behind the head-master. It was the school nurse, and Dr Langford, with a stethoscope round his neck.

The headmaster called for silence and stillness. 'As you can see, we have a visitor. Many of you may already know Dr Langford.'

There was an outbreak of chatter as the children compared notes on visits to the doctor. Johnny started telling Ernest how he'd had a ride on Dr Langford's bike only that morning. The teachers, who were sitting on chairs all round the edge of the hall, shushed everyone quiet. Mr Wilson leaned forward and slapped Johnny on the head to shut him up.

The headmaster continued, 'Dr Langford has informed me that the family of one of our pupils has become infected with a serious illness.'

There was another buzz of talking, quickly stopped by the staff.

'Silence,' barked the headmaster. 'This is a most important matter. We have no reason to suppose that any of you are ill, but it is necessary for you to be checked straight away. You must all strip down to your underwear and make your way to the stage. Fold your clothes neatly, and leave them to mark your place.'

Johnny was horrified. He hadn't expected to have to undress today. He was wearing his oldest pants and vest. They were full of holes, and badly needed a wash. He knew he'd be teased by the other boys, especially Albert Taylor who, because of the alphabet, was right next to him. He expected Ernest Roberts on his other side to have a go at him too. Ernest lived a few doors down from the Swansons. He had been Johnny's friend and playmate until that term, when Mrs Roberts had taken him to the optician and he'd been prescribed thick spectacles. The boys at school were no kinder to Ernest than the girls had been to

Olwen. Constant jokes about Ernest's glasses had made him crack. Now he did Albert Taylor's bidding in return for his protection. He'd become Taylor's shadow, doing his homework and doling out insults and menace on command. If that meant persecuting his old friend, Johnny, for being short and poor, it was a price Ernest felt he had to pay.

Shivering with fear rather than cold, Johnny slowly pulled off his jumper and shirt. He saw Mr Wilson advancing again, ready to strike. Johnny winced, but Wilson reached across him and wrenched at Albert Taylor's arm instead, revealing an inky trail that ran from his wrist to his elbow.

'What's this, boy?' shouted Mr Wilson. 'See me after school.' He gave Taylor's arm a quick twist as he flung it down again, and Albert huddled into himself, trying to hide the list of biblical names he'd written on his skin: Jamin, Ohad, Jachin, Zohar, Shaul, and many more. From the stage, the headmaster sent one of his nasty stares across to the group of boys around Taylor. It promised trouble in the future.

But the head had more pressing business. 'Right,' he said when everyone was undressed. 'Now come up, class by class, one by one, to see the doctor. Then go back to your places and get dressed again.'

Another murmur ran through the hall. 'Silence!' cried the headmaster. 'The doctor needs quiet. He has to listen to your chests.' Everyone except Taylor obeyed. He was whispering threats into Johnny's ear, blaming him for Mr Wilson's attack. 'If you weren't so small, he'd never have been able to see me,' he said, while Ernest Roberts surreptitiously ground his heel onto Johnny's foot as they stood in line. Johnny looked round the hall to see if Olwen was being taunted too. He spotted Mrs Palmer's class, but she wasn't among them.

Dr Langford came to the front of the stage and explained what he was going to do. 'Now, children, I am going to listen to your lungs, but you're also going to have a special test, which will show us very soon whether you have been infected. All I have to do is make a little scratch on your wrist . . .'

There was a mass cry of '*Urggh!*'

'. . . No, really, you will hardly notice it, and in two or three days I'll be able to tell whether any of you might need treatment. But don't worry. That's very unlikely indeed.'

The doctor briskly examined each child. Occasionally he asked the school nurse to make a note of something, or had a little chat with a child he knew well. When Johnny's turn came he smiled. 'Well, I never thought I'd be doing all this when I saw you this morning,' he said.

'What are you checking for?' asked Johnny.

'TB, I'm afraid,' said Dr Langford, scraping Johnny's wrist while he was distracted. He lifted Johnny's vest and listened to his stethoscope. 'But I'm sure you've got nothing to worry about, my boy. Your chest is nice and clear.' The school nurse put a tick against Johnny's name, and moved the line on.

When everyone had been dealt with, the headmaster had a quick conversation with the doctor while the last of the children got back into their clothes. Then he called for quiet again and addressed the school. 'I'm sure we're all very grateful to Dr Langford for giving up his time to come here today. Now, there's no more time for lessons, so we'll stay here in the hall until home-time. Mr Wilson, perhaps you would like to lead us in some prayers.'

Mr Wilson stepped forward and prayed for the safe recovery of sick people everywhere. As the bell went to mark the end of the day, everyone burst into the same question: who was the child whose family illness had caused all this fuss?

In the playground, Albert Taylor's sister rushed up,

flushed with pride at being able to tell her big brother the news. 'It's that new girl,' she said. 'The one I told you about. The Owl. Mrs Palmer says she's gone back to Wales. Good riddance to bad rubbish, that's what I say.'

'What's wrong with her?' asked Taylor.

'It's TB,' said Johnny, glad to have inside information, and hoping it would earn him some credit with Taylor. 'The doctor told me.'

'And what's that, then?'

'I don't know,' said Johnny. 'But Olwen told me her family were ill.'

Taylor sneered, 'Yes. You were talking to The Owl last night, weren't you, Quacky?' He pulled his sister away from Johnny. 'Better keep away from you. You might have it too. We all might catch it.'

'But the doctor says I'm all right,' said Johnny as the crowd of children ran off.

Mr Wilson approached. He was trying in vain to catch Albert Taylor before he dodged his punishment for trying to cheat in the scripture test. Johnny plucked up the courage to ask him what TB was.

Mr Wilson shook his head. 'It's a very grave disease. A very grave disease indeed. It attacks the lungs. It can be deadly. We've had it here once before – a bad outbreak during the war. Several families were affected. We lost some pupils. That's why they built the big sanatorium at Emberley. But there hasn't been a case in this school since. Let's hope this is just a false alarm.'

Johnny ran to pick up his bag of newspapers at the shop. He took a detour through the graveyard towards the end of his paper round. This time he looked at the dates on some of the gravestones. There were a lot from 1916. He noticed some family groups. Three of the Roberts family were buried in one plot, and there were four Dangerfields, all children, who had died within months of each other. Could they be relatives of Miss Dangerfield up on the hill?

A voice started shouting: 'Hey! You boy! You boy. Get out of there!'

Johnny spun round. Through the branches of a holly bush he could see a black hat on the other side of the graveyard wall. A netting veil covered the face of the short, dumpy woman who was wearing it, but he knew at once that it was Miss Dangerfield herself. She was angry. 'Get away from those graves,' she cried. 'What do you think you are doing?'

'I was only looking,' said Johnny. 'I was just wondering if they were your family – if it was TB.'

'That's none of your business,' snapped Miss Dangerfield, raising her walking stick.

'But I just wanted to ask—'

'How dare you? You nasty little squirt. They were worth a hundred of you. Be off with you.'

Johnny ran away to finish his deliveries, wanting to know more about the bodies under the slabs, but too frightened to ask again.

Chapter 5

LETTERS

Johnny asked his mother about Miss Dangerfield and the TB, but Winnie had not lived in Stambleton in 1916, and knew less about the epidemic than Johnny did. She reassured him about the disease. If Dr Langford said Johnny was healthy, she was sure he was right. But other children had been told more lurid stories, and for the next few days the talk in the playground was all about TB, with graphic descriptions of victims gasping for breath, coughing up blood, and wasting away or just dropping down dead. Everyone was watching their wrists for signs of a reaction to the test. Dr Langford had said he'd be looking for a red bump at the point where a tiny trace of bacteria had been introduced. In art class, Ernest Roberts dabbed on some paint to make it look as if his scratch had flared up into a livid inflammation, but in fact everyone was boringly clear.

Johnny was still worried about Olwen. But when he asked at school whether anyone had heard anything about her they just teased him, so he kept quiet. He wondered in secret what had happened to Olwen's family. This disease was so bad that she had been sent away, and yet everyone said there was no cause for concern. Johnny was confused. But he was excited as well, hoping every day that he would get a reply from Box 23 containing the Secret of Instant Height. He met the postman in the street, and asked if he had seen an envelope addressed to John Swanson Esq. No, said the postman, there hadn't been any letters for Johnny's house that week. Even Hutch was concerned. He could see that Johnny was unusually anxious.

'Have you heard from that aunt of yours yet?' he asked.

'No. Nothing,' said Johnny. 'I hope she's all right.'

'Is she your mother's sister?' Hutch paused for thought. 'I suppose she must be. I knew your father all his life, and he never had a sister. Does she live where your mother comes from? Nottingham, isn't it?'

'Yes,' said Johnny, feeling he should at least tell the truth about his mother's origins, even if everything else was a lie. He was saved from further questions when a customer came in, but he realized that he would have to sort out this Auntie Ada business pretty soon. Maybe he should say that she had died. But then Hutch might send condolences to his mother. And Hutch might mention Ada to her anyway, dead or alive. It would be only natural if Winnie went into the shop. Johnny would have to keep Hutch and his mother apart. He needed yet another plan.

That night, Johnny got home first. There were two letters on the doormat, one addressed to him in his own handwriting, the other an official-looking brown envelope, with his mother's full name, 'Mrs Winifred May Swanson', typed boldly across it. As Johnny picked them up, he heard his mother coming. He just had time to stuff his own envelope into his pocket before she reached the front door.

'What have you got there?' she asked.

'It's a letter. For you,' he said. 'It looks important.'

Johnny was desperate to get away to read his own letter, but he stayed and watched while Winnie opened hers. She was still wearing her hat and coat, standing by the dim oil lamp in the kitchen. If you'd been looking through the window, you might have thought she was Johnny's sister. Like him she was short and slight. From a distance it was hard to

41

believe that she was thirty. But close up, her puffy hands, raw with housework, and the worry-lines on her brow told a different story. The wrinkles grew more pronounced than usual as she took a single typed sheet out of the envelope. Then she flopped down onto a chair.

'What is it, Mum?' asked Johnny, still grasping the letter in his pocket. 'Is it bad news?'

He could see that she was trying to compose herself, to reassure him that there was nothing to be concerned about. Then she looked him straight in the eye. 'Johnny,' she said, 'I think you're old enough to know. It's from the landlord. The rent's going up after Christmas. We're going to have to find an extra three shillings a week.'

'But that's more than I make from the paper round in a fortnight,' said Johnny.

'Oh darling, I wouldn't ask you to pay it. I'll just have to try to find an extra job.' She started mumbling to herself: 'But there's not much work around. Maybe I could take in some washing. But how would I pay for the soap, and the fuel to heat the water?'

Johnny couldn't help it. His eyes went to the Peace Mug on the high shelf.

'No,' said his mother. 'We're not touching the

Christmas money. I'd sooner go without breakfast than use that. Anyway, it would only last a few weeks. It's staying up there. I'm not even going to count it till December.'

Johnny was half relieved that his mother was unlikely to find out he had taken money from the mug, and half ashamed at what he had done. But at least he had his own letter, almost throbbing in his pocket, begging him to open it. At least Box 23 had replied. The money from the Peace Mug hadn't been wasted.

Winnie pulled herself up from the chair, took off her hat and started slowly unbuttoning her coat. Johnny knew he should find some words of comfort, or come up with an idea for raising money, but he couldn't wait to open his letter.

'I'm just going to the lav,' he said, striding out to the yard, where a tiny, damp shed housed the lavatory. It was getting dark, and he could only just make out the writing on the envelope. He tore it open. Inside was a piece of paper that looked as if it had been ripped from a notebook. It was folded into four, with *The Secret of Instant Height is* . . . written in heavy black ink on the outside. Now Johnny was scared. What would it be? Would he have to take medicine, or mix some chemicals? Where would he get them from? How would he pay for them? He couldn't bear to open the note. But he had to know the secret. He had to find out how to grow taller. Maybe then he would be able to do jobs that brought in more money. Then he could help his mother with the rent. The lavatory seat didn't have a cover, but he sat down without lowering his shorts and looked again. *The Secret of Instant Height is . . .* He unfolded the paper. There were just four words written inside: *Stand on a box.*

He couldn't believe it. That was all it said. He had been tricked. He could feel the blood pumping round his ears as he blushed with shame. Two shillings and sixpence had been wasted – plus the cost of the envelopes and the stamps. He had stolen his mother's money, and thrown it away just when she needed it most. And that wasn't all. At any time Hutch might ask Winnie about 'Auntie Ada', and Johnny would have a lot of explaining to do. Everything would come out. He would be shown up as a fool, a liar and a thief. And now there was another thing. He had wet himself.

Chapter 6

CLEARING UP

Johnny stood with a blanket round his middle while his mother filled a tin bath with warm water, to wash him, and then his clothes. Winnie was sympathetic. She thought Johnny's 'accident' must have been brought on by worry about the rent, and she blamed herself for telling him about it. He said nothing of how he had been tricked over the advertisement, and covered his embarrassment by babbling on with ideas for raising more cash.

'I could do more work at the shop,' he said. 'Hutch is always complaining that he's too busy. I'll ask him tomorrow.' As he spoke, Johnny thought of another advantage. He could keep his mother away from Hutch, so she wouldn't find out about 'Auntie Ada'. 'And if I'm working there,' he added, 'I can bring our groceries home with me. You won't have to go shopping at all. That will give you more time to take on extra work, if you can find it.'

Winnie was wringing out Johnny's sopping shorts.

45

'I don't know how we'll get these dry in time for school tomorrow,' she said. 'I think I'll have to light the fire again.'

So Johnny felt even more guilty, seeing money go up in smoke because of him.

He didn't sleep much that night. For the first time in years, he took his old toy rabbit to bed with him, clutching its floppy body for comfort as he worried about the rent, the Peace Mug money, and his new friend Olwen, somewhere in Wales, possibly facing death. Every time he felt close to sleep a new anxiety arrived and he was wide awake again, imagining homelessness, shame and disease. At one a.m. he was weeping, trying to think of ways to get back at the people at Box 23. Should he tell the *Stambleton Echo* about the Secret of Instant Height? Shouldn't they know that a scam was being run from their own paper? He might not be the only one who had been tricked into sending a postal order. The person who put in the advert might be making a fortune . . .

And that's when the idea came to him: so clear and exciting that he sat bolt upright in bed. *If they can do it, so can I*, he thought. *If I could fall for a trick like that, surely plenty of other people would too!*

He spent the rest of the night thinking out his plan. At first he was full of enthusiasm. He got out of bed and paced the room, muttering to his toy rabbit. He would have to find out how the advertising pages worked, but that wouldn't be difficult. After all, he had plenty of papers in his delivery bag every day. There must be something printed in them to tell you how to place an advert. He'd put one in as soon as possible, and sit back to wait for the replies.

The replies! How would he get them? He couldn't have them sent to his house, or Winnie would find out what he was doing. He knew she wouldn't approve. He'd need a box number, like the Instant Height people. But then he'd have to find a way to slip over to the newspaper offices to collect them. And he'd need to work out how to cash postal orders without arousing Hutch's suspicion.

By half past one it all seemed too complicated. Johnny got back into bed. How could he hope to organize such an intricate scheme when he already faced the problem of disposing of 'Auntie Ada' in a way that would stop Hutch mentioning her to his mother? Surely he should see to that first . . .

He nuzzled up to the rabbit's threadbare fur, breathing in its familiar dusty smell as he tried to work out what to do. Maybe he should just own up and tell Hutch that 'Auntie Ada' had never existed ... Or maybe ... Maybe ... He yawned, and felt himself drifting off to sleep at last, only to be jolted awake again by the sound of the town hall clock striking two, and the arrival of another idea.

Maybe 'Auntie Ada' should stay in his life. Perhaps she could be part of his advertising plan. Johnny would explain to Hutch that his mother couldn't do her own shopping any more because she was busy looking after her invalid sister. And he would account for the postal orders by saying that he was cashing them on behalf of his aunt.

It was brilliant. But Johnny knew it was wrong. At a quarter to three he resolved to abandon the whole thing, deciding it would be simpler to admit what he had already done, and to face his mother's anger and (worse) her disappointment. He wiped his tears on the rabbit's ears, envisaging the scene as he confessed to stealing the money. Then he imagined what would happen if the advertising scheme worked. He pictured himself cashing postal orders, replacing the money in the Peace Mug, and even contributing to the rent. That felt better. At three o'clock he changed his mind one last time. He would risk it after all.

He snuggled under the blanket and started thinking up adverts that might trick the readers of the *Stambleton Echo*. He wanted to find things people were embarrassed or ashamed about so that, like him, they wouldn't want to tell the world how they had been swindled.

His own experience that day gave him his first idea: *Stop your baby wetting the bed.*

He wouldn't be too greedy. Perhaps he'd only ask one shilling for the answer to that. And the answer would be: *Make him sleep in a chair.*

Johnny was desperate for morning to come. He couldn't wait to get started. His legs wriggled uncontrollably every time he thought about the money that stupid people would send him. Somehow, soon after half past three, he finally slipped off to sleep with a smile.

But success didn't seem quite so certain in the chilly morning mist when, almost too tired to walk, he set off for the shop with his damp shorts chafing against his skin.

Chapter 7

THE LANDLORD

Johnny was glad to see that Hutch was in a good mood, whistling as he unpacked a delivery and stacked cans of tinned peaches into a pyramid on the shelf behind the counter.

'Hutch?' said Johnny. 'Is there any chance you could find me some more work here? I could come on Saturdays if you like, and in the holidays, too.'

'So you've had the letter then,' said Hutch, without looking up.

'What letter?' asked Johnny, panicking for a moment at the thought that Hutch might somehow know he'd been fooled into buying the Secret of Instant Height.

'The rent letter. There were some folk in the pub last night complaining about it. It looks as if he's gunning for all of you.'

'Who? Who's gunning for us?'

'Young Mr Bennett, up at the big house on the hill. I never liked the boy. Though he's a man now, of course. Just back from Cambridge University, so they say. He's inherited everything from his father. The factory, the farm, the whole estate. He owns your house now.'

'And he's the one who's putting up the rent?'

'Yes. Yours and everyone else's. He owns an awful lot of property round here. His family always have. But you people on Dagmouth Lane will get the worst of it.'

'Why us?'

'Because his father – old Mr Bennett, God rest his soul – kept all your rents specially low. He built those little houses just before the war. He did it to make money of course. Dagmouth Lane was just a bit of old wasteland then, and he saw a chance to make a profit out of it – renting out homes to factory workers and getting back the wages he paid them. But when the war came, and so many husbands and fathers were killed, he had a change of heart. He made sure Dagmouth Lane went to people like your mother. People who were suffering.' Hutch took out his handkerchief and blew his nose. Johnny hadn't noticed that he'd got a cold. 'Poor Winnie was only a girl then. She and Harry had been married just a few months, and I doubt whether your dad even knew she

51

was expecting you when he went off to fight. After he was killed, Winnie needed a roof over her head, but with you on the way she couldn't get enough work to pay much rent – so old Mr Bennett let her have the house you live in now. She still had to pay, but much less than that house could have fetched. He did the same for lots of other families. He was a good man.'

'I know,' said Johnny. 'Mum talked about him when he died. But she didn't expect the rent to go up.'

'Well, she knew the father, but she doesn't know the son. He was only a lad in the war. He didn't have to fight, and he's not interested in the sacrifice people like your father made. He can only see those houses as a drain on his income. And to be fair, some people could pay a bit more now. Look at Mrs Roberts – she's married again. Her Alf's got a good job.'

'But my mother hasn't. She has to look after me, and the house, and go out to work. She works all the time. She can't afford to pay more.'

'I understand, son,' said Hutch, more warmly than he had ever spoken to Johnny before. 'And now she's got that sister of hers to worry about too.' Johnny flinched at the reminder of Auntie Ada.

Hutch continued, 'I'll see what I can do for you. I won't be able to pay you much, mind. But it might be enough to help a bit. And I'll expect you to work hard.'

'Don't worry, I will.'

'You can stay on after your evening paper round every day and sweep up. And you can help me unpack some of the deliveries.' As he said that, Hutch's hand slipped, and the pyramid of tins fell to the floor. Johnny collected them up and started rebuilding the display.

'This can's got really badly bashed,' he said. 'And the label's ripped.'

'Put it to one side,' said Hutch. 'I'll have to sell it at a discount. No one's going to want to pay full price for that.'

Johnny put the dented can under the counter.

Albert Taylor and Ernest Roberts were waiting outside with their pocket money. Strictly speaking, Hutch didn't let customers in till nine o'clock, but everyone knew he could be persuaded to sell a newspaper or two earlier, and today was the day the comics arrived. Hutch let the boys in. They were polite to him, but when his back was turned they made coughing noises at Johnny.

'Heard from your girlfriend?' said Taylor. 'Is she dead yet?'

Johnny pretended not to notice, and raced out of the shop to deliver the morning papers.

At the end of the day, when Johnny had helped tidy up, Hutch reached under the counter and handed him the damaged tin of peaches. 'Take this home to your mum,' he said. 'Tell her it's not charity. It's your pay for the extra work you've done.' Then he looked sternly at Johnny. 'I won't always be so generous, mind.'

But Johnny saw it as the start of a new role for him. From now on he would take stuff home from the shop whenever he could. That way his mother wouldn't go in there and Hutch would never get the chance to ask her about Auntie Ada. It had been a good day. For on his paper round he had looked in all the newspapers to find out how to place adverts. He reckoned he could get his secret business up and running with just one more raid on the money in the Peace Mug. He would write out his first advertisement in bed that night.

Chapter 8

THE SANATORIUM

The next morning Dr Langford gave Johnny another exhilarating bike ride down the hill. Hutch was not there when they arrived at the shop. The doctor propped his bicycle against the wall and waited with Johnny.

'I might as well pick up my paper here,' he said. 'I'll be at the sanatorium all day, and there's no point in you taking it to my house if I'm not in.'

'Is that a flat tyre?' Johnny asked, pointing to the front wheel of the bike.

'Oh dear. It looks as if we went over something sharp,' said Dr Langford. 'Yes, here's the culprit.' He showed Johnny a tiny nail sticking into the rubber. 'Never mind, I'll have it fixed in no time.'

The doctor opened the saddlebag and handed Johnny a long tin with rounded ends. Johnny wriggled the lid off. Inside there were some metal levers, sandpaper, assorted patches, a tube marked RUBBER SOLUTION, a crayon, and a few bits and pieces Johnny couldn't identify at all.

The doctor turned the bike upside down and asked Johnny to pass him one of the levers. Soon he'd worked the inner tube of the tyre out from under the rubber tread. It hung like an empty sausage skin. Dr Langford unclipped the pump from the bicycle frame and inflated the tube. 'Come here, Johnny,' he said. 'Keep quiet and tell me if you hear a hiss. With a bit of luck we'll find the hole pretty quickly. If not, we'll have to dunk the tube in a puddle and look for some bubbles.'

Johnny put his head close to the doctor's and listened. 'There it is!' they cried together.

'Crayon!' said Dr Langford, as if he were talking to a nurse in an operating theatre. Johnny passed it to him, and Dr Langford marked the spot.

As the doctor got to work on the puncture, Johnny found the courage to talk to him more freely than he had before. It was easier when they weren't looking directly at each other. Johnny cleared his throat. 'Dr Langford?' he said. 'Can I ask you an embarrassing question?'

The doctor seemed uncomfortable, too. 'I'll be happy to talk to you, Johnny,' he replied, without looking up. 'But you will have to come and see me at my old surgery. I can open it up specially for you, if you've got something on your mind.'

'Oh no,' said Johnny. 'I didn't mean that sort of embarrassing. It's just that I'm ashamed that I don't know this already. You said you were going to the sanatorium. My teacher talked about it too. What exactly *is* a sanatorium?'

The doctor laughed, and asked Johnny to pass the sandpaper. 'Oh, is that all? What a relief. Well, if they taught Latin at that school of ours, you'd be able to work it out. It comes from the verb *sanare*, meaning "to cure", or "to heal", and the adjective *sanus*, *–a*, *–um*, meaning "healthy". It's a place of health: a kind of hospital. But a special one. It's just for people who've got tuberculosis. That's the disease I was checking you for at school the other day. We sometimes call it TB, or consumption.'

'Everyone's talking about it at school. They say it makes you cough up blood and shrivel away to skin and bone.'

'That's one way of putting it, yes,' said Dr Langford. 'It usually affects the lungs, but it can strike other organs, too. It can give you a very nasty condition called scrofula – horrible purple lumps on the neck.'

Johnny automatically put his hand to his own

throat and started feeling for bumps, rolling the sound of the word 'scrofula' round his mouth.

'Rubber solution!' said the doctor. 'It's the little yellow tube.' Johnny gave it to him, and he continued working on the bike with the dexterity of a surgeon, chatting on about diseases. 'In the olden days they thought scrofula could be cured by a touch of the King's hand. They called it the King's Evil. But it was really just another kind of tuberculosis.'

'And tuberculosis is TB?'

'Yes, but we doctors have yet another name for it. Here's a special word for you, Johnny. This one's from ancient Greek: *phthisis*. It's one of my favourites. Just eight letters, but quite a tongue-twister – and only one vowel, if you don't count the "i" twice.' He spelled it out for Johnny. 'Remember that word, son. Try it out on your teacher and see if he knows what it means. You might need it in a crossword puzzle one day.'

As the doctor stuck a patch over the repair, Johnny tried to fix the word in his memory, saying it again and again; flicking from the first 'f' sound of the 'ph' into the 'th' and then on to the hiss at the end. 'It sounds like a curse,' he said.

'Well, the disease certainly is,' said Dr Langford.

'I'm sorry to say that it's often fatal. Some people get better, but there's no absolute cure. We do our best for patients with fresh air, good food and exercise. And we keep them away from other people, so that they don't pass on their germs. Last time there was a TB outbreak in Stambleton we had a big collection to build our sanatorium a few miles out in the country, so there would be less risk in the town.'

'Was that when all the Dangerfields died?'

'How do you know about that?'

'I've seen the gravestones in the cemetery.'

The doctor shook his head. 'Poor Miss Dangerfield. First her beloved brother and his wife were taken by the disease, then their children died, one by one. She nursed them all, you know. I'll never forget the sight of her weeping over the tiny body of her last dead nephew. And after all that, she lost her fiancé in the war. She was already getting on a bit then. It was her last chance of happiness. She's the only Dangerfield left now. It's no wonder she looks so much older than she really is.' He changed the subject without a pause. 'Any chalk in that tin? We need it to stop the repair sticking to the inside of the tyre when the tube goes back in.'

Johnny passed the chalk. 'Why didn't Miss Dangerfield catch TB? Why haven't you?'

'Well, you know, Johnny, we doctors have a way of staying healthy. And it's like all diseases. Not everyone who comes into contact with a nasty bug gets sick. If they did, the human race would have been wiped out long ago. But some people – babies especially – can pick up tuberculosis very easily. And they can die from it. Anyone can. Mind you, some French doctors have come up with a vaccine . . .'

'A what?'

'Vaccine – that's another good word for you (double "c" – you don't get that very often). It's a special medicine to stop you getting a disease in the first place. It's a wonderful thing – made of living cells. But it's very hard to produce – they have to grow it in a special liquid made from potatoes.'

Johnny laughed. 'Potatoes?'

'Yes, I know it sounds comical, but it's actually a very tricky process.' The doctor picked up the lever again, and carefully manoeuvred the inner tube back inside the tyre. 'It's not something you can just boil up in your kitchen. You need controlled laboratory conditions. But if you get the process exactly right, the vaccine contains a tiny dose of the disease.'

'Isn't that what was in the test you gave us?' Johnny held out his wrist to show that he was in the clear.

'A vaccine's much more potent than that. It's strong enough to teach the blood to fight against invading germs, but it doesn't make people ill. Do you want some more strange words? This vaccine's called Bacille Calmette-Guérin. We make it easier for ourselves by calling it BCG. It's named after the Frenchmen who developed it – lucky devils.'

'Lucky?'

The doctor wiped his hands on his trousers. 'Oh Johnny,' he chuckled. 'There's nothing a medic wants more than his name attached to something: a piece of equipment, or a disease.' He screwed the nozzle of the bicycle pump back onto the valve. 'That way your memory lives on even after your death. I knew them both, you know – Calmette and Guérin – when they were starting out on their research, long before the war. In fact that's how I met my wife. She's a distant relative of Professor Calmette.'

'Mum told me she was French,' said Johnny, looking longingly at the pump. 'But she doesn't sound foreign, does she?'

Dr Langford turned round. 'Would you like to do this bit?' he asked, and Johnny gladly got to work re-inflating the tyre. The doctor set an empty apple box on its end and sat down. 'Well, she's been living here for more than forty years, remember. And her English was pretty good to start with.' He smiled, and his eyes grew moist as he thought back. 'It was the first thing I noticed at that dinner party in Lille all those years ago. She's very well educated. From a fine background. It was good of her to give it all up for a humble English doctor.' He cleared his throat and slapped his knees. 'Still, as it turned out, her family lost everything in the war, so it's probably just as well that she married me.' He reached over and felt the wheel. 'That's enough now. Leave it for a bit to make sure it doesn't go down again.'

'But the professor,' said Johnny; 'the one who made the vaccine – did he survive?'

'Oh yes. He's still around – though, like me, he's ageing now. I saw him quite recently. My wife and I went over to visit the laboratory where they produce the vaccine. France has gone overboard for it. They're giving it to babies – free.'

'Why don't we have it here?' asked Johnny, collecting up all the bits and pieces from the pavement, and putting them back in the tin.

Dr Langford sighed. 'It's complicated. There's a law

against bringing new medicines into this country unless they've been approved by the government.'

'So why don't they approve it?'

'All sorts of reasons. Some people are against vaccination on principle – they think it's wrong to interfere with Nature; and there are big-wigs here who aren't convinced that the BCG works. But the fact is, Johnny, we British have never liked being taught anything by the French. Our government is paying British scientists to search for a British treatment. They haven't come up with anything yet, and I don't think there's any need for them to try.'

'Couldn't you tell the government to let us have the French vaccine?'

'Oh, I'm a nobody as far as they're concerned.' Dr Langford dropped his voice. 'But, as it happens, I do have a little plan for something that might change their minds.' He looked around, cautiously. 'Now you mustn't tell anyone, Johnny, but when I last went to France I didn't come back empty-handed.'

Johnny was excited at being let into a secret. He pulled up a crate of his own and sat down close to the doctor. 'You brought the vaccine with you?' he whispered.

'Not exactly. I brought some of the culture – the

cells from which it's made – and I've passed it on to someone who has access to a laboratory. We're trying to keep it alive and grow it on to create a reliable supply. If we can, we're going to run a little trial – just enough to prove to the authorities that it works, and to persuade them to use it here.'

'But aren't you breaking the law? Suppose they find your lab. Won't you get into trouble?'

'Possibly, Johnny. But I'm an old man. I'm happy to take that risk, just in case I can save some lives with the vaccine.'

'And you could give it an English name. It could be called after you: "the Langford Treatment", or something like that.'

The doctor laughed. 'That does have an attractive ring to it. But I don't think it would be fair. I'm only copying what the French are doing. I think we'd still have to call it BCG.'

'Can I come and see it? Will you take me to the laboratory?'

'No, Johnny. I've already told you too much. And anyway, the lab is far, far away from here, out in the wilds. The project is entirely in the hands of my associate at the moment.'

'When will the vaccine be ready?'

'If all goes well, we may have a little before the end of the year, but it will be a long while before we can produce enough to get the government to change their policy. For the time being they'll just have to keep on building special hospitals, like our sanatorium.' Dr Langford rose and turned his bike the right way up, wheeling it backwards and forwards along the pavement to check that the repair was good.

Johnny was enjoying getting to know the doctor better. Now that they were at ease with each other, he plucked up the courage to ask a question he'd had in mind all along but had kept to himself, for fear of appearing love-struck, or nosy. 'Dr Langford,' he said, cautiously, 'do you know anything about Olwen? Is she all right?'

To Johnny's relief, the doctor answered without a trace of amusement or disdain. 'The little Welsh girl? When I examined her, she was perfectly well. But she's gone back to Wales to stay with relatives. She'll be safe there, and I've passed on the name of an excellent sanatorium nearby that will take her in if she does develop symptoms. I'm afraid her parents and her sister were too sick to travel with her. They're in the sanatorium here. I'm sorry to say that the baby is desperately ill.'

'Can't you give it some of your vaccine – as soon as it's ready – even just a little bit?'

'It's too late for that, Johnny. You have to take the vaccine before you get sick. But I wish I could give it to all the other babies in the country. I really do.'

Johnny heard a wheezing noise behind him. It was Hutch, hurrying towards the shop, panting, and carrying a cardboard box.

'Has he got phthisis?' Johnny whispered to the doctor anxiously.

Dr Langford laughed. 'No, he's just out of breath.' He steadied the bike against a lamppost and walked towards Hutch. 'Can I give you a hand with that, Mr Hutchinson?'

'Thank you, sir,' Hutch puffed, handing the box to the doctor as he fumbled in his pocket for the keys to the shop. 'It's the poppies for the Remembrance Day collection. There was a bit of a mix-up, and I had to go and collect them at the station. I got held up.' He tapped his bad leg. 'I'm not as fast on my feet as I'd like to be.'

Inside the shop, Hutch hurriedly sorted the newspapers. 'I'm sorry, Johnny,' he said. 'This is going to make you late for school. There's no way you'll finish the round before the bell goes. And people will be furious that their papers are late. Don't let them take it out on you. It's all my fault.'

'Don't worry about that,' said the doctor. 'No one will be angry with me if I'm delayed getting to the sanatorium. I'll take Johnny on his round on my bicycle.'

So Johnny hoisted himself onto the crossbar, and the two of them delivered all the papers in record time. The doctor told him more about the sanatorium, and passed on another new word – *haemoptysis* (or spitting up blood). Not many people were out at such an early hour, but those who were waved happily at the old man and the boy. All except Dr Langford's neighbour, Miss Dangerfield, who always had a sharp contempt for anything out of the ordinary. She was polishing the brass numbers on her garden gate as Johnny and the doctor reached the end of the paper round.

Dr Langford rang the bell on his bike and shouted, 'Good morning, dear lady. Behold! Your paper!' as Johnny thrust it into her arms.

That was bad enough for Miss Dangerfield. Anyone might have seen. But it got worse. Johnny and the doctor both stuck out their legs and cheered as the bike freewheeled down the hill back to the shop. Miss Dangerfield had one word for it: 'Really!'

Johnny got to school just in time, and in class his mind slipped from images of illness back to his money-making scheme. He thought ahead to what he would do after he had raised enough cash to pay the rent. He would keep going with the adverts until he could afford to buy himself a bicycle.

Chapter 9

THE ADVERTISER

While Winnie threw herself into looking for extra work, Johnny got down to business. That night, after his mother had gone to bed, he raided the Peace Mug again and wrote out his Stop Your Baby Wetting the Bed advert, following the pattern of the one for the Secret of Instant Height, which was painfully imprinted on his memory. After school the following day, he hurried through his evening paper round and ran to the headquarters of the *Stambleton Echo*, a tall building by the canal. He could hear printing machinery thumping away below him as he climbed the steps up to an entrance marked OFFICE.

Johnny pushed open the heavy double doors, panting for breath, just as the woman in charge of the advertising department was getting ready to leave for the day. He'd already worked out what to say. Auntie Ada was going to help him out again. He had taken great care to make his handwriting look as neat and grown up as possible.

'Excuse me,' he puffed, standing on tiptoe to see over the high counter that separated the staff from the visiting public. 'Excuse me, madam. I've been sent with a message. My aunt wants to put an advertisement in your paper.'

'Which paper?' said the woman, impatiently.

Johnny was mystified. 'The *Echo*,' he said.

'Which *Echo*? The Hampton, the Balgrave, the Stambleton . . .'

'Stambleton,' said Johnny. 'I didn't know you did the others too.'

'Those, and the *Dorford Chronicle*, the *Mardly Trumpet*, the *Nethercross Express*—' It sounded as if she was ready to go on for a long time.

Johnny interrupted, 'They're all written here?'

'They're all printed here. And your aunt can advertise in any or all of them.'

Johnny was ecstatic. He had no idea that his adverts might be seen by so many people. 'Oh, all of them. I'm sure she'd want that.'

He handed his advertisement to the woman. She put on her glasses and started counting the words. Johnny had already done that several times. He knew that *Stop Your Baby Wetting the Bed. Send a postal order for one shilling and a stamped addressed envelope to Box*

X added up to twenty-one words. It would cost him one shilling and sixpence. He had the money in his pocket. He was slightly worried that it might cost more if the box number was in double figures, like the horrible 'Box 23'.

'That will be sixteen shillings and ninepence,' the lady said, as if it weren't a small fortune.

'Oh, I thought it would be one and six,' said Johnny, sheepishly. 'Twenty-one words. It says so in the paper.'

'That's for one advert, for one week, in one paper – and without a box number,' said the lady.

'Oh, but Auntie says she must have a box,' Johnny gulped, on the verge of tears. 'She doesn't want strangers to know where she lives. She wants you to collect the replies.'

'I quite understand,' said the lady, lifting her glasses to peer down at Johnny. 'A woman can't be too careful these days. But a box is sixpence a week.'

'But I've only got one and six,' said Johnny, putting his coins on the counter. 'And I have to get the advert in. She told me to run here. I don't know what to do.' He could feel his eyes starting to sting.

For once, being small and pale worked wonders for Johnny. The woman smiled sympathetically, put her glasses back on and examined the advert again.

'Well, you could have twelve words in one newspaper for a shilling,' she said. 'Let's see if we can cut this down.'

She showed Johnny how 'stamped addressed envelope' could be abbreviated to 'SAE'. 'One shilling postal order' could be written as '1/– PO'. She assured him that everyone would know what that meant. Like the box number, and 'SAE', it would count as just one word.

They ended up with: *Stop Your Baby Wetting the Bed. Send 1/– PO & SAE to Box 5.*

'I shouldn't really be showing you that,' said the lady, who was getting ever more friendly. 'Strictly speaking, I ought to encourage you to write more, so that we can charge extra. The other week someone came in with a little advert like this, and I persuaded him to spell out everything in full and put in the whole address of the paper. It pumped the price right up. I think I even got him to pay for a border round it. But he wasn't a nice man. He was really rude. I don't see why I should have to put up with discourtesy.'

Johnny thought back to the Instant Height advert. He hoped the lady was talking about the person who had tricked him into parting with money for that. 'Well, my auntie will certainly be very grateful that you have been so helpful to me,' he said in his best voice. 'Now I really mustn't hold you up any longer. Goodbye, madam.'

'Goodbye,' said the lady, smiling at his politeness. 'Tell your aunt she can collect the replies on any weekday during office hours.'

'She'll probably send me,' said Johnny.

He was on his way through the door and the lady was putting on her coat when she added, 'Oh, how silly of me. I forgot to take your aunt's name and address.'

Johnny hoped his panic didn't show as he made up a fictitious address on the spot. Auntie Ada was becoming ever more real. And she had a surname now. It seemed to come to him from nowhere, but afterwards he thought it fitted her rather well. From now on she was Mrs Ada Fortune. She'd have to be married. 'Miss Fortune' just didn't sound right.

Chapter 10

IN BUSINESS

After a week, Johnny returned to the newspaper office. He was late again. There was no way he could deliver all the papers and get there much before five o'clock. As before, the lady was in a hurry to leave.

'I have quite a journey,' she said. 'I live in Mardly. The bus goes at twenty past.'

'I'm sorry,' said Johnny, concealing his delight that she was not a Stambleton resident. He'd been worrying for days that she would realize he'd given a false address. He turned on the charm again. 'Do forgive me for coming at this hour. My aunt has sent me to collect the replies to her advertisement. It's Box Five.'

The woman turned to a rack of pigeonholes and took out a large envelope. She peeped inside, then sealed the flap. 'Take care of it,' she said. 'There are a few letters in there. They might have money in them. Mind how you go.'

Johnny couldn't wait to get away and open the

package. 'I won't hold you up any longer, madam,' he said, nodding politely on his way out. He dashed down to the edge of the canal and hid there until the woman had locked the door and set off for her bus stop. Then he tore open the big envelope. There were four smaller packets inside. Each of them contained a postal order for one shilling and a stamped addressed envelope for Johnny's reply. Johnny remembered how he had felt, assembling his letter to the people offering the Secret of Instant Height. For a moment he pictured the senders of these letters, desperately hoping for the solution to their babies' bedwetting, not suspecting that they were being tricked. But then he gathered up the postal orders. Four shillings. It was enough to cover the cost of this first advert, and to fund another, with money to spare to go back in the Peace Mug. He put the image of the anxious parents to the back of his mind, tucked everything back in the big envelope, and stuffed it down his jumper.

Up in his bedroom that night he wrote *Make him sleep in a chair* on four pieces of paper, and put one in each of the stamped addressed envelopes. Next morning, he popped them in the post box outside Hutch's shop. All day he checked and rechecked that the postal orders were still in his pocket. After school, when the post office was open, he asked Hutch to cash them on behalf of Auntie Ada. The sound of the four shilling bits jangling together as he ran cheered his journey home through the rain.

Over the next couple of weeks Johnny had a run of successes with:

Free yourself from rats . . .
Free yourself from mice . . .
Free yourself from spiders . . .
Free yourself from noisy neighbours . . .

and

Free yourself from nosy neighbours . . .

All of which had the answer,

Move house.

Not only were there no complaints, but one woman even sent in for the solution to her spider problem when she had already been tricked over the mice. *Get into Films* did well. There seemed to be a lot of would-be starlets around. For a shilling Johnny told them to *Go to the cinema*.

It was all very time-consuming. But Johnny had more time on his own now. His mother had found an extra job behind the bar at a run-down pub on the other side of town, and Johnny spent most evenings alone at home, making up adverts and practising Auntie Ada's flowing handwriting.

There were disappointments. No one seemed to want to know how to scratch itches without leaving unsightly marks (*Wear gloves*), but there was a huge demand for a way to stop your husband disturbing you with his snoring (*Sleep in a different room*). That one brought the Peace Mug back to its original level. Hutch seemed to believe that all the postal orders belonged to Auntie Ada. Johnny had told him that she did needlework in her sickbed, and sold it by post.

Some of the people who answered Johnny's adverts didn't send postal orders, but paid with unused postage stamps. At first Johnny was annoyed by that because, despite his growing business, he hardly ever sent any letters of his own. Then he had the brainwave of using the stamps for a different kind of scam. He put in an advert saying:

I will pay your rent for a year.
Send 15/– PO to cover expenses.

Eight people fell for it. They each received their rent for a year. Unfortunately for them, the year was 1066, and all they got was 3d. in stamps, which Johnny reckoned would have been enough for a fairly handsome property in those far-off days. There was one angry letter of complaint, sent to the box number. At first Johnny was worried. What if the disappointed customer told the newspaper what was going on, and they tried to track down Ada Fortune? Then (since he had plenty of stamps) he hit on the idea of writing back, using some of the language he'd seen in the law reports in the papers. He added in one of the best words Dr Langford had taught him: *haemoptysis*. He thought it sounded important, and he guessed that anyone stupid enough to think that a stranger would pay their rent for a year wouldn't know that it meant 'spitting blood'. Johnny used some of his earnings to buy thick paper and envelopes, and in his ever-improving handwriting he concocted a polite but firm letter, from a false address in London, in which he said that his legal advisers, and those of the newspaper, were in agreement (having consulted authorities on the law of haemoptysis) that there had been no deception, since no year had been specifically mentioned in the advertisement. He generously offered not to charge for the administrative costs that had been incurred in responding to the un-justified complaint. Johnny hoped that the angry man wouldn't try to contact him again. He didn't.

But, lucrative though it was, Johnny knew he had been lucky to get away with the rent scam. He under-stood now that people were much more likely to complain if they had paid a lot of money; and fifteen shillings was too much to ask for anything. It was safer to lure twenty people into parting with a shilling than to trick one into paying a pound. So he got rid of the remaining stamps with a cheap – but successful – offer:

Official Portrait of the King. 1/–.

Johnny had meant to be a little more honest, and to say 'miniature portrait', but he wasn't sure how to spell 'miniature', and anyway, it was always good to save a word in an advert. There were no complaints, even though the suckers had at least ended up with a stamp (worth anything from one penny to sixpence) to put on their angry letters. No doubt they agreed with Johnny that they would have looked pretty daft if they'd admitted falling for that trick. But it was a good one. Johnny worked out that once his costs were covered, he was making a profit of anything from 100 to 1100 per cent, depending on the value of the stamps he sent to his patriotic customers. True, the actual amounts that reached the Peace Mug were very small, but he was beginning to dream of bigger projects, with mighty returns.

And there was one unexpected side effect of all the effort. Winnie ran into Johnny's form teacher, Mrs Stiles, in the street one Saturday morning.

'Oh, Mrs Swanson,' said Mrs Stiles. 'I'm so very pleased with Johnny this term. His work has improved immensely. It's very neat indeed.'

'I'm delighted to hear it.'

'Yes, and it's not just his presentation. His maths is coming along in leaps and bounds. He's especially good at money sums.'

Later that day, when Winnie told Johnny what his teacher had said, she thought he was blushing out of proud embarrassment. She knew nothing of the guilty secret that was burning his cheeks.

Chapter 11

UMCKALOABO

Just before half-term, Dr Langford came to school again, to check that everyone was still clear of TB. He got Johnny's class off Geography this time. He was becoming rather popular. Then, during the week of holiday, Hutch gave Johnny jobs in the shop every day. Johnny saw Hutch at work in the stockroom, behind the counter, and in the post office. They had time to chat, and got to know each other better.

The store was always busy, with customers wanting everything from groceries to knitting patterns. There was a wooden booth near the door with a bench and a telephone inside. People came from all over town to use it. Some stayed inside for ages, and it smelled strongly of stale cigarette smoke. Johnny tried not to listen to the muffled, one-sided conversations seeping out through the sliding door, but sometimes he just couldn't help it. So he knew all about the deputy headmaster's attempt to get another job, and the vicar's daughter's entanglement with someone called

Michael, who appeared to be married. One day he heard Mrs Slack on the phone to some distant relative, droning on about her health and how she couldn't cope at home. At first he was appalled to find the old lady virtually begging for money, but he felt better about her when she continued:

'I don't know what I'd do without Mrs Swanson. She comes in every day to see that I'm all right and never asks for a penny. She's a marvellous woman. Sometimes I think she's all that's keeping me alive.'

He never told his mother what he had heard. He thought she would be angry with him for listening in. In the weeks to come, he was to wish that he *had* said something. But by then it was too late.

When it was quiet in the shop, Johnny had the chance to study the newspapers, looking at the advertisements for ideas. He knew the best adverts were in the Sunday papers, but he could never get a good look at them on the day, because the shop was shut; he just saw the headlines as he posted each copy through a letter box. To read them properly he had to wait till Hutch threw his own copies away; so when Johnny fished *Reynolds's News* out of the bin on the Monday of half-term, it was covered in brown circles from the bottom of Hutch's teacup.

Johnny opened out the huge newspaper. It took up almost the whole counter. He had to move aside the charity collection tin and a jar of Liquorice Allsorts to make room for it. He turned the pages, leafing through news and fashion tips, the sheet music for a popular song, a short story, cartoons, theatre reviews, and display adverts for cars and London department stores. Among the small ads, one entry caught his eye immediately. It was headed: CHEST DISEASES, and it went on:

'Umckaloabo acts as regards Tuberculosis as a real specific'
(Dr Sechehaye in the 'Swiss Medical Review').
It appears to me to have a specific destructive influence on the Tubercule Bacilli in the same way the Quinine has upon Malaria.'
(Dr Grun in the King's Bench Division).

If you are suffering from a disease of the chest or lungs – spasmodic or cardiac asthma excluded – ask your doctor about Umckaloabo, or send a postcard for particulars of it to Chas. H. Stevens, 204–206 Worple Road, Wimbledon, London, S.W.20, who will post same to you Free of Charge.

Readers, especially TBs, will see in the above few lines more wonderful news than is to be found in many volumes on the same subject.

Johnny read the advert through several times, trying to get his tongue round the strange word 'Umckaloabo'. It sounded like something from Africa. With his practised eye, he couldn't help calculating the price of such a wordy advertisement in a high-circulation paper. With all the special layout to make it look like a news story, you wouldn't get much change from three pounds. Chas. H. Stevens of Wimbledon must have great faith in what he was selling, particularly as he wasn't asking his customers for any money up front.

Johnny's heart quickened. Maybe this advertisement was indeed the 'wonderful news' it claimed to be. Perhaps Mr Stevens really had found a cure for TB. If that was so, shouldn't Dr Langford be told? Perhaps he could use Umckaloabo to help Olwen's family. Johnny knew the Langfords didn't take *Reynolds's News*. They wouldn't have seen the advertisement themselves. He took out some scissors from the drawer under the counter and carefully cut it out.

*

After work, Johnny went straight up the hill to Dr Langford's house to tell him about Umckaloabo. Mrs Langford opened the door. She was tall and slim, like her husband, but while his limbs tended to flail around in an ungainly way, hers moved with an effortless grace, even though she sometimes put her hand to her back, as if it hurt to bend. Her steel-grey hair was twisted up at the back in a chignon. Johnny knew that was what it was called because he'd seen a diagram showing how to do it in the paper only that morning. Winnie had often admired Mrs Langford's clothes, saying how well-made they were, and how well co-ordinated. Johnny had no opinion on how Mrs Langford's skirt and blouse were constructed, but he could see that they matched. Both were a deep shade of blue.

'Hello Johnny,' said Mrs Langford. 'Are you looking for your mother? She went home hours ago.'

'No. I've brought something for Dr Langford,' said Johnny, pulling the crumpled cutting from his pocket. 'It's important. I think Dr Langford ought to know. Someone's found a cure for TB.'

'Well, if they really have, he'll be fascinated. Not to say amazed. Let me have a look at that. You'd better come in.' She took the cutting and showed Johnny into the drawing room. 'You sit by the fire and get warm. Now, where are my glasses?'

Johnny watched her search the room, which had more places to lose things than in his entire home.

She ran her hand along the bookshelves, shook out plump cushions, dug down the back of the soft sofa and shuffled though piles of newspapers and magazines. 'I don't know where they get to. I must have had them just before I came to answer the door. Now, let's see. What was I doing when you arrived?' She paused and thought back. 'That's it. I was sewing. I was sitting just where you are now.'

'Oh, I'm sorry,' said Johnny, jumping up. 'I didn't know this was your chair.'

'Don't be silly. You're my guest. You can sit where you like. Just forgive me a moment.' Johnny heard her knees click as she bent down and scrabbled on the floor behind his feet. She pulled out a work basket. An old sock dangled from under the lid. 'I remember now. I slid it there when the bell rang – just in case it was the vicar or someone like that. I wouldn't want him to catch me darning holes!'

Johnny held the basket while Mrs Langford, sighing, hauled herself back up again. Then she took it back, and lifted out her spectacles. 'If I had sixpence for every time I've lost these, I'd be a very rich woman,' she joked. 'I've seen people with their glasses on special strings round their necks. Rather an ageing effect, I've always thought. But perhaps the time has come for me.'

Johnny was already mentally composing a new advert: *Never Lose Your Glasses Again*. He was wondering whether to send people real string, or just the suggestion that they could tie up their glasses themselves. Maybe he could charge more if he used coloured ribbon . . .

Mrs Langford straightened out Johnny's cutting, and looked at it through her spectacles. 'Oh, Umckaloabo. I've heard of this. There was a big row about it a few years ago. This Charles Stevens was struck off because of it.'

'Struck off?'

Mrs Langford explained: 'Struck off the Medical Register. It means the authorities took away his right to practise medicine. He's not allowed to call himself a doctor any more. He was making wild claims about an unproven drug. He's what we call a quack.'

'A what?'

'A quack. A fake doctor.'

'They call me Quacky at school,' said Johnny. 'But it's nothing to do with doctors. It's because of my name: Swanson. It makes them think of ducks.'

'That's not very nice of them,' said Mrs Langford. 'But boys will be boys, I suppose. They called my husband Longfeet when he was at school, because he was so tall.'

'What's all this?' said Dr Langford, who had just entered the room. 'Oh, hello Johnny. I wasn't expecting to see you. Nothing wrong, I hope?'

'No,' said Johnny miserably, unable to disguise his disappointment at finding that the advertisement was a trick.

Mrs Langford passed the cutting to her husband. 'It's Umckaloabo again,' she said.

Dr Langford patted his pockets. 'Can I borrow your glasses a minute?' he asked. His wife passed them over, with a wink to Johnny. The doctor sighed. 'So he's still making money out of it. It's a disgrace, giving false hope to worried people and pocketing the proceeds. I thought we'd seen the back of this Stevens character.' Dr Langford was still reading the advertisement. 'He lives a long way away. Wimbledon.' He looked up at Johnny, grinning. 'You know what Wimbledon is famous for, don't you, son?'

Johnny shrugged. 'Don't ask me.'

'Tennis.' There was an awkward pause. The doctor seemed to be waiting for something. 'Do you see? Do you get it? Has the penny dropped?'

'I'm sorry?' said Johnny, embarrassed and confused.

'It's just that . . . well . . . you know . . . this Umckaloabo stuff. It's a Wimbledon racket.' The doctor paused again. Eventually Johnny got the joke, and mustered a half-hearted laugh.

Mrs Langford threw the cutting on the fire.

'I bet hundreds of people will answer that advertisement and pay good money for rubbish,' said Dr Langford. 'It's not right.'

'Why don't you put your vaccine in the paper then?' asked Johnny.

The room fell silent, and Mrs Langford gave her husband a stern look. The doctor, shamefaced, put a finger to his lips. 'I shouldn't have told you about that, Johnny. It's absolutely secret. I could get into a great deal of trouble if anyone finds out what I'm doing.'

'You mustn't mention it to anyone,' said Mrs Langford, trying to sound kind, but looking more agitated than Johnny had ever seen her. She turned to her husband, muttering something under her breath.

Johnny felt embarrassed, and cross with himself for getting the doctor into trouble with his wife. He interrupted. 'Don't worry. I won't tell anyone. But I still don't understand. Why is it all right for this man

Stevens to advertise something that doesn't work, and against the law for you to sell something that does?'

'Because real medicines have to be controlled, Johnny. Powerful drugs can do harm as well as good. You can bet your life that almost everything you see advertised in the paper is useless. You'd be astounded at what people will fall for in the small ads.'

Johnny didn't say that he knew only too well. He could feel himself blushing as his mind flashed back to that moment by the canal, when he had last thought of his customers as real people who were being tricked. Dr Langford had put that feeling into words: *It's a disgrace, giving false hope to worried people and pocketing the proceeds.*

Johnny wanted to get away from the awkward atmosphere. It wasn't just his hidden shame over the adverts. He didn't want to get trapped in between two quarrelling adults, and he felt guilty that he had made such nice old people angry with each other. 'I think I'd better go home now,' he said, as politely as he could. 'I'm sorry to have troubled you.'

'That's quite all right, Johnny,' said Dr Langford, showing him to the door. 'I know you were only trying to help.'

'I was thinking of Olwen,' said Johnny. 'I know it's too late for your vaccine to work on her, but it sounded as if this Umb ... Umber ... whatever it's called, might help. But if that's no good, what will happen to her?'

'I'm afraid I can't say. I don't even know exactly where she is. She's not my patient. She's probably not even ill at the moment. All I know is that she's with relatives in Wales.' The doctor lowered his voice. 'Now remember, son. Mum's the word. Don't tell anyone about the vaccine. Understand?'

The door closed behind him, and Johnny could hear raised voices. He crept round to the drawing-room window, hoping to be able to make out what the Langfords were saying, but he could only catch fragments of the argument.

Mrs Langford was furious: '... couldn't resist it ... totally unnecessary risk.'

The doctor was trying to reassure her: 'He won't tell anyone ... Who's going to listen to a boy? ... doesn't know where the laboratory is.'

'I just wish you'd never got involved ... not even going to make us any money ... scrimping to make ends meet ...'

Johnny heard a door slam and the voices disappeared.

He set off down the path, only to find Miss Dangerfield waiting at the gate. After seeing Mrs Langford in her trim clothes, Johnny noticed how Miss Dangerfield's shapeless old-fashioned layers of black swept along the muddy ground, and how short and stooped she was underneath her funereal fringes and flounces. Even so, her fierce nasal voice was chilling.

'I've been watching you,' she said. 'I saw you hovering by that window. Hoping to break in, I shouldn't wonder.'

'No, Miss Dangerfield. I wasn't. I was just listening—'

'Listening!' She grasped Johnny's shirt and pulled him towards her. 'Eavesdropping – that's what I call it.'

'No. Not that,' said Johnny, shaking. 'I'd just been inside, talking to Dr Langford.'

Miss Dangerfield was spitting with contempt. 'You? Inside? Don't be ridiculous. Why should Dr Langford want to talk to you? What were you talking about?'

Johnny had only just promised to keep quiet. He could see how concerned the Langfords were that no one should know they had brought the BCG to Britain. He said nothing. But he knew Miss Dangerfield would take his silence as a sign of guilt.

'I thought as much!' she said when Johnny failed to speak. 'You're a liar as well as a thief.' She pushed him away. He wanted to run, but his legs wouldn't move. She grabbed his hair and shook him till his eyes watered with pain. 'You get away from here, and don't come back!' she yelled, turning him round and poking her walking stick into the small of his back. 'I'm warning you.'

After what the doctor had told him about Miss Dangerfield's sad past, Johnny had begun to feel a bit sorry for her. But not now. Not after how she had just treated him. To Johnny she was a miserable old woman once again. Instead of walking away, as he knew he should, he did something he'd never done in the presence of an adult. He made a very rude sign and said an even ruder word. Then he ran.

Chapter 12

THE PRIVATE BOX

Every afternoon a man with a wide moustache came up to the post office counter to ask if he had any mail.

'Why does he do that?' asked Johnny. 'Why doesn't the postman take him his letters?'

'Oh, he's got what we call a private box,' said Hutch. 'He has all his letters addressed here, and he collects them himself.'

'Why would he want to do that?'

'Well. There could be all sorts of reasons. He might be travelling, and picking up letters from several post offices on his route. Or he might not like the folk he lives with to see what letters he's getting. Or perhaps he doesn't want the people who send the letters to know exactly where he lives.'

'But they could come here and ask you,' said Johnny.

Hutch stood tall and took a deep breath. 'They could, Johnny, but I'd never tell them,' he said in his official 'post office' voice. 'I'm a servant of the Crown, and a private box is called a private box for a reason. That man's identity and his address are a confidential matter. The very fact that he has a private box is private. I probably shouldn't even be talking to you about it now.'

Johnny could instantly see the advantages of a private box at the post office. He wanted one. If the replies to his adverts were delivered to the shop, he wouldn't have to walk to the newspaper offices so often. He was getting worried about the lady there. She seemed to like him, but that was becoming a problem. He always tried to collect Auntie Ada's letters just before closing time, but even then she wanted to chat. Once, she had suggested that they should walk to her bus stop together, and recently she'd raised her eyebrows at some of the adverts he took in. How long could he trust himself not to say something that would make her suspicious? What if she herself responded to one of the adverts? She had already seemed rather too interested in *The Answer to Smelly Feet* (*Wear a clothes peg on your nose*).

Since her company owned most of the newspapers for miles around, Johnny couldn't avoid the lady, even when he moved his business from one local paper to another. But if his post could be sent to Hutch's shop, he might be able to start advertising in different places – perhaps even the national papers, which had more readers. Now that he had more money, Johnny could send in his advertisements by mail, paying for them with postal orders and stamps he received from his customers. He might even be able to phone the advertising departments. His voice was still high. They would believe he was Ada Fortune.

'I think Auntie Ada should have a private box,' he said to Hutch casually. 'She must worry about the people who buy her needlework knowing our address. The last thing she needs in her state of health is surprise visitors. And if her letters were delivered here in the first place, I could cash her postal orders with you and take the money straight home. She wouldn't have to wait so long to get it. How much does a private box cost?'

'Not much,' said Hutch. 'But listen, the poor woman's an invalid, and I know your family's having a rough time at present. I won't make her pay. I'll cover the costs myself.'

Johnny tried to protest. But before he got the words out, he realized that he couldn't offer to pay the fee himself. He mustn't let on that he had a stash of money at home.

'No, I'll pay,' said Hutch, interrupting Johnny's garbled rejection of the offer, which he took as simple politeness. 'I insist. It will be a pleasure. But it must all be done properly. You take this form home and get your aunt to fill it in.'

So, that night, Johnny created Ada Fortune's first official document, beautifully signed. The next day, Hutch marked it with his rubber stamp and filed it away.

'Tell your auntie that her address is now PO Box Nine, Stambleton, Warwickshire. In future I'll keep her letters aside, and you can take them home with you.'

Even though the new address would add a few pence to the cost of each advertisement, Johnny knew the private box was going to make his life a lot easier, and he spent the rest of half-term dreaming up new projects. When he looked through the national papers he saw that most of the advertisements were about health and self-improvement. It was obviously a lucrative market, and although Dr Langford had struck a nerve with his criticism of quack medicine, Johnny could see that sending out remedies offered a solution to another problem. He needed to convince Hutch that Auntie Ada really *was* doing needlework in exchange for all those postal orders. It was time to be seen posting parcels on her behalf. But there was no need for Johnny to sew anything. Hutch would never know what was inside the packages, so Johnny could fill them with 'cures' for everything from sleeplessness to sore toes.

He had no trouble finding a list of illnesses: years of accompanying his mother on her visits to Mrs Slack had exposed him to the human version of a medical encyclopaedia; and the graveyard on his paper round had everything he needed to fulfil the orders. He pulled the juiciest leaves off the evergreens, and collected the most beautiful fallen autumn foliage from the ground. There were seed husks, conker shells, acorns, and twisted pieces of twig.

He was tugging the feathers off the corpse of a pigeon when he heard a rapping noise. It was Miss Dangerfield, bashing her walking stick on top of the wall.

'Hey! You boy! What do you think you are doing?'

Johnny had to think fast. 'Oh, hello, madam,' he said, playing for time. 'I'm ... I'm ... It's Nature Study. I have to collect some specimens for school.'

'Don't you "madam" me! And don't you "Nature Study" me! I know the school is on holiday. Nature Study indeed! You're up to no good. And where's my paper?' Johnny put his hand into his bag to get it for her. 'Not here, you fool! I don't want it here, do I? I want it at home. And you're late. Mr Hutchinson pays you to deliver the newspaper to my house. And you're late!'

Somewhere inside himself Johnny knew that it was pointless to argue, but after her unkindness the other day, and with the safety of the graveyard wall between them, he couldn't resist pointing out the flaw in what Miss Dangerfield was saying. 'But I'm on my way. And anyway, you're not there, are you? I mean, you're here. So you wouldn't know I was late, would you? If you were there, I mean. Which you're not.'

'Don't you answer me back, boy.'

'I wasn't answering back—'

'Yes you were, and you're doing it again now. I've got a good mind to report you. Now get off up the hill and deliver my paper.'

Johnny placed a few more leaves in the bag.

Miss Dangerfield banged her stick on the wall again. 'Do it now, I tell you! And if there's any dirt on that paper, I'm cancelling my order. I've got my eye on you, boy. Indeed I have.'

Johnny ran off up the hill and finished his deliveries. He'd enjoyed the brief moment of standing up for himself, but he was worried about Miss Dangerfield. Suppose she had gone straight from the graveyard to the post office? She might be telling on him now. He might lose his job just when the rent was about to go up. He needed his base at Hutch's, with its postal orders, stationery and stamps, to keep the money coming in. He had to get back, to talk his way out of trouble.

Hutch was sweeping up, looking stern. 'I've had a complaint.'

'I know. Miss Dangerfield told me she was going to talk to you.'

'Talk! She ranted. She raved. Lucky for you, she knocked over the display of sugar with that stick of hers, and she flounced off before I could make her any promises. But I'm warning you, Johnny. Stay on the right side of her. I won't be able to defend you for ever.'

'I'll try,' said Johnny, meaning it, because he knew his business interests could be smashed by one blow from Miss Dangerfield's cane.

He had no time to lose. He must make the most of the post office while he still had access to it. So he bought a notepad and some brown paper from Hutch and went home to compose a host of adverts to put in right away, and to wrap up his stock of 'cures' ready for a quick dispatch. He had no idea whether any of the leaves were poisonous, so he put a note in each parcel saying FOR EXTERNAL USE ONLY. He'd seen that written on the tin of Dr Sampson's Patent Ointment for Cuts, Burns and Stings.

According to the nature of the problem, he told his customers to slip the leaves, husks and feathers under their pillows, in their underwear, or down their socks. To his horror, his first victim wrote straight back to say that the 'cure' had worked. His heartburn had disappeared as soon as he had put dried potato peelings down his vest.

Chapter 13

RAKING IT IN

The TB scare had died down by the end of half-term. Normal lessons seemed even more tedious after the brief burst of excitement, but that wasn't the only reason Johnny was sad to go back. It meant a pay cut from Hutch, and reduced the time he could spend running his business. Even so, he got some profitable ideas at school.

On the first day back, they were studying light waves in Mr Marshall's Science class. The teacher pointed to Ernest Roberts, who was sitting next to Johnny.

'Roberts. Take off your glasses.'

'But I won't be able to see the blackboard then, sir.'

'That's the point, Roberts.'

Ernest took off his specs, and the teacher threw a square of cardboard in his direction. Without his glasses he couldn't catch it, and it dropped to the floor. Johnny picked it up.

'Well, Swanson. Tell us what that is.'

Johnny was bemused. 'It's just a piece of cardboard, sir.'

'Look carefully. Do you notice anything special about it?'

Johnny examined it closely. 'It's cut from a packet of hair restorer, sir.' He read out the label. '*Vivatone Radio Active Hair Restorer. Grey banished. No dyes. No stains.*'

Everybody laughed.

'The other side, Swanson. Look at the other side.'

'It's just plain, sir. But there is a little hole in the middle.'

'Exactly, Swanson. A hole. What we call a pinhole. And why do you think it's called that?'

'Because you made it with a pin?' shouted Albert Taylor.

'Well done, Taylor. I made it with a pin. Now, Roberts. Look through that pinhole and tell me what you can see.'

Ernest Roberts shut one eye and looked through the pinhole with the other.

'I can see you, sir. Perfectly clearly.' He read the heading off the blackboard: '*Optics*. It's magic, sir.'

'No, Roberts, it's not magic,' said Mr Marshall. 'It's science,' and he drew a diagram on the board to show

how the pinhole concentrated the light waves so that they hit Roberts's retina at just the right spot.

'Cheaper than a pair of glasses, eh, Roberts?' he said. 'Someone should put it on the market. Talk about money for old rope.'

Johnny was already devising a new advert in his head: *The Secret of Instant Sight.* There was plenty of old cardboard in the shop. He knew Hutch would let him have it for nothing.

And the remark about 'money for old rope' wasn't lost on Johnny either. He found some twine in the graveyard. He cut it up into short lengths and tied them into bracelets, to be worn on painful wrists and ankles. The potato-vest man bought one, and wrote again, convinced that his arthritic joints were much relieved.

Despite being back at school, Johnny couldn't stop himself. He saw financial opportunities everywhere. *Reynolds's News* had a popular feature:

MAUD DAWSON'S LOVE ANSWERS
Is your burden too hard to bear? Let me share it!

The answers to the questions seemed like down-right twaddle to Johnny. He was sure he could do better than Maud Dawson, and charge people for his advice. He put an advert in the *Saturday Post* (calling himself Ada Ardour), offering advice on anything, in return for a shilling and a stamped addressed envelope. He was overwhelmed with requests for help. Some of the letters were several pages long, and went into embarrassing detail about love affairs. This was typical, if less explicit than most:

Dear Miss Ardour,

I am engaged to be married next year. My fiancé says he loves me, but he is insisting that I must give up cycling when we are married, and he says we cannot have any pets, though I love dogs and cats. We argue about all these matters. Should I give in? I worry that if we continue in this way he may cease to consider me sweet natured, and that we may be getting into a habit of dispute which will continue after the wedding.

Yours in desperation,
Anxious of Ambleside

Johnny had no doubt that Maud Dawson would advise 'Anxious of Ambleside' to be dutiful and to yield to her fiancé's demands. He took a different view, and wrote back:

Dear Anxious of Ambleside,

This man does not sound very kind. Leave him, keep your bike, and get a dog. This may cause you embarrassment now, but you will thank me in years to come.

Confidentially yours,
Ada Ardour

He was pleased with his reply, and let his mind play with the scene in Ambleside as 'Anxious' told her boyfriend to get lost. But then he had visions of the jilted lover tracking him down, and added at the bottom:

Of course, this is only advice, and your decision will be entirely your own. Ada Ardour takes no responsibility for the eventual outcome.

He liked the expression 'Confidentially yours', and it went on to become the regular heading on his 'agony' advertisements. And he added that extra sentence on the bottom of all his advice letters – just in case.

'Confidentially Yours' was entertaining (and educational) for Johnny, but it was also tiring work, with each letter needing an individual reply. He dreamed up another scam where his customers would do most of the work. 'The Poetry Police' offered to send critical advice to aspiring poets at two shillings a time. Johnny read the poems, but he sent all the poets the same few words of encouragement: *A good effort. Do not be afraid to experiment.* And he kept the poems. One came in handy for English homework. Then he spotted a competition in the Sunday paper. Underneath 'Maud Dawson's Love Answers' was a column headed 'For the Chicks'. It was a sickly item, aimed at children, written by someone who called herself 'Aunty Betty'. She was offering prizes for 'Fairy Verse'. Johnny just happened to have a poem about fairies amongst his haul. He sent it in under his own name, and his mother was awash with pride when a letter arrived from the paper, enclosing a five-shilling postal order for Johnny. She was moved when he insisted on putting his winnings towards the rent money. She didn't know that he was hiding even more cash inside the floppy body of his old toy rabbit, which sat on top of the wardrobe in his bedroom. And she had no idea that he was buying food at the shop. Whenever Johnny came home with something for the larder, he always said that Hutch had sent it, because otherwise it would just have to be thrown away.

Every morning, Johnny set off with a stash of letters in his school satchel. Most were replies to his hapless customers, but there were always at least three new adverts, destined for papers all over the country. Soon he couldn't get to sleep at night until he had everything in order for the next day. He began to take a pride in his 'work'. Only once did he have a real attack of conscience. It came as the result of one of his least sophisticated efforts, based on the simple formula of the Secret of Instant Height. Anyone who sent Johnny a shilling to find out how to *Make Your Money Go Further* was told to *Roll it down a hill*. Twenty people fell for it, and so Johnny would have made a pound; but there was one postal order he felt he couldn't cash. It was from Mrs Langford. This wasn't the first time Johnny had been given the chance to trick someone he knew – Albert Taylor's mother had fallen for the snoring scam, and he'd been glad to take her money – but the doctor was so generous with his bike rides that Johnny felt it would be unforgivable to cheat his wife out of a shilling. He remembered Mrs Langford darning socks on the day he'd visited them, and her harsh words to her husband about how poor they were becoming. He put her postal order straight into the stamped addressed envelope and sent it back.

But the other nineteen applicants all got the silly answer. And none of them complained.

Chapter 14

REMEMBRANCE DAY

Not long after the half-term break there was another day off school. That year, 1929, 11th November fell on a Monday, and everything closed down for a big parade and religious service to honour those who had died in the Great War. But the papers still had to be delivered, so Johnny was up early as usual. When he got to the shop, Hutch was polishing his medals. He had three, hanging from multi-coloured ribbons, and a round silver badge with a crown and the King's initials intertwined. Around the edge, it said: For King and Empire. Services Rendered.

Johnny picked it up. 'Mr Murray's got one of these,' he said. 'He wears it all the time at school.'

'It's what you got if you were discharged from the army because you were wounded,' said Hutch. 'I must have been one of the first to have it. I got shot right at the beginning of the war.' He slapped his leg. 'I was one of the lucky ones. I only saw one battle, and I survived.'

'Mr Murray doesn't seem to think he was lucky.'

'Well, he wasn't really. He got hit in the face. It ruined his whole life. Turned him into such a bitter man. I'm OK. I'm still doing what I did before. Everything changed for him.'

'What? Do you mean he wasn't a teacher before the war?'

'Him? A teacher? Do you think he'd ever have wanted to be a teacher? He hates it. Surely you've noticed that?'

'I've noticed that he hates me,' said Johnny. 'He's so mean and cruel.'

'He doesn't really hate you, I'm sure,' said Hutch. 'But he's angry. He never wanted to fight. He didn't volunteer like me. He was called up towards the end of the war. He was a good-looking man – hoping to become an actor, you know. He can't do that with half his face shot away, and now he's stuck with a job he doesn't like and can't afford to give up.'

'But why take it out on me?'

'He probably doesn't mean to. You probably just make him feel guilty.'

'Guilty? Why?'

'Because your father died and he survived. It's hard for us veterans, you know. I don't think many of us are going to take pride in being able to march in the parade today. We'll be thinking of all the dead men who deserve to be there. And there'll be plenty of others angry that we're still around, when their loved-ones are gone. That Miss Dangerfield lost her sweetheart. Your own mother lost your dad. She'd be a saint if she wasn't jealous of the women who got their husbands back.'

'But she's proud of how Dad died. This morning she got out the little plaque with his name on, and the scroll the King sent when he was killed. She keeps them in a special box, you know, with the letter they sent about how his body couldn't be recovered. Mr Murray says that means he was blown to bits.'

Hutch winced. 'Who knows, Johnny? Who knows? It was chaos out there. Half the stories about what happened to people must be lies or guesswork. But whatever happened, your mother is right to hang on to her pride. The trouble is, it's all wearing off a bit now. During the war we were heroes. Now I'm just a man with a limp, and your Mr Murray is a bitter bully with an ugly face. We'll have our parade, but some people won't even bother to go. And next year there'll be even fewer who'll brave the cold. There's plenty of folk who think we should put it all behind us. Maybe they're right. The war's been over for more than ten years now, after all.'

Hutch was staring into space, and Johnny felt awkward seeing him so emotional, so he picked up the bag and set off on his paper round. The square was being prepared for the ceremony, and the band was rehearsing stirring marches and sad laments for the dead.

At ten o'clock, Johnny and Winnie took their place by the war memorial. Johnny quickly found his father's name, but this year he noticed two Hutchinsons and a Murray there too. He hadn't realized before that those two had lost brothers. Gradually other people joined the crowd – all of them well wrapped up in winter clothes, stamping on the stone cobbles to keep their feet warm. Towards half past ten, Dr Langford and his wife arrived. They both looked smart. She was wearing a stylish black coat with a wide fur collar, bought in the days when they still had plenty of money. Her hair was pulled back into a tight bun under her hat, showing off the fine features beneath her wrinkled skin. Even Johnny could tell that she was naturally elegant. Maybe it was that French blood the doctor had told him about.

Mrs Langford exchanged some pleasant words with Winnie as they waited for the parade to begin. Dr Langford quietly shook hands with several of his former patients. He pinched Johnny's cheek in his well-meaning, but painful, way.

The bandsmen were just lifting their instruments to start playing when a large black car swept into the square. Johnny was collecting cigarette cards with pictures of all the latest models, and he recognized it straight away as the most luxurious of the set: it was a Rolls-Royce Phantom II. A whisper ran through the crowd as people realized who had arrived. It was young Mr Frederick Bennett, the new landlord, making his first public appearance in Stambleton since his father's death. Seeing the parade about to start, he strode over to find a place at the front of the spectators, followed by a very thin woman whose long fur cloak flapped open to reveal a startlingly short dress. She squealed as her high-heeled shoes slithered on the uneven cobblestones. The couple wriggled in between the Langfords, right opposite the vicar, who was about to signal the start of the service. Frederick Bennett kept whispering to Mrs Langford during the hymns and between the prayers. No one else said anything, but it was as if a shout of disapproval rang around the square. At eleven o'clock Johnny could sense that his mother was having trouble holding back tears, and he took her hand for the two-minute silence. The atmosphere was ruined by several bouts of coughing from Mr Bennett's companion, whose automatic 'Pardon me' came out louder than even she could have expected.

After some marching by the old soldiers, and the laying of wreaths, the Mayor made a short speech. Then the crowd dissolved into little pockets of chatter. Johnny overheard more than one comment that Frederick Bennett wasn't a patch on his father; but he couldn't help being impressed by the car. He watched as Mr Bennett and his companion climbed back into the huge automobile. He saw them lighting cigarettes and giggling together before Bennett turned the wheel and the car screeched away towards his big house.

Dr Langford put his hand on Johnny's shoulder. 'There goes your new landlord, Johnny,' he said. 'What do you make of him?'

Johnny tried to be polite. 'He was a little rude,' he said. 'Do you think his wife is ill?'

'No. And I don't think she's his wife either, Johnny. Don't worry. That cough of hers probably has more to do with the cigarettes than any disease.'

'So she hasn't got phth . . . phthis . . . whatever it's called?'

'Phthisis . . . TB . . . No.' Dr Langford chuckled. 'She's not going to end up in the sanatorium.' And he winked, adding, 'I'm pleased to say.'

'Actually, I wanted to ask you something about the sanatorium,' said Johnny. 'I was wondering if I could visit Olwen's family there? I thought they might know how she's getting on in Wales. I've been worrying about her a bit. I could ask them for her address. I could write to her.'

'That's very sweet of you,' said the doctor, making Johnny blush. 'But I'd advise you to stay away. You'd probably be safe, but it's best not to take any risks. In any case, the sanatorium has very strict visiting rules. It's usually relatives only. This Olwen isn't a relation of yours, is she?'

'No. Just a friend. And I haven't known her very long. I've never even met her parents. They wouldn't know who I was.'

'Why don't you leave it to me, then? I still go to the sanatorium from time to time. If you want to send them something or write them a note, I'd be happy to take it with me next time I'm called in to help with a case. Just come to my house and drop it off.'

Chapter 15

MISSING

next evening Johnny got home from his
und to find his mother on her hands and
g out the cupboard under the sink. It was
sign. Whenever Winnie was worried or
ould take refuge in unnecessary cleaning.
rong, Mum?' he asked.
she said unconvincingly. She turned and
er her bucket of soap suds. Johnny
mop and soaked up the water before any
e, but Winnie was already in tears.
led out a chair and sat her down at the
the kettle on,' he said. 'Now, what is it?'
robably just being silly,' said Winnie,
hose. 'It's the Langfords. They've dis-
en I got to their house this morning the
ed and the shutters were closed. I rang
cked. There was nobody there.'
haven't cancelled their newspapers. I
as usual, morning and evening.'

Johnny said thank you, and promised to take something round in the next few days. Then he rejoined Winnie, who was talking to Mrs Langford. Mr Bennett was the subject of their conversation, too.

'The family were my husband's patients,' said Mrs Langford. 'So of course we've known him most of his life. His father and my husband were very close, you know, particularly towards the end.'

Johnny hoped that Winnie would steel herself to ask for a pay rise. He thought that perhaps, since Mrs Langford had just been reminded of how his mother had been widowed so young, she might show some pity. Winnie had sensed the moment too. 'You've heard that Mr Bennett's putting our rent up, I suppose?' she began, nervously. 'We may have to move out of the house.'

'Yes, dear,' Mrs Langford cut in, patting Winnie's hand. 'Times are hard. Hard even for us, I'm afraid. We're all going to have to tighten our belts.'

Winnie understood the signal. There was no prospect of more money from the Langfords; so she tried asking for something else. 'I'm going to have to get extra work elsewhere,' she said. 'I wonder if you could possibly write a letter of recommendation – for me to show to people I ask for jobs?'

Mrs Langford seemed relieved that Winnie had taken the hint. 'Of course,' she said. 'I'll do it today. Maybe you would like to come round to collect it? In fact, come anyway – shall we say about four o'clock? I've just asked Mr Bennett and his young lady to supper, and you can help me prepare.' Johnny noted that there was no mention of any payment for the unexpected work. Without waiting for a reply, Mrs Langford turned to call her husband. 'Come along, Giles,' she said, not wanting to raise her voice on such a solemn occasion. 'We'd better be getting home.' There was no response, so she sent Johnny. 'Run along and ask my husband to come here, dear,' she said, and Johnny did as he was told,

The doctor was caught up with chit-chat, but he understood Johnny's sign language, and Johnny returned to tell Mrs Langford that her husband wouldn't be long.

Mrs Langford pulled Johnny to one side and whispered to him. 'About the other day,' she said. 'That advertisement and what my husband was talking about. You understand, don't you – whatever happens, whoever asks you, however much you feel like boasting' – she squeezed his arm so tightly that he couldn't doubt her seriousness – 'not a word.'

118

'Of course.'
'I mean it, Johnny. I
back to your mother. S

Johnny could see that
sadder than he had
towards the memorial,
the letters that made
This wasn't the mome
could make their live
have to wait until he
doing in a way that w
he was happy, becau
were about to get bet
But then, suddenl

The very
paper ro
knees, sortir
always a bad
upset, she w
'What's w
'Nothing,'
knocked ov
grabbed the
harm was do
Johnny pu
table. 'I'll put
'Oh, I'm
blowing her
appeared. Wh
door was lock
the bell. I kno
'Well, they
delivered them

120

'Did you notice anything?'

'No. I just put the papers through the letter box.' Johnny didn't mention that he liked to get up and down that hill as fast as possible since all the trouble with Miss Dangerfield. 'Maybe they've just gone to visit friends or something?'

'But I'm sure they would have told me. I was there yesterday afternoon, remember? They didn't say anything about going away. In fact Mrs Langford suggested I should leave my basket and my apron there, since I'd be back again so soon. That's one of the things I'm worried about. I need my basket. I need my apron. I need my money too. They should pay me on Friday. What if they're not back by then?'

'They probably will be. And anyway, we'll manage,' said Johnny, tempted to tell her about the secret hoard of cash upstairs. 'I bet you'll go round in the morning and everything will be just as it should be.'

'Well, let's hope so. I'm sorry, Johnny. It's just with the worry about the rent and everything . . .' She wiped her eyes on her sleeve. 'Oh my! Look at the time. I'd better get going or I'll be late for the pub. There's some cheese on the windowsill for your tea. Will you be all right?'

'Of course. I've got lots of homework to do,' said

Johnny, who wanted to get cracking on his latest brainwave (*Send 2/6 for the Secret of Living to the Year 2000. Full refund guaranteed in the event of failure.*)

'You're such a good boy – working so hard. Now don't be afraid to turn the light up. We're not so poor that we can't afford a drop of oil. I won't have you ruining your eyes in the dark.'

'Don't worry about me, Mum. I'll be fine. You run along, and I'll come with you in the morning to see what's going on at the doctor's. I bet everything will be back to normal.'

But the next morning the Langfords' house was still locked up. Before the evening paper round, Johnny wrote a note to Olwen's parents, wishing them well and asking how to contact her in Wales. He even enclosed a stamped addressed envelope for their reply. He chose a box of toffees for the doctor to take to the sanatorium with the note. Since it was early closing day Hutch was busy in the stockroom, so Johnny put the money for the sweets under the cash register and set off to deliver the papers.

Johnny knocked on the Langfords' door, hoping that the doctor would be back, so he could pass over the present for Olwen's parents. There was no answer, and the shutters were still closed. He posted the newspaper through the letter box. It was too high for him to look through, so he couldn't tell whether the previous day's papers had been picked up. Johnny wondered where the Langfords could have gone, but then another thought struck him. What if they were inside, locked in? Suppose they were sick, or even dead? He clambered onto a window ledge, and tried to climb the drainpipe to look in upstairs. The pipe wobbled and pulled away from the wall. As he struggled to keep his balance, he felt a sharp blow across his back. It was Miss Dangerfield's walking stick.

'Got you! You little burglar,' she said as he dropped to the ground.

Johnny tried to explain. 'I'm not breaking in, Miss Dangerfield. I'm not a thief. I'm worried about the Langfords. There's no sign of them. I thought they might be trapped inside.'

'Trapped inside? Don't give me that! You know they're not there. You wanted to get in and steal something while they're away.'

'Are they away?' said Johnny.

'That's no more any of my business than it's any of yours.'

'But it is my business in a way,' said Johnny. 'They haven't cancelled their papers.'

She prodded him with her stick. 'Now get up. And talking of papers, get on with delivering them. Have you got mine?'

Johnny opened his bag to get Miss Dangerfield's copy of the *Evening Echo*. She spotted the toffees nestling alongside. 'And how do you explain these?' she asked, grabbing the box. 'Where did you get them? Stolen from Mr Hutchinson's shop, I shouldn't wonder!'

'No. I paid for them. I was bringing them to Dr Langford.'

'What! You were giving the doctor a present? Credit me with some intelligence!'

'No, they're not for him. They're for a friend. Well, for her parents actually.'

'Oh really? And what's the name of these people?'

Johnny realized he'd never known Olwen's surname. 'I'm not sure—'

'Ha! You're not sure. You're giving a box of expensive sweets to people you don't know! You expect me to believe that?' She steered him towards the gate, bashing his legs with her cane. 'Come with me. I'm taking you back to the shop.'

'But—'

'Silence! You can explain yourself to Mr Hutchinson. He's got a telephone down there, hasn't he? I may even ask him to call the police.'

She marched Johnny down the hill, and battered on the door of the shop. Hutch unlocked it, and let her in. Miss Dangerfield slammed the box of toffees down on the counter.

'Proof!' she cried. 'I tried to tell you the other day. I said this boy was up to no good, and I was right. I caught him climbing into the doctor's house, and now this. He's been stealing from you as well.'

Hutch picked up the box and looked up to the shelf. There was indeed a gap in the display.

'But I paid for them, Hutch!' Johnny croaked through the tears he had been fighting all the way to the shop. 'I tried to tell her. I paid for them. They're mine.'

Miss Dangerfield looked at Hutch. 'Is that true? Did you sell them to him?'

Hutch fumbled with the box. 'To be honest, I don't remember doing that.'

'It's a police matter,' said Miss Dangerfield. 'The boy should be locked up.'

Johnny, still crying, was trying to explain. 'You were

in the stockroom,' he sniffed. 'I had to go on the paper round, so I took them—'

'What did I tell you!' cried Miss Dangerfield,

'I took them, but I put the money under the till. It's probably still there now.'

'A likely story!' scoffed Miss Dangerfield as Hutch ran his hand along the counter and found the two-shilling piece.

'Here it is!' he said with relief.

'Ha!' said Miss Dangerfield. 'A trick. The boy's even more devious than I thought.'

Hutch took control. He opened the shop door. 'Thank you, madam, I'm sure you were only trying to help, but I will deal with things from here. Leave the boy with me, and I will talk to him.'

'You should sack him. Don't forget, I saw him breaking into the Langfords'—'

'I will ask him about that, too,' said Hutch in a polite, but firm, tone. 'Goodnight, now, Miss Dangerfield. I really must close the shop.'

She left, mumbling complaints, and Hutch bolted the door. Johnny expected him to laugh about the old woman, but he was furious.

'After all I've done for you! After all that. She says she caught you red-handed. You were trying to break in.'

'I wasn't. I was trying to have a look to see if something had happened to the Langfords. Their house is all locked up.'

'So? Maybe they've gone away for a few days.'

'Why didn't they say they were going?'

'How should I know?

'Suppose they're locked in? Suppose they're sick or something?'

Hutch was getting exasperated. 'Don't be daft. He's a doctor. And they've got a telephone. What are the chances of them being stranded inside their own house? You're just letting your imagination run away with you. Miss Dangerfield was right about one thing. It's none of your business.' He took a deep breath. He looked stern. 'Now, I've promised her I'll deal with the matter.'

'No!' Johnny's nose began to run. 'No! Don't sack me, Hutch. Please.' He looked at Hutch with desperate pleading in his streaming eyes.

Hutch was calming down. 'I'm not going to sack you, but I'm taking you off that part of the paper round, and I'm knocking sixpence off your pay. I'll deliver Miss Dangerfield's papers myself until the Langfords get back and all this blows over. You keep away from there.'

'All right,' said Johnny.

Hutch handed him the box. 'You'd better take these. But remember, you're not going to have so much money in future. You certainly won't be able to spend it on fancy sweets.'

'They weren't for me,' said Johnny, and he explained about Olwen's family at the sanatorium, and how the sweets had been a present.

Hutch's mood softened. 'And you paid for them out of your own money?'

Johnny sniffed. 'Yes,' he said, letting Hutch believe he had been saving up his wages.

'Well, that's very good of you, Johnny,' said Hutch, handing over his handkerchief so that Johnny could dry his eyes. 'I'm impressed. I think Miss Dangerfield has misjudged you, and if there's one thing I can't stand it's people making false accusations. But you keep away from her – and from the Langfords' house until they get back. She might go straight to the police next time, and trouble with the police is the last thing your family needs at the moment.' Hutch put the toffees back on the shelf, and gave Johnny his two shillings. 'Charity begins at home, son,' he said. 'Give this to your mother, if you feel you can spare it. Now, get off home, and don't be late tomorrow.'

Johnny was almost exhausted with relief, but he ran home, hoping to catch Winnie before she left on her long walk to the pub. He met her as she was closing the front door, and he walked with her, trying to explain what had happened before she heard about it from Miss Dangerfield. Winnie understood how horrible it was for Johnny, being accused of something he hadn't done, and why he'd wanted to see in through the Langfords' upstairs windows, but she was angry with him for climbing and breaking the drainpipe.

'It was a stupid thing to do,' she said. 'Dangerous, too. That house looks good, but everything's starting to fall apart. If you wanted to look in upstairs, you should have gone up a tree or something.'

'I still could,' said Johnny, inspired by Winnie's throwaway remark.

'But you can't risk being seen by Mrs Dangerfield. She'd be back at the post office complaining about you all over again.'

'Not if you come with me. She wouldn't dare tell me off if you were there.' Johnny was getting excited about his plan. 'Come on. You want to know what's inside, too, don't you? Let's go together.'

'What, now? said Winnie, startled. 'But it's dark.

And it will still be dark before you go to school in the morning.'

'All right then – later tomorrow. When it's light. I'll get out of school at dinner time. Meet me at the Langfords' and I'll climb a tree in the garden and tell you what I see.'

'I'm not sure,' said Winnie. 'I'll sleep on it.'

She did, and in the end her concern over her basket, her apron, and whether she would ever get her wages over-rode her natural caution. Johnny climbed an old pear tree. He'd hardly had time to steady himself before he heard the sound of a sash window opening. But the noise was coming from over the road.

'You boy!' shouted Miss Dangerfield. 'You, boy, get away from there!'

'Oh no,' said Winnie, quivering with fear. 'You'd better come down, Johnny. She's seen you.'

'Just a minute, Mum,' said Johnny. 'I'm up here now. I might as well carry on. You pretend you're angry with me, and I'll stay up here till I've had a good look.'

So Winnie started shouting at Johnny while he clambered through the branches, looking into the Langfords' house. He tried to sound as if he was answering back rudely, but he was really giving Winnie a running commentary on what he could see. They made a good team, but all Johnny had to report on was a row of empty bedrooms and a tidy study.

'Well, that was a waste of time,' said Winnie as they strode back towards the gate. 'I feel terrible now. That was really wrong, looking in someone's windows. We'll just have to accept that the Langfords have taken off without paying me. Maybe they'll explain it all if they ever come back, but until then, Hutch wants you to stay away from here, and so do I. Promise me you will.'

'All right. I promise.'

'Good boy,' said Winnie, taking his hand. 'We'll just put all this behind us.'

Miss Dangerfield was still watching from an upstairs room, muttering to herself about 'that Swanson woman'. It seemed that she was just as bad as her nasty little son.

Chapter 16

THE CLONG

The weekend came and went, and the Langfords were still away. Nobody apart from Johnny and Winnie seemed bothered, so Johnny decided to use his new advertising skills to try to find them. He was already intrigued by the 'personal columns' in the newspapers, where people put in strange messages that meant nothing to anyone but themselves. He'd seen: *Masham. Contact Dawkins. Something to your advantage*, and, *Cad. I don't care. So there. Flopsy*. Now he composed one of his own: *Langford. Please contact Swanson. Worried*. At threepence a word, he had to drop something to get the cost down to a shilling. He decided to lose the 'please', but keep 'worried', which he had already substituted for 'urgent'. Even at a shilling it was expensive compared with his other adverts, because of course it wasn't going to bring in any money. He knew from his deliveries that the Langfords read the *Stambleton Echo* and the *London Times*. He put his advert in the London paper, since they could get that anywhere, and he was pretty sure they weren't in Stambleton.

A fortnight later, there was no response.

But the rest of Johnny's advertising business was booming. Letters were still coming in from the lovelorn and the poets, one of whom was now writing to 'PO Box 9' with a new creation, and two shillings, every few days. A new advertisement – *Make Your Shoes Last Twice as Long* – was a big hit in a Norfolk newspaper. There were no complaints about the answer: *Hop everywhere. Remember to change legs.*

The rabbit on top of the wardrobe was becoming quite heavy with money. One Tuesday in December, almost a month after the Langfords had disappeared, Johnny thought he would cheer up his mother on her night off from the pub by spending some of his cash on a cake for tea. He told Hutch that Auntie Ada was paying for it, but he planned to knock it about a bit on the way home, and pretend to Winnie that Hutch had sent it because it was damaged and would otherwise be thrown away.

Both Hutch and his mother had forbidden him to approach the doctor's house, and for weeks Johnny had gone home the long way round; but tonight it was raining and the wind was rising, and he couldn't resist taking his old route past the Langfords'. The days were so short now that it was dark whenever he wasn't at school, and he was sure that in the bad weather Miss Dangerfield wouldn't be outside to spot him, even if she still cared what he did.

Did he imagine the light? He walked up the hill into the December gale, with his head down most of the time to keep the sharp sleet out of his eyes. But he looked up now and then, trying to make out the shape of the Langfords' house against the moonless sky. He'd always thought that the house must have been built by someone who'd made up the plans as he went along. From one side it appeared to have four floors; from another, only two. Wings stuck out in all directions, each with its roof sloping at a different angle. By day it was easy to spot the house, but in the dark, with nobody home, nothing was clear.

But maybe the Langfords were back? Johnny was sure, even from halfway down the hill, that he saw a glow in one of the upstairs windows. He started running towards it, but it was gone. Then it was back again, lower down now, and moving. He caught a glimpse of a silhouette. Was it a person, or the shape of one of the branches between him and the house, bouncing in the strengthening wind? He ran to the front gate.

Usually it squeaked as it opened, but tonight the sound couldn't be heard above the din of the storm. There was a noise from the back of the house. Was it a car, or another blast of wind? The gale was so strong now that Johnny struggled simply to walk forward, clutching the cake inside his coat; trying to keep it dry.

He banged on the front door. There was no answer, and the shutters were still closed across the windows, but he had a feeling that something had changed – that someone had been there just before him. The drift of leaves that had collected on the front step over the past month had almost disappeared. Had it been blown away by the storm, or had somebody kicked it aside to open the door?

Johnny thumped again, rang the bell, and waited. But nobody came, so he set off for home, still protecting the cake, and bursting to tell his mother that someone might have been inside.

He arrived dripping wet and full of babble. Winnie stood silently by the table as he jabbered about what he thought he had seen. At first he didn't notice that she wasn't speaking – that she didn't seem to be taking in what he was saying about the Langfords and the light. Then he sensed that she was angry. Of course! She had told him not to go there. She must be cross. He stopped talking. She still just stood and stared down at the table.

It was laid for three. That was strange. They never had visitors. It was always just the two of them, if that. More often these days they each ate alone, because Winnie was out at work so much. Johnny looked around. There was no one else in the room.

'Is someone coming to supper?' he asked. Then he saw a chance to get back his mother's favour – he unbuttoned his coat and took out the cake. 'What a stroke of luck!' he said. 'Hutch gave me this as I was leaving the shop. He was throwing it out because – well, you can see. It's got a bit squashed. No one would want to buy that now, would they?' He knew he was talking too much – saying too many words too quickly to sound as casual and convincing as he wanted to. But at least the cake really was soggy and deformed after its journey home in the rain.

Winnie still said nothing.

Johnny felt he had to fill the gap. 'Who's coming, Mum? Who's the extra place for?'

'Can't you guess?' said Winnie, in a voice laced with a bitterness Johnny seldom heard.

Johnny was stumped. How could he know who she'd invited to share their meal?

Winnie's voice had a note of sarcasm now. 'It shouldn't be too difficult for you. After all, you know her better than I do.'

'Who? I don't know, Mum. Tell me. Don't make me guess. I can't think of anyone.' His mind raced through the women they knew, but none of them ever came inside the house, let alone to tea. Could it be someone important? One of his teachers perhaps? Please, no. Not that. Mrs Slack? Or worse, Miss Dangerfield? Was Winnie trying to make peace with her?

Winnie stood still, stern and smouldering. Then she snatched the cake from Johnny and slid it out of its wet paper bag straight onto the table. She picked up the bread knife and thrust it towards him so hard that for the first time in his life he thought she might really want to hurt him. 'You cut it,' she spat. 'Does she like cake? How much does she want? You decide. You're the one who knows all about her.'

With a blow of physical horror, Johnny realized why his mother was so angry. A few days before, in the shop, Hutch had named the sensation that Johnny was experiencing now. They had been quietly unloading a delivery when Hutch had stopped dead and clapped his hand to his mouth. Johnny had wondered if he was ill, but Hutch explained that he wasn't unwell, he had just had a terrible 'clong'. A 'clong', he said, was 'a rush of cold sick to the heart'. It was what happened when everything was going well, and you suddenly realized that you should be somewhere else, or had let somebody down, or were about to be found out. For Hutch, that day, the clong came when he recalled a promise to provide refreshments for the Mayor and Mayoress as they paid an official visit to the Chamber of Commerce. The event had already started, and Hutch had done absolutely nothing about it. It had slipped from his mind completely. Until the clong.

Now Johnny felt that same chilly, electric sickness. There was a metallic buzz in his joints, and his body seemed to be gearing up to run, though his feet were too heavy to move. He could feel his brain lurching to invent explanations, but failing to find even two coherent words. He wished he was still outside, with that wonderful expectation of how happy his mother would be to hear about the lights at the Langfords', and to see the wonderful cake. But there was no chance of happiness now. Because before his mother spoke again, Johnny knew what she was going to say:

'Go on, Johnny,' she shouted, with a catch of hysteria in her voice. 'Cut her a slice. Go on. Cut a nice slice of cake for your Auntie Ada!'

Chapter 17

THE ROW

'**H**ow could you?' cried Winnie. 'What were you thinking of? How could you make me look so . . .' She couldn't find a word for the humiliation she had felt when she'd run into Hutch in the street, and he had asked after her invalid sister. 'I didn't know what he was talking about.'

'He didn't tell me that he'd met you when I did the papers after school,' Johnny mumbled.

'Well, let's hope that means he doesn't know you're a liar. But he must have thought I was terribly rude.'

'What exactly did he say?'

'He said that Ada's needlework seemed to be selling very well. I just stood there, wondering who Ada was. Then he said how good I was to take my sister in when times are so hard. I thought he'd mistaken me for somebody else.'

Stupidly, Johnny seized on that as an opportunity to try to wriggle out of trouble. 'Maybe he had. Maybe there's someone else with a sister called Ada—'

'Someone else! Someone else who also has a son called Johnny who delivers Hutch's papers for him? Oh, and who also, I hear, sends letters for this Auntie Ada, and deals with all her money.'

Johnny stuttered out the beginning of a limp explanation: 'It's not . . . I haven't . . . It's just . . .'

His mother kept talking. 'I just stood there. What could I say? Thank goodness it was raining. In the end I rushed away, pretending I was cold. How could you, Johnny? How could you lie like that?' She didn't wait for an explanation, but carried on. 'Do you think for one minute that I would have stayed in this town if I'd had family somewhere else? Do you think I would have let old Mr Bennett put me in this cheap house if I'd had relatives to help me pay my own way properly? Oh, I wish I'd had a sister – or anyone to help me out when your dad was gone. Now everyone will think I was turned out by my own family. They'll think you're a . . .' She paused and wiped some spittle from her mouth. 'They'll think I had you without being married at all. They'll think that's why I'm on my own.'

'I'm sorry,' said Johnny weakly. 'I was trying to help.'

'Help? How does it help to invent an extra person?

140

What were you trying to do? Did you make up this story to get Hutch to give you all that food you've been bringing home from the shop?'

'No!' Johnny was outraged at the idea that he'd been begging for charity. 'Not that. Hutch hasn't . . .' He was about to tell her that he'd been buying the extra food. But then he realized that would mean revealing another lie – about the adverts and the money he'd been making. Instead, he tried to explain how the myth of Ada had come about. 'It just got out of hand. I needed a postal order—'

'A postal order? What would you need a postal order for?'

How could Johnny explain it all? How could he tell her about sending off for the Secret of Instant Height? About stealing from the Peace Mug? About telling Hutch that the money was for Auntie Ada's ticket to visit them? How could he account for all the other postal orders, or admit that, for more than three months, he had been placing trick advertisements in newspapers all over the country?

His mother kept on at him. 'What does a postal order have to do with this "Auntie Ada"?'

'It's just . . . It's just . . . It's just I said to Hutch that we needed to send her some money, so she could get a train and come to stay, because she was ill. And stamps for the letter. He wouldn't have opened the post office specially if it was just for me.'

'Opened up specially? What on earth did you need the post office for anyway? You're a child, Johnny! Children don't need postal orders and stamps. What were you up to?'

Johnny decided to tell part of the truth. 'I needed to place an advertisement,' he said.

'A what? You? *You* needed to place an advertisement?'

'A personal message. I've seen them in the papers. It's how people get in touch with each other when they don't have an address.'

'But why would you want to send a personal message?' She changed her voice to make 'personal message' sound la-di-dah.

'To find the Langfords,' said Johnny. 'I asked them to contact us. *Langford. Contact Swanson. Worried.* It cost me a shilling.'

'A shilling of your own money?'

Johnny, his heart pounding with guilt, stood still, staring at his feet, letting her believe it was.

'And you told Hutch it was for this auntie – this Ada?'

'Yes,' muttered Johnny, still not looking up.

Winnie thumped the table. 'Well you shouldn't have. You mustn't tell lies, Johnny. I've always told you that. It only leads to trouble.' She was still cross, but she was calming down. 'First thing tomorrow you're going to put this right. You're going to tell Hutch what you've done, and you're going to apologize. Do you understand?'

Johnny sniffed. 'Yes,' he said, though he had no idea how he would find the words to untangle everything. 'I was only trying to help. I thought if the Langfords came back you could get your wages and have your job with them again. I'm sorry.'

Winnie picked up the knife and fork she had set on the table for Ada. She turned to put them back in the drawer. 'Well, perhaps you thought you were doing your best,' she said. 'But it hasn't worked, has it?'

'What?'

'The advertisement. The Langfords haven't been in touch?'

'No.' Johnny slumped down into a chair.

Winnie took the seat on the other side of the table. Her voice was almost normal now. 'I've been trying to find the Langfords too, you know. When I ran into Hutch today I was on my way back from the sanatorium. I went there on the bus after you'd gone to school.'

'You didn't tell me you were going,' said Johnny, hoping to switch the blame and make Winnie feel guilty now.

'I wasn't sure I would go until the last minute,' she said. 'I thought they'd just turn me away and say I was being nosy if I asked if they knew where Dr Langford was. But then I had an idea. I had that letter of recommendation from Mrs Langford. I could pretend I was going to see if they had any cleaning jobs.'

Johnny stopped himself pointing out to Winnie that what she'd done was a kind of lying. 'Did they know where the Langfords have gone?' he asked.

'No. In fact they hadn't even noticed that Dr Langford was away. He doesn't have any work there just now. That case he was helping with . . . well, I'm afraid the little baby' – she paused, and tried to break the news kindly – 'passed away.'

Johnny felt another blow to his stomach. 'It was Olwen's baby sister, wasn't it?'

'Yes. I'm sorry, Johnny, but I think it must have been.'

'Does Olwen know? What about her mum and dad? They're in the sanatorium too, you know.'

'I wasn't going to ask about them, was I, Johnny? I don't even know them. Neither do you. I don't know why you're so obsessed with them. You only talked to that Olwen once, didn't you?'

'Yes, but I liked her. She was nice to me. We could have been friends. And it must be horrible for her, worrying about her family, all alone and far away.'

'At least she won't be ill, if they got her away in time. But listen, Johnny. I've got something else to tell you. It turned out that I didn't have a wasted journey.'

'What?'

'Well, as it happens, they *do* need cleaners. I'm going to start work at the sanatorium tomorrow.'

Johnny was horrified. 'What? You can't!'

Winnie began to sound enthusiastic. 'You should see it, Johnny. It's a really nice place – huge wards, and workshops, a library, a gymnasium, gardens. And it's good money. They have to pay well there. People are too frightened to go.'

'Of course they are! And they're right. It's dangerous. Dr Langford as good as told me that himself. He told me not to visit. You might get their disease. Phthisis. It's TB – consumption. You might die. Olwen's sister died!'

'I've got no choice, Johnny. The rent goes up in a couple of weeks.'

'But I can get us money,' said Johnny, desperate to tell her about the advert scam, but terrified of making her as angry as she had been before.

'You? How? Don't be silly. I'm the one who should be providing for you.'

'I won't let you go to the sanatorium,' Johnny insisted, throwing in his own bit of news. 'And anyway, what if the Langfords are back? You can work for them again. Remember? I told you. I saw lights up at the house tonight.'

Now Winnie was angry again, with a rage that had been buried by the fury over Auntie Ada. 'That's another thing!' she yelled. 'You shouldn't have gone there. You promised you wouldn't.' She was almost crying. 'Oh Johnny, what's happening to you? You've lied to Hutch. You've invented this silly aunt. You've disobeyed me. Don't we have enough troubles without all this?'

They were both weeping now, and both furious. Johnny picked up the cake and threw it against the wall. His mother jumped to her feet, knocking over her chair. She grabbed her coat from the hook on the back of the door.

'I'm going out,' she said. 'I'm going to look for those lights of yours.'

'I'll come too,' said Johnny, reaching for his jacket.

Winnie pushed him back. 'Oh no you won't. I want to be by myself. I may be a while. You get off to bed. I'll see you in the morning.'

She slammed the door behind her, and strode into the storm.

Chapter 18

WINNIE'S WALK

Winnie stomped up the hill. The wintry rain was even harder than before. In her rage, she'd forgotten her hat and gloves, and she was soaked and freezing before she reached the Langfords' house. Water was cascading from a gutter above the drainpipe that Johnny had pulled away from the wall nearly a month before. The windows were still tightly shuttered. Winnie rang the bell and thumped the door with her fists; then she went all round the house banging on windows, rattling the back door and peering though the misty glass of the conservatory. She shouted the Langfords' names, yelled hellos and, as she was overtaken by tears, gave out animal wails of anger. But there was no one there. She wandered aimlessly down the other side of the hill, away from home, towards the shops. She slipped on some mud and landed awkwardly, hurting her wrist as she tried to save herself. Back on her feet, she pushed wet strands of hair out of her eyes, smearing dirt across her face.

There was no one on the streets. They were all warm and snug in their homes – those who weren't in the pub of course. Winnie could hear the tinny plink of the piano before she turned the corner and saw the lights. She never went to that pub. She saw enough of the one she worked in, on the other side of town, and she couldn't afford to be a drinker anyway. But tonight she had a little money in her pocket – the change from her bus fare to the sanatorium. She was cold and unhappy. She pushed open the door. She recognized most of the faces, though she knew none of the people well. Everyone stopped speaking as Winnie walked to the bar, muddy and dripping. Mr Murray from the school was there. Winnie tried not to stare at his hideous wounded face, but she didn't want to seem repelled by it either.

He was equally thrown by her wild appearance. 'Good evening, Mrs Swanson,' he said, awkwardly.

Winnie couldn't reply. She was too shaken by the argument, and too embarrassed by the knowledge of what she must look like, to engage in conversation with one of Johnny's teachers.

The pub chatter gradually got going again, and the pianist restarted his tune. Everyone ignored Winnie as she huddled in a corner, sobbing, and struggling to make one little drink last for the rest of the evening.

Johnny went to bed in tears, and listened out for his mother's return. He wanted to tell her how sorry he was, and he decided that if she wasn't too angry when she got back, he would try again to stop her going to the sanatorium. If that meant coming clean about the adverts and the money in the rabbit, he would have to do it. He tried to stay awake, but somehow he missed the click of the front door and Winnie's soft steps on the stair. Very early next morning he was woken by his mother's voice outside his bedroom.

'Johnny, I've got to go,' she said. 'Don't be late for your paper round.'

It took him a moment to wake properly and get out of bed. By then she had left. He thought she must still be angry. He couldn't have known that she didn't want him to see her setting off for her new job looking pale and dishevelled, in a wet and muddy coat.

Chapter 19

NEWS

The rain had stopped, and Johnny made it to the shop in good time, prepared to be brave and to apologize to Hutch about Auntie Ada. But Hutch was cheery. He didn't mention his conversation with Winnie the previous day, and Johnny decided that it must have made much less of an impression on him than it had on her. He decided to leave his explanation until the evening, when the shop was shut and Hutch wasn't so busy. He got his deliveries done and went to school, where he spent the day mentally rehearsing his speech to Hutch, and thinking of ways to make peace with his mother. By the end of the last lesson, he felt ready to come clean.

As soon as he was outside the school gates, he knew that something strange was going on. There were groups of women gossiping in the street. No one was ever collected from school by their parents, but today Mrs Taylor was there, waiting for Albert and his little sister. She took them aside and started talking in a frenzied whisper. Albert looked alarmed, but excited. Johnny tried to listen in, but he couldn't make out any details before Mrs Taylor pulled her children further away. What had happened? Hutch would know. The shop was a great place for news, and as it was early closing day, he would have time to talk. Johnny ran all the way there.

A car was parked outside. Johnny had never seen it before. He peered through its windows. The back seat was covered with clothes, messy papers, maps and empty cigarette packets. Hutch came out. He put his hand on Johnny's shoulder.

'I was only looking,' said Johnny.

'That's all right, son,' said Hutch, in a tone that was meant to reassure him, but was so kind that it gave Johnny a jolt of panic. Hutch steered him towards the shop. 'Come inside,' he said. 'I've got something to tell you.'

A man in a brown suit and a soft hat was leaning half in and half out of the wooden telephone booth, just inside the door. He was lighting a cigarette. Johnny noticed it was the same brand as the ones in the car.

'May I have another word with you, Mr Hutchinson?' the man called as they went past.

'I'll be back with you in a moment, sir. This is my delivery boy. We just need to sort a few things out.'

Johnny didn't understand. The bag of newspapers was always ready for him, behind the counter. Why was Hutch taking him through to the stockroom?

'Sit down,' said Hutch, pointing to a tea chest. 'Johnny, lad, I've got some bad news.'

'Mum?' cried Johnny, terrified that something had happened to her at the sanatorium.

'No, Johnny. I'm sure your mother is all right. It's Dr Langford, Johnny. I'm very sorry to be the one to tell you this, but I'm afraid Dr Langford has died.'

'Where? How do you know?'

'He was found up at his house a couple of hours ago. Miss Dangerfield called the police when she noticed a window had been broken. She thought there might have been a burglary. But when the constable got in to have a look, he discovered the doctor's body.'

Johnny buzzed with shock, excitement and indignation. 'So Dr Langford was in there, dead, all this time, while everyone thought he was away? I told you. I said—'

'Well, no, Johnny. That's what I thought at first too. But that gentleman out there is a newspaper reporter, and he's told me the police are sure that Dr Langford died last night.'

Johnny thought back to the lights he had seen; then his mind started running on. 'What did he die of? Where's Mrs Langford? Was she there too?'

Hutch silenced him. 'Calm down, Johnny. I don't know many details yet, but I think it's right for me to tell you this. According to that reporter, the police think that Dr Langford was murdered.'

'Murdered? How? Why?'

'I don't know. The detectives are still up at the house. But I thought that since you knew Dr Langford well, you should hear the news from me.' Johnny was staring ahead. Hutch wasn't sure whether he had taken everything in. 'Would you like me to come home with you to tell your mother?'

'She won't be there. She's working at the sanatorium at Emberley today, and she's going to go straight on to her job at the pub tonight.'

'She'll probably hear about it there, poor woman. I'm so sorry. I know the doctor was very kind to you both.'

Johnny was stunned. He could hear his blood pumping round his ears, and his arms and legs were tingling. He remembered that he was supposed to be doing his paper round. 'I'd better go,' he said, jumping up and strapping on the bag. 'People will be waiting for their newspapers.'

'Only go if you're sure you're all right,' said Hutch. 'But Johnny, I think it will be best if I do the round in the morning. There's nothing in tonight's paper, but this business is bound to be all over tomorrow's. I wouldn't want you to have to handle the . . . the details . . . if you see what I mean.'

Johnny left with the newspapers, and Hutch went to talk to the reporter again. The news was already sweeping the town, and as Johnny passed from house to house, more people spoke to him than usual. Some even came to the door to take the paper from him rather than waiting for it to drop through the letter box. They were all disappointed that the discovery of Dr Langford's body had come too late to get into print, but they gave Johnny titbits of gossip, and he passed on the rumours as he went. By the end of his round he knew a little more: there were four police cars and an undertaker's van up at the house; the body still hadn't been removed; and the neighbours were being questioned.

Even though it meant breaking his promise again, Johnny couldn't resist climbing the hill to see what was going on; but a constable was holding back a growing crowd, and it was too dark to see the Langfords' house at all. So, since he'd finished his deliveries, he turned back towards the shop. He was overtaken by a bicycle racing downhill at speed. For a moment he thought it was Dr Langford, and he recalled those thrilling early morning lifts, perched on the crossbar. But it wasn't Dr Langford. It was a policeman. That was when it hit him. The charge of shock and excitement that had carried him through the past half-hour drained away. It was replaced by a sad emptiness he had never known before. He would never see Dr Langford again. There had been a murder. Here. In Stambleton. And the victim was someone he knew.

Chapter 20

QUESTIONING

When Johnny got to the bottom of the hill, the policeman's bicycle was outside the shop. Hutch opened the door and let Johnny in. The reporter was leaning on the counter. The constable was standing stiffly, with his helmet under his arm.

Hutch spoke first. 'Johnny, the officer wants to have a word with you. Strictly speaking, your mother should be here, but I've explained that she's at the sanatorium. They've sent a fast car for her, but I don't think she'll arrive for a while. Would you like me to stay with you while the policeman asks you some questions?'

'Yes,' said Johnny, taking off his bag. He turned to the officer. 'Do you know who killed the doctor? Is Mrs Langford all right?'

'I'm the one asking the questions, son,' said the policeman. He coughed, and gestured towards the reporter. 'Would you mind waiting elsewhere, sir?' he said, and the reporter grumpily went out to sit in his car.

Hutch bolted the door behind him. Then he brought out the high stool from behind the post office grille, and helped Johnny up to sit on it. The policeman put his helmet on the counter and took out his notebook.

'Now then, Johnny,' said the policeman, 'I'm told you knew Dr Langford well?'

'All my life,' said Johnny. 'And my mother is their cleaner.'

'Yes, your mother. We'll get to that.'

Johnny wondered what he meant.

'When were you last at Dr Langford's house?'

Johnny could feel himself blushing with guilt. 'Last night,' he said, looking at his shoes. Hutch let out a sigh. Johnny hoped he wouldn't tell the policeman that he'd forbidden him to go there.

'Were you there with your mother?' asked the officer.

'No. I was on my own. I was on my way home from the shop.'

'What time was this?

'About half past five. I thought I saw a light inside.'

'A light? Where?'

'Upstairs at first, just for a moment. And then downstairs, I think. I went to look, but there was nobody there.'

'You're sure of that? You didn't see or hear anything else?'

'It was raining, and windy. I might have heard a car.'

'You might have heard a car. A big car? A small car?'

'I don't know,' said Johnny. 'It was just a noise really. I'm not even sure it was a car.'

'And where was your mother while you were at the Langfords' house?'

'At home. She was already there when I got back.'

'And you both stayed at home for the rest of the evening?'

'Yes. Well, I did. She went out.'

'Where did she go?'

'I don't know.'

The policeman looked up from his notebook. 'You don't know? She didn't tell you? She doesn't tell you where she is when she goes out?'

'Yes, she does usually. But last night was different. I don't think she knew where she was going. She was angry. We'd had a row.'

'A row. What about?'

Johnny didn't know what to say. He couldn't explain all about Auntie Ada, especially with Hutch sitting there listening. But he knew he should tell the

159

truth, even if it wasn't the whole truth. 'It was about money. And I was cross because she was going to work at the sanatorium.'

'And why were you cross about that?'

'Because she might catch a disease there. But she said she had to go, because we need the money now that she's not getting paid by the Langfords.'

The officer licked his pencil and started writing again. 'So the Langfords had sacked her?'

'Oh no. But they went away. They've been gone for about a month. But they didn't say they were going, and Mum hadn't been paid when they left.'

'And she was angry about that?'

'Well, a bit. But not just angry. Worried. We both were. And she needed her basket and her apron. She'd left them at the Langfords' house, you see.'

'An apron, you say. What was it like?'

'Pink. And embroidered with flowers. She made it herself.'

The policeman paused to make some more notes, then he asked, 'And what time did your mother go out last night?'

'I don't know. It might have been about seven o'clock, I suppose.'

'And she was angry when she left?'

'Yes. Very angry.'

'And what time did she come back?'

'I've no idea. I tried to stay awake, but I'd fallen asleep.'

'So it was late?'

'It must have been. I was lying there for ages, till long after the wind died down. I know I'd heard the clock strike ten.'

'And this morning? Did she tell you where she'd been?'

'No. I didn't see her. She had to leave early for her new job.'

They were distracted by the bell of a police car speeding along the High Street.

'That will be them bringing your mother here now,' said Hutch. 'We'll soon get all this cleared up.'

But the car sped past the shop and onwards up the hill. The reporter started the engine of his own car and followed it.

Johnny turned to the policeman. 'Was my mum in that car?'

'Probably,' said the policeman. 'I think the detectives up at the doctor's house want to speak to her.' He turned to Hutch. 'This is a serious business, Mr

Hutchinson. The investigation may take some time. We'll have to make arrangements for this young chap to be cared for.'

Johnny was horrified at the thought of being taken away, but Hutch told the officer that wouldn't be necessary.

'The lad has an aunt at home,' he said. 'I'm sure she'll keep an eye on him.'

Johnny knew he should speak now. He should tell Hutch that he'd never had an auntie. But then he would have to explain about the postal orders and the adverts, and he couldn't do that in front of a policeman. And if the officer knew there was no one at home, Johnny might be sent away to be looked after by strangers until Winnie got back. His mouth was dry, his chest was heaving with every breath. He jumped down from the stool and raced for the door. 'I want to see my mother,' he cried, tugging on the handle. It was no use: the door was locked. 'Can't I go where she is?'

'No,' said the policeman firmly. 'That's out of the question.'

Hutch could see that Johnny was getting distressed. He put his arm round him and moved him back into the middle of the shop. 'I'll give you the makings of supper for you and your Auntie Ada,' he said. 'It's best that you wait at home for your mother to come back. Have you finished with Johnny, Officer?'

'For now, yes,' said the policeman. 'But think hard, Johnny, and see if you can remember anything else about last night. If you do, tell Mr Hutchinson here, and he can phone us at the police station or up at the Langfords' house. And don't talk to anyone else, Johnny – especially that reporter I saw here before. Make sure any information comes straight to us.'

Hutch saw the policeman out, then did as he had promised, gathering together the ingredients to make supper for two. Johnny started the speech he had memorized at school, relieved at last to have the chance to explain what he had done: how there was no Auntie Ada, and how he would be alone at home without his mother. 'Hutch,' he began, 'Hutch, there's something I've got to tell you—'

A car zipped to a halt outside. It was the reporter, back again from the crime scene. He battered on the door, asking to be let in to use the phone. Johnny's confession would have to wait.

Hutch and Johnny listened in as the reporter rang his news desk. He was twitching with excitement, holding the receiver between his shoulder and ear as he tried to light a cigarette while jabbering to his editor. Clearly some of the policemen had broken their own rule about not talking to the press. 'It's better than I thought,' the reporter panted down the phone. 'There may be two victims. They've got a suspect who had a motive for killing both the Langfords. They're ransacking the house, and they're going to search the garden in the morning. The suspect's denying everything, and refusing to say where the second body's hidden, but they're going to question her all night . . . What? Yes, that's right: *her*. The suspect is a woman.'

At that moment Johnny realized why the policeman had been asking him so many questions. His mother was in very deep trouble indeed.

Chapter 21

THE SUSPECT

It was clear the reporter had no idea that Johnny was the suspect's son. Before Hutch could steer Johnny out of earshot, the man rattled out his story for the next morning's paper to the person on the other end of the phone.

'OK. If you're ready, I'll start dictating,' he said. 'It'll need a good headline: BARMAID QUIZZED IN BLOODY DOUBLE MURDER, or something like that.' He took a drag of his cigarette and began, occasionally consulting scribbled notes, but obviously composing his article as he went along:

'*Mystery surrounds the discovery, in Stambleton yesterday, of the corpse of retired doctor Giles Langford. At first light today police begin the grim search of the Langfords' garden for the remains of his wife, Marie, feared to be the second victim of a savage double killing.*'

He paused to let the typist catch up.

'*Dr Langford was found in a pool of blood yesterday afternoon, after a neighbour observed a broken window on the first floor of his house. She suspected a burglary, but when police arrived at the scene they found that the hole in the window was too small and too high to climb through, and that there was no sign of forced entry elsewhere. They believe that the Langfords may have let their killer into the house. Both front and back doors were locked from the outside, suggesting that the murderer might be someone, such as a domestic servant, who had access to a key. A barmaid, who was once the Langfords' cleaner, was being questioned by police last night.'*

Johnny lurched towards the phone box, trying to interrupt the man; to say that Winnie wasn't really a barmaid and had never been given keys to the Langfords'. If she had, she would have gone inside weeks ago to see if everything was all right. But Hutch grabbed hold of Johnny, stopped him speaking and pulled him into the stockroom as the reporter flipped to another page of his notebook and continued:

'Giles Langford (seventy-two) was well respected in the area for his work during the tuberculosis outbreak in 1916. Trained at St Bartholomew's Hospital in London, and Lille University in France, he . . .'

Hutch closed the door. 'You mustn't talk to that man,' he whispered. 'Remember what the officer said.' He handed Johnny the bag of food. 'Now, you get home to your auntie. I'll stay here to close up.'

'Hutch . . .' said Johnny, thinking that he really should say that there was no aunt, and that he would be going back to an empty house. 'Hutch . . .'

But Hutch shooed him out of the back door. 'Go now, Johnny, before he gets off the phone. You don't want him asking you any questions.'

So Johnny ran home, and sat at the table with food enough for two but absolutely no appetite at all. There was nothing unusual about him being alone – these days Winnie was often out working in the evenings – but Johnny felt her absence more than ever. His mind raced over what he had heard. He tried desperately to persuade himself that the evidence didn't point towards his mother, but he could see that it might. And yet never, not even for a second, did he believe that Winnie was guilty of the crime. When he closed his eyes, he imagined Dr Langford on the floor surrounded by blood. He was worried about Mrs Langford too. Was she lying somewhere in the garden? Poor Mrs Langford. Had she already been there when he went up to the house in the storm? Had he walked past her body? Had he seen the murderer silhouetted against the light?

He went upstairs to his room. He needed something to do, to take his mind off the horrors up on the hill and the image of his mother in a cell. Usually, he'd have had a clutch of replies to PO Box 9 to deal with, but Hutch hadn't given him any that night. He understood now why Winnie fell to cleaning and sorting when she was worried. He tidied up his few possessions and made his bed. He unpacked his satchel. He'd already done his homework (during a History lesson) to give himself time to write out some new adverts at home. On any other night, that would have filled the hours till bed time. But he couldn't do it now. He couldn't think up silly jokes to trick people out of money. Because it was all his fault. Johnny could see that. If he hadn't invented Auntie Ada; if he hadn't done the adverts; if he hadn't lied, Winnie would never have stormed off that night, and none of this would be happening.

He opened the door to his mother's bedroom. These days he hardly ever went in there, but he remembered how he used to climb into bed with her when he was little, and how she would cuddle away his nightmares and kiss away his fears. The room was perfectly tidy. There was nothing to do in there. Winnie's nightdress was hanging on the bedstead. It still smelled of her. He spread it out on the bed and lay down alongside it. Then the tears came. He cried till he ached.

And suddenly it was morning. Johnny was still wearing yesterday's clothes, the pattern of Winnie's bedspread was imprinted on his cheek, and it was time to get up.

Chapter 22

GUILTY

He went to the shop even though Hutch had told him not to, but Hutch wouldn't let him deliver the papers. While Hutch was out doing the round, Johnny read the copies kept on the counter for sale. Most of them had brief versions of the story that added nothing to what he already knew. Several ended with a phrase he had seen in papers before. He'd always thought it rather comical, but today it had an ominous ring. *A woman is helping the police with their enquiries.* That was his mother they were talking about.

He desperately wanted to see her: to tell her that he knew she was innocent, and to find out whether she needed anything. It wasn't far to the police station. He was sure he could get there and back before Hutch had finished the paper round. He felt bad about leaving the shop unlocked, but he thought Hutch would understand.

*

Johnny had never been in the police station before. From time to time he'd seen people going in or out, but the doors always swung shut behind them. He'd imagined the scene beyond those doors: rows of cells, with frantic prisoners shaking at the iron bars, and fierce guards snarling, truncheons at the ready, making sure that no one escaped. So it was a bit of a disappointment to discover that the inside of the police station looked rather like the office at the Stambleton Echo. There was no sign of any criminals at all.

Johnny found himself in a small room with a dark wooden counter. There was no one behind the desk, just a silver bell and a sign saying: RING FOR ATTENTION. Johnny rang the bell. Nothing happened. He didn't know what to do. He didn't want to get into trouble for ringing it twice, but what if no one had heard it? He decided to wait, and sat down on a hard wooden bench, reading a poster about the penalties for riding a bicycle without lights.

He was just about to reach for the bell again when the door behind the counter opened, and a large policeman came through, backwards, pushing the door with his bottom. He was holding a teapot and a mug, and had a thick slice of bread and jam gripped between his teeth. As he swung round, he noticed Johnny. He let the bread drop onto the counter and put down the pot.

'I didn't know you were there,' he said, gruffly. 'You should have rung the bell.'

Johnny was about to say that he had rung, but then he thought it might sound like answering back, and he could sense that the policeman wouldn't like that.

'What do you want?' asked the policeman, angrily picking up the bread, which had fallen jam-side down.

'I'd like to see my mother, please.'

'And who might she be?'

'Winifred Swanson,' said Johnny. 'She's helping the police with their enquiries.'

At the sound of Winnie's name, the policeman drew himself upright and adopted a more formal tone. 'Mrs Swanson is here, yes. But I'm afraid you can't see her. We don't let children in to see the prisoners. This isn't a playground. Only adult relatives or legal representatives.'

'But she hasn't got any adult relatives.'

'Don't be silly, boy. Everyone's got adult relatives.'

'But . . .' Once again Johnny got the silent message that arguing would only make things worse. He tried asking a question instead. 'When will she be coming home?'

'Not for some time, I should think, son. Though it's not my place to say. Your mother is in a great deal of trouble. Murder is a capital offence.'

A capital offence. Johnny knew what that meant, but hearing the policeman say the words made him admit to himself, for the first time, that there was a chance that Winnie would be put to death. A capital offence meant the gallows. Murderers were hanged. In all the agony of last night, Johnny had never imagined that he might lose his mother for ever. He was suddenly drenched in sweat. There was a rush of sickly acid from his stomach to his throat. Surely, now that the police had talked to Winnie all night – now that they could see how quiet and gentle she was, and she'd had a chance to explain everything – surely they couldn't believe that she was guilty? And yet this policeman seemed to think it was possible. It was all a dreadful mistake. Johnny tried to say so, but the officer silenced him.

'Now be on your way. I'm a busy man.'

'Please would you tell her that I came? Tell her Johnny was here?'

'Do I look as if I have time to pass on messages?'

Johnny stopped himself saying yes. 'But if she asks . . .'

He had gone too far. The policeman had had enough, and wanted to get back to his breakfast.

'Look, son. I've got work to do. And you should be getting off to school, shouldn't you?'

'But . . .' It was no good. 'Please give her my love,' Johnny called as he went back through the swing doors. He ran to the shop in tears, imagining his mother alone in a cell, facing the death penalty.

Hutch returned looking ashen, and mumbling swear words under his breath. 'You're going to have to be careful, Johnny,' he said. 'There are people out there who have decided your mother is guilty before she's even been charged. I don't dare repeat some of the things I've heard this morning.'

'She didn't do it, Hutch.'

'I know, son. I'm sure she can't have done. But the police seem to think they have enough evidence against her. They're not looking for anyone else. If we knew as much as the police, perhaps we could prove that they should.'

'How can we find out?'

'Well, if your mother could afford a fancy lawyer,

he'd check everything. But I know there's no money for that. It looks as if it's down to you and me, son.'

Someone was tapping on the shop door.

Hutch shouted, 'We're not open till nine o'clock,' without looking up. The knocking continued. It was the reporter again, signalling with fancy hand gestures that he wanted to use the phone.

'I'd better let him in,' said Hutch. 'And anyway, he might have some new information. You go and sit in the stockroom. I don't want him to know you're here.'

Hutch tried to get on the right side of the reporter as soon as he opened the door. 'Sorry, I didn't realize it was you,' he said. 'You're up early.'

'I've got to move fast on this one,' said the reporter. 'I want to get everything I can into the early edition. If they charge her, we won't be able to print much until she comes up in court.'

'And how long will that be?'

'Well, there'll have to be a remand hearing very soon if they want to keep her in custody, but the magistrates can put big restrictions on how much of that we can report. The police will make their case for holding her in jail, but we can't put all the evidence in the paper in case it influences a future jury.'

'And have the police got a good case?' asked Hutch.

'Seems like it to me. She was seen there on the night of the murder, and her apron was found at the scene, soaked in the doctor's blood. It certainly sounds as if she's the criminal type. I've been talking to that Miss Dangerfield. She's told me all about her.'

Johnny was tempted to burst out of his hiding place and punch the man, or at least to tell him what a nasty, cruel woman Miss Dangerfield was. But he stayed where he was, listening, as the reporter continued:

'And this Swanson woman had a motive. The police know why she went to the Langfords' house. They owed her money.'

Johnny had another clong. He felt shaky, and his mouth was dry. He realized why the police thought his mother had a motive for murdering the Langfords. He had told them. He had explained to the constable the night before that Winnie hadn't been paid, and he had said that she was angry, though he hadn't dared say why. He'd even described Winnie's apron: the pink one with the dainty daisies. So Johnny was as much to blame as Miss Dangerfield. He had given the police a reason to believe that his own mother was a killer.

The reporter went to the phone. He closed the

door on the little kiosk, but Hutch and Johnny could still make out what he was saying to his editor. He was relishing the story. It involved High Society now: for the suspect had revealed that the Langfords had entertained young Mr Bennett and his fiancée to supper on Remembrance Day – the last day that anyone had seen them alive. Now the detectives were planning to drive over to the Bennett mansion to talk to the most powerful man in town.

'I'd better hurry,' the reporter yelled down the phone. 'I want to get there before the police do.'

It gave Johnny an idea. This was his chance to get close to the men in charge of the investigation – to find out what they knew, and to persuade them that Winnie couldn't possibly be guilty.

Chapter 23

HIGH-CLASS INFORMATION

Without a word to Hutch, Johnny ran out of the shop before the reporter had even put down the receiver. He dived into the back of the reporter's car, cramming himself down onto the floor and pulling some of the rubbish from the seat on top of himself in the hope of being camouflaged. A minute later the reporter jumped into the front, lit up a cigarette, and accelerated away. With his ear pressed against the floor of the car, Johnny heard the rumble of the main road, dull thumps as they turned onto a country lane, splashes as the wheels rocked through puddles, and then the crunch of gravel as the car drew up outside Mr Bennett's grand house.

The reporter got out, leaving his door open. Through a gap under the seat, Johnny saw him walk across to talk to a man who was washing Mr Bennett's car.

The reporter stroked the bonnet. 'Quite a beast. A Phantom Two, isn't it?'

'Watch it,' snapped the man, wiping the part the reporter had touched. 'I've just polished that bit.'

'Sorry. Takes a bit of looking after, I should think?'

'The engine's fine, but it's like any other car: if you drive through the countryside, you have to clean off the mud. Mr Bennett wants it spick and span for this afternoon.'

'Where's he off to?'

The handyman stopped rubbing the car and looked quizzically at the reporter. 'Who wants to know?'

The reporter drew closer to the man, and offered him a cigarette. Johnny couldn't hear everything now, but from the tone of the mumbled words he guessed that the reporter was trying to get information about Mr Bennett, and to talk his way into the house. Johnny was scared that it wouldn't work. If the reporter was sent away, his own journey would be wasted. So he wriggled over to the other side of the car and opened the door as quietly as he could. Then he slithered out and crawled into some shrubs by the front door. The winter leaves were sparse. If the reporter turned round he would be certain to spot Johnny curled up there, trying to hide. But Johnny was saved when a police car rolled in and pulled up right by the flowerbed.

A man got out and planted his huge foot within inches of Johnny's head. He was wearing ordinary shoes, not the boots that uniformed policemen had. His brown raincoat almost brushed against Johnny's face. Johnny was frightened, but he was glad he'd come. These were real plain-clothes detectives: the top men. Fortunately the man by the flowerbed didn't detect Johnny. He strode straight over to the Rolls-Royce, and after some stern words the reporter got back in his car and drove away. Another policeman rang the doorbell and spoke to the butler, who let the visitors in and closed the door. Johnny crept round the outside of the house, trying to get out of sight of the handyman, who was polishing the car again. He was hoping to find another way into the house.

The back door was open, and there was no one around. Johnny could hear the butler in the distance, talking to the policemen.

'If you would be so good as to wait in here, gentlemen, I will tell Mr Bennett that you wish to see him.'

Johnny made his way in the direction of the voices. He followed a dark corridor leading from the servants' area to the front of the house, and stopped where the drab linoleum met the polished marble of the circular entrance hall: a vast open space, with doors all round the edge, lit by a dome of glass. He saw the butler emerge from a room on one side of the ring and walk across to another, directly opposite. Johnny guessed that the policemen were in the first room and Mr Bennett in the second. There was an ornate coat-rack on the wall to his left, not far from the door to the policemen's room. He recognized the overcoat Bennett had worn on Remembrance Day, and his girlfriend's long fur cloak. He heard voices: Mr Bennett and the butler were about to come out and cross the hall. If Johnny stayed where he was, they were bound to see him. If he went back down the corridor, he might not be able to hear what they were saying. On impulse, he ran round the edge of the room and slid behind the fur cloak. It almost covered him, but didn't quite reach the floor. He reached up, grabbed the hook, bent his knees and pulled his feet out of view just in time. It was just as well. The policemen heard Bennett coming and strode into the hall to meet him. Johnny had to stay very still. His arm ached with the strain of supporting his weight, and he wedged his feet against the wall to get steady. With his other hand, he felt a slit in the side of the cloak, where the lady would have put her arms through. He slowly pulled it up to his face. The fur tickled his nose, but he could see now. The butler looked annoyed. No doubt he thought the policemen should have stayed where he had put them, but Johnny was glad they hadn't. In the echoing rotunda he could hear every word.

'That will be all, Maxwell,' said Bennett, and the butler nodded an automatic 'Very good, sir.' He strode off, almost brushing against the fur cloak on his way to the servants' corridor.

Frederick Bennett had not been up long, and was still in his dressing gown. He'd been toying with his breakfast when Maxwell had announced that the police wanted to see him, and he'd come to meet them with the newspaper in one hand and a piece of toast in the other.

'A bad business,' he said, using the toast to point to the story about the murder. 'Langford was our family physician, you know. Perhaps that's why you've come?'

'Indeed, sir,' said the older of the two detectives, who introduced himself as Inspector Griffin. 'We were wondering if you might be able to throw some light on the Langfords' whereabouts for the past month. We gather that you and your fiancée dined with them on November the eleventh.'

'Absolutely,' said Mr Bennett, 'though Miss Carmichael and I are not engaged to be married, Inspector. We never were, and I'm pleased to say that we never will be. Miss Carmichael has returned to her job at the Gaiety Theatre in London.'

The inspector gave Bennett an understanding smile. The tale of a rich young man temporarily infatuated with a show girl was a familiar one. He returned to the point. 'It seems that you may have been the last people to see the Langfords before they disappeared.'

'Disappeared?' Bennett sprayed crumbs from his mouth as he finished the last of his toast. 'They didn't disappear, Inspector. Whatever gave you that idea? No. They went to France. They may have left a bit abruptly, but they told me they were going.' The junior detective got out a notebook and started writing as Bennett continued. 'They talked about it over supper that night. I remember clearly. Mrs Langford received a telephone call while we were there. One of her relatives – a cousin, I think – was seriously ill. They were going over to visit her – to see if they could help. I imagine it's quite useful to have a retired doctor in the family at a time like that.'

'I dare say,' said the inspector. 'So you are sure they both went?'

'Yes, but Mrs Langford wrote to tell me that her husband was on his way back. The letter came only the other day. I may still have it. Would you like me to try to find it?'

'That would be very good of you, sir,' said the inspector. Johnny could tell he was trying not to show too much enthusiasm about a possible lead.

'Come this way, then, gentlemen,' said Bennett, leading them into a third room, right next to the coat-stand. When they were all inside, Johnny let his feet drop to the floor and shook out his aching arm. Then he edged along to look round the door-frame. It was Mr Bennett's study. He was facing the window, rummaging through large piles of papers on the desk. The two detectives stood on either side of him. To Johnny's relief, all three had their backs to him.

'It should be here somewhere,' said Bennett, 'unless I threw it out straight away. To be honest, I only glanced at it when it arrived. It didn't seem very important at the time.'

'I quite understand, sir,' said Inspector Griffin, 'but do please have a look if you don't mind.'

'I've had a tremendous amount of correspondence since my father died: letters of condolence, family business, and so on. Things still aren't straight after more than a year. There are rather a lot of bills, I'm afraid – what with the state of the stock market, and death duties, of course. You know how it is.'

The inspector grunted sympathetically as Bennett leafed through his paperwork.

'Ah! We're in luck,' said Bennett, holding up a sheet of paper. 'There's no address, I'm afraid. Just a date – Friday the thirtieth of November nineteen twenty-nine.' He lifted a silver-framed calendar from his desk. 'So, let's see, that's two weeks ago tomorrow.'

'Exactly so,' said Inspector Griffin. 'It should give us an idea of the whereabouts of Dr and Mrs Langford on that day at the very least. Would you be so good as to read us the rest of the letter?'

Bennett continued: '*Dear Frederick, Do forgive me for taking so long to write, but as you know we left for France in rather a hurry. Giles and I both want to tell you formally how grateful we are for your generous donation towards the work of the sanatorium at Emberley.*'

Bennett cleared his throat with mock modesty. 'I was very impressed with what Dr Langford and his colleagues were doing there. TB is such a wretched disease. One has to give what one can.' The policemen nodded. Bennett continued reading. He was walking around the room now, and every now and then Johnny had to dart back to avoid being seen.

'It was quite unexpected, and I assure you that my only motive in inviting you to supper was to enjoy the pleasure of your company, and that of your charming friend— Well, not quite so charming, as it's turned out. But never mind . . . My cousin's health – Ah, I was right: it was a cousin – My cousin's health is improving somewhat, and my husband feels that he should be able to return to England in ten days or so.'

The younger policeman, more smartly dressed than Griffin but rather quiet, Johnny thought, for a detective, spoke for the first time. 'It all fits. He was killed on Tuesday. That's ten days exactly after the letter was written.'

Inspector Griffin still had his back to the door, but Johnny could tell from an angry flick of his wrist that he disapproved of the interruption. The polite wave that followed indicated that Mr Bennett should continue reading:

'I, however, will stay in France to help with her convalescence. We will leave Avignon – Ah, Avignon. That was it. That's where they went – leave Avignon next week for a country hotel where I intend to stay until after Christmas. Once again, thank you for your generosity. Your friend, Marie Langford.'

He folded the letter and offered it to Inspector Griffin. 'You may keep this if it is of any interest to you.'

The inspector took it with a grateful bow. He looked over the letter. 'So we can assume that Mrs Langford is abroad.'

'Yes. That's a relief, anyway,' said Bennett. 'It means you can be pretty sure she's safe.'

Johnny was thrilled to hear it. At least that was one worry off his mind.

Inspector Griffin nodded. 'As you probably read in the paper, we have been looking for another body, just in case, sir. I think we can stop that search now. But we need to inform the poor lady that her husband is dead.'

'How will you find her?' said Bennett. 'She must have left Avignon already. All we know from the letter is that she's at a country hotel somewhere in France. That's not much to go on.'

The second detective spoke again. 'No. And we don't even know where she was staying in Avignon. If we did, we could ask the people there where she and her aunt moved to.'

Griffin interrupted him. 'Do you still have the envelope, by any chance, sir? Perhaps an address was written on it. It's the continental way. Even a post-mark might help.'

'I'm afraid not, Inspector. I put envelopes on the fire as soon as I open them. Otherwise I would be drowning in paper here.'

'I quite understand. But what a shame. I fear it may take some time to locate Mrs Langford.'

'I only hope she doesn't read the English news-papers, wherever she is. It would be awful for her to hear about her husband's death from the press.'

'Indeed, sir. But we will do our best to find her, and to break the news as gently as we can. I don't think we need detain you any longer.'

Mr Bennett started ushering them towards the door. Johnny slid back under the fur coat just in time. As Bennett opened the front door he said, casually, 'It says in the paper that you have a suspect. May I ask who it is?'

'Well, strictly speaking, I shouldn't tell you, sir. But I'm sure we'll be charging her today. It's the Langfords' cleaning woman, sir. A Mrs Swanson. Do you know her?'

'Not to speak to. But she's one of my tenants. She lives in one of the houses on Dagmouth Lane. I'm plan-ning a lot of improvements on that part of the estate.'

Johnny would have liked to add that any building works were an excuse to drive up the rent, but he held his tongue as Bennett stopped on the doorstep and continued: 'Funnily enough, now I think about it, I remember Marie Langford mentioning Mrs Swanson over supper that day. She said the woman was looking for extra work. She asked me if there were any jobs here. Apparently Winnie Swanson is a bit hard up.'

'That's what we've heard too, sir,' said Griffin, holding out his hand to say goodbye. 'It seems that money may be at the heart of all this.'

'The things people will do for cash,' said Bennett, shaking his head. 'It beggars belief.'

Johnny wanted to talk to the detectives, to convince them that his mother was innocent. It was why he had come. But now he could only do it if he revealed that he had been hiding and listening in to everything they'd said. For a split second the brave part of him – the part that would do anything for his mother – urged him to show himself; but in an instant his fear of getting into trouble triumphed. He even persuaded himself that being caught would make things worse for Winnie. He stayed hidden under the cloak.

He heard the door close, and the police car pull away. He regretted his decision straight away. The chance to meet the inspector had gone, but he was still at risk of being caught. He was trapped for as long as Mr Bennett stayed in the hall. Johnny sensed that Bennett was walking towards him. He peeped through the slit again, only to see Bennett staring straight back, his eyes filled with contempt. Johnny held his breath; then Bennett broke the tension, turning to shout down the corridor to the butler.

'Maxwell! Some fresh coffee in the morning room!' Johnny relaxed as Bennett started walking away to restart his breakfast, but then he stopped, and yelled again: 'And Maxwell, get rid of that fur coat. Miss Carmichael won't be coming back.'

A distant shout of 'Very good, sir' came from the kitchen. Johnny panicked. He couldn't leave his hiding place while Bennett was in the hall, but there was no way he could risk staying there till Maxwell re-entered and tore the cloak from its peg. He watched Bennett walk slowly back to the breakfast room, but a heartbeat later he heard Maxwell coming up the passage. The butler turned towards the coat-stand and looked the fur up and down. But his hands were full. He sniffed. No doubt he'd deal with the coat after he'd put down his tray.

As soon as Maxwell was in attendance on his master, Johnny ran for the back door. He didn't want to risk meeting the handyman, or walking on the noisy gravel at the front of the house, so he crossed the grounds till he found a wall. It was a long walk back to the post office, but he was elated to have got away, and glad to be carrying Hutch the good news that Mrs Langford was safe.

Chapter 24

THE HEARING

Winnie was due to appear in court on the next Wednesday afternoon. Wednesday was early closing day in Stambleton. All the shops shut at noon, including Hutchinson's General Store and Post Office, and Hutch told Johnny that he would go to the court to see what happened. Johnny, he said, wouldn't be allowed in, and must go to school as normal.

Of course, nothing was 'normal' at school now. Johnny had never been paid so much attention; but it wasn't the kind of attention he enjoyed. The other pupils stared at him and whispered about him, but no one came near. Some had been told by their parents not to have anything to do with him. The teachers were stiff and formal, and didn't know what to say. Only Mr Murray made any reference to Winnie's arrest. Johnny's class were in the gym, using the wall-bars and climbing ropes. Mr Murray curled a rope into the shape of a noose, and lolled his head to one side with his tongue hanging out. Everybody laughed.

On the day of the hearing, Johnny was stuck in a classroom, trying to imagine what was going on. Hutch had explained that this wasn't the big trial: it was to decide whether the police had enough evidence against Winnie to justify keeping her in prison, so that the case could go on to a more important court. Johnny knew what that meant, though Hutch didn't spell it out: a court that could impose the death penalty.

Hutch got to the court as early as he could, determined to find a seat in the public gallery. There was quite a crowd. With all the shops closed, lots of other people were free too, and everyone wanted to hear why the police were so sure that Winnie had killed Dr Langford. If they had gone to see a monster, they were disappointed. Winnie looked tiny, standing alone in the shabby shift dress she'd had on when she was arrested. She stayed still, with her head down and her hands clasped in front of her, throughout the proceedings. Her mousy hair flopped forward, hiding her face. Hutch had hoped to catch her eye – to give her a reassuring nod, at least – but she didn't look at the public gallery once. Her voice was so weak when she confirmed her name that the magistrate had to ask her to speak up.

The policeman who had discovered the body described the scene. Then a doctor testified that the victim had definitely not died of natural causes, but from a blow that had opened a blood vessel in his head. It was possible that he had been punched, and had fallen against the mantelpiece. In his opinion, the state of the corpse suggested that the murder was committed some time between five and eight o'clock on the night of Tuesday 10th December.

Then Miss Dangerfield was called to the stand. There was a titter as she confirmed her full name: Letitia Euphemia Gladys Dangerfield. Dressed in black, as ever, she looked stern and trustworthy as she swore to tell the truth. The prosecuting lawyer asked her why she had called the police on 11th December.

'Because I had noticed a broken window at the Langfords' house.'

'And at what time did you notice it?'

'At about ten in the morning. I called the police immediately, but it took them rather a long time to come.'

'That's as may be, Miss Dangerfield. One can perhaps forgive the police for not expecting a broken window to be important.'

'But I told them I thought there might have been a burglary.'

'And what made you think that?'

'Because the night before I had seen someone behaving strangely in the garden.'

'And do you see that person here today, Miss Dangerfield?'

'I do, sir.'

'Would you be so good as to point them out to us?'

Winnie, pale and weak, flinched as Miss Dangerfield lifted her walking stick and waved it at the dock. 'That's her,' she bellowed. 'Mrs Winifred Swanson.'

'Thank you, Miss Dangerfield. Now tell us, at what time did you see her?'

'It must have been between seven o'clock and seven twenty. I had finished my supper, and I had not yet turned on my radio-gramophone.' She said the word 'radio-gramophone' with great relish, glad to boast to the court that she owned one. 'I can be sure of the time. That night I listened in to a talk by Professor W. W. Watts on "The Origins of Life". I have consulted the *Radio Times*. It began at seven twenty-five.'

'And why do you say that the accused, Mrs Swanson, was behaving strangely?'

'Because she was. It was pouring with rain, and she

was running around with no hat on, shouting abuse and wailing.'

'And what, exactly, was she saying?'

'I couldn't hear. The rain and the wind were too loud.'

'But you said it was abuse.'

'I could tell by the tone. And anyway, I know the kind of woman she is.'

'Yes. I'll come back to that. But first, could you tell us, had you seen Mrs Swanson near the Langfords' house before?'

'Many times. She was their cleaner. She came every day.'

'And was it customary for her to behave in this manner?'

'No, sir. But there had been some strange episodes lately.'

'What do you mean by that?'

'Ever since the Langfords went away, I'd seen the accused and her son loitering around the house. On one occasion her son was trying to break in. On another he was climbing a tree in the garden. His mother was with him. I got the impression that they intended to burgle the property while it was empty.'

'Did you inform the police?'

'No, sir. Of course, now I wish I had.'

'And on the night when Dr Langford died – did you actually see the accused enter the house?'

'No, sir. It was dark and stormy. I did not have as good a view as usual.'

'But in your opinion, could she have gone inside?'

'Yes, sir.'

'And did you see her leave?'

'No. Obviously it was still dark, and the weather was bad, and as I said, from seven twenty-five onwards I was sitting down, listening to my radio-gramophone. I would not have been able to hear her. My radio-gramophone is a Lissenola New Era. That model is equipped with an extremely powerful loudspeaker.'

The lawyer stifled a smile. 'So I believe, madam. Now, you said the house was empty. But as we know now, Dr Langford was at home. How long had the Langfords been away?'

'I'm not sure, sir. They didn't tell me they were going.' She sounded rather put out about that. 'I know they were still there on November the eleventh, because I saw Mr Bennett visit them in his big car.'

'And when did Dr Langford return to the house?'

'I don't know.'

'You saw nothing to suggest he was back?'

'No, sir – and I keep a good eye out.'

There were some more giggles from the public gallery. The lawyer hushed them with another question.

'I'm sure you do, madam. Now, tell me this. During your observation of the house over the years, have you formed an opinion of the accused and her relationship with the Langfords?'

'I dare say Mrs Langford treated her kindly. But I thought the accused got on rather better with Dr Langford. Lately I'd sometimes see them meeting and talking together, very early in the morning, outside the house. Dr Langford even gave that son of hers rides on his bicycle.'

'Are you implying that the relationship between Mrs Swanson and her employer might have been too close?'

'You might infer that, sir, if you choose to.'

Winnie wasn't too sure what all this 'imply' and 'infer' stuff meant, but she could tell what Miss Dangerfield was suggesting, and she cried out, 'No. That's not true.' But it was too late. Miss Dangerfield had managed to introduce an extra element into the case against her.

The lawyer followed it up. 'Miss Dangerfield, in your long observation of the accused, have you noticed anything else about her character?'

'Well, I know she works in a pub. Some way from our part of town.'

'In a rough area?'

'Indeed. And I know she can't control her son. That time he was up a tree in the Langfords' garden, she was there, shouting at him, but she didn't seem able to make him come down.'

'Could you hear what she was saying to him?'

'No, I can't quite recall. I believe my radio-gramophone may have been on at the time. But whatever she was saying, it wasn't having any effect.'

Hutch sat in the public gallery, trying to be hopeful. Despite all the bad things Miss Dangerfield had said, as far as he could tell all she'd really proved was that Winnie was outside the doctor's house on the fateful night. And how much notice would the court take of a sour spinster's picture of Winnie's character? If Miss Dangerfield was the only witness the police had against her, perhaps things weren't as bad as they'd seemed.

But she wasn't the only witness. Hamish Alexander Murray was called to the stand. It was the PE master from school, wearing a suit rather than his usual sports kit. The lawyer asked him to state his name, and then confirmed that he was a teacher, and that his facial injuries had been sustained in the war. Hutch could see why he was doing that – to make Murray sound like a hero so that his evidence would be more convincing.

'Mr Murray,' said the lawyer, 'on the night of December the tenth – that is, the night before Dr Langford's body was discovered – where were you?'

'I was in the Black Horse public house, sir.'

'And in the course of the evening, did you see the accused?'

'Yes, sir.'

'Now let us be clear. She was not serving behind the bar?'

'No, sir. She doesn't work there. I believe Mrs Swanson works in an altogether different class of establishment. She came into the Black Horse for a drink.'

'And what time was that?'

'About seven thirty. Maybe seven forty-five.'

'And you are sure this was on December the tenth?'

'Yes, sir. It was the night of the storm. She was soaking wet when she arrived, rather bedraggled, and behaving strangely, I remember.'

'And she was alone?'

'Yes, sir. I noticed that. I'm sure everybody did. Not many respectable women go into pubs by themselves.'

'Indeed,' said the lawyer, hoping the magistrate would draw the obvious conclusion about Winnie's character. 'And how would you describe her demeanour?'

'She looked distressed. Wild, I'd say. Her hair was all over the place, and she was covered in mud. She wouldn't meet my eyes when I tried to say hello. I would say she was in a real state.'

'A state? A state of shock?'

'More agitation . . . as if something had just happened to her, or as if she had just done something exciting. Desperate, if you get my meaning. More like an animal than a human being.'

The public gallery took in a collective gulp of breath. The lawyer raised one eyebrow just a little, and carried on. 'Did she speak to anyone else?'

'Just to order a drink.'

'An alcoholic drink?'

'I believe so. Then she sat alone in the corner. She was trembling. I was surprised. You'd think she'd be at home, looking after her son. After all, there's no man in the house.'

*

Hutch left the court. Even though it was early closing day, the evening papers had to be sorted and delivered. It was just as well that he had to go. He was seething at the picture of Winnie that was being painted, layer by layer; and he knew he should get away before he said something and landed himself in trouble. He wished he'd got to know Winnie better over the years; but she hadn't lived in Stambleton before her marriage, and after Harry Swanson's death Hutch had been afraid of being too forward – of seeming too interested in a young war widow, new to town. Yet Hutch knew enough about Winnie and about her son to find it impossible to believe in her guilt. He could think of nothing he could do to help her, but he was determined to shield Johnny from the worst of the evidence, and from the public reaction to her plight.

Even so, when he got back to the shop and found Johnny outside waiting eagerly for news, he had to be honest. 'You'll have to be strong, son,' he said. 'It isn't over yet. I don't think your mother will be home for Christmas.'

Chapter 25

ALONE

Hutch was right. The court decided that Winnie should face a full trial at the end of January. Johnny knew that would bring more torture at school. He'd already been given a new nickname: 'Swingson', which constantly reminded him that his mother might hang. He couldn't face new taunts, so he composed a letter from Auntie Ada, saying that 'under the circumstances' it might be appropriate for him to start the Christmas holidays a little early. The headmaster agreed, with relief.

So Johnny had some free time; but he wasn't allowed to visit his mother, and anyway the prison was two bus rides away. Hutch said he would go next Tuesday, when he'd be closing at lunch time, because it would be Christmas Eve. He told Johnny to make Winnie a card, wishing her well. Hutch would take her a present: something nice to eat, from the shop. But there was the best part of a week to wait until then, and no more school for Johnny.

When Winnie was arrested, he had worried constantly that someone would find out he was living on his own; but far from being troubled by busybodies, Johnny was frozen out by the people of Stambleton. No one visited. Nobody came to their door when he delivered their newspapers. People crossed the street rather than stop and talk to him. He couldn't tell whether it was embarrassment or contempt that made them do it. He could feel himself being stared at, but no one came near enough to insult him or sympathize. He didn't want to talk to them either. He stopped playing in the street. Alone in the house, he'd lost the urge to keep busy by tidying up, and even before the hearing he had found himself writing out adverts again. He'd felt guilty at first, after his realization on that terrible night that they had been the cause of the trouble, but he just couldn't stop himself; and he wanted to keep Auntie Ada alive so that he wouldn't be taken away to a children's home.

But Johnny had plenty of time to think, and his determination to persuade the world that his mother couldn't be a killer was gradually matched by an obsession that the real murderer must still be on the loose. Johnny realized that he knew something the police did not: Dr Langford had been working on the

BCG vaccine – or at least someone at a laboratory 'out in the wilds' had been doing it on his behalf. Suppose that was the reason he had been killed? Johnny remembered how determined the Langfords had been to keep it a secret – how worried they were that someone might find out. What if somebody had? Johnny agonized about his promise not to say anything. Mrs Langford had been unambiguous: *Whatever happens, whoever asks you, however much you feel like boasting – not a word.* Did that mean he shouldn't tell the police? Dr Langford was dead. He couldn't suffer any more. But what about Mrs Langford? She might get into trouble if Johnny spoke out. But maybe she was in danger anyway. Suppose the killer found her in France, or was waiting for her to come home, so that he could strike again? Johnny decided that he would have to break his silence. After all, the police were used to keeping secrets themselves. Then he remembered how much the reporter had found out about his mother from officers who couldn't resist passing details on. Was it worth the risk? In the end he decided that if it might save his mother, it was. On his first day off school he steeled himself to go back to the police station.

*

This time the desk sergeant recognized him straight away. He was just as hostile as before.

'What do you want? Your mother's not here any more. She's in the big prison now.'

'I know. I want to talk to you. I want to help you find the real killer.'

'We already have the real killer, son.'

'No you don't. My mother could never hurt anyone. Someone else did it.'

'And you know who, do you?' The swing doors opened, and a man came in from the street. The policeman broke off from talking to Johnny. 'I'll be with you in a moment, sir. This won't take long.' He turned back to Johnny. 'Well? Do you have a name to give me?'

'Not a name, exactly,' said Johnny. 'It's a bit more complicated than that.'

The newcomer was leaning against the counter and looking down at Johnny with a patronizing smile. Johnny felt he couldn't go into details of Dr Langford's secret in front of a complete stranger.

'It's private, too,' said Johnny, hoping the policeman would take him somewhere they could speak without being overheard.

The policeman laughed. 'If it's so private, you'd

better keep it to yourself, son. I've got better things to do with my time. Now this gentleman would probably appreciate a little privacy. You'd better be on your way.'

'But it's important.'

'I said get out of it.'

Johnny stood for a moment, stuttering, but the policeman just pointed to the door. 'Now, sir, what can I do for you?' he asked the man.

'I want to report a lost dog.'

The policeman started making a note. Without even looking up, he bellowed at Johnny again. 'Go!'

Johnny knew there was no point in staying. He ran away, not letting the tears of fear, anger and dismay break through until the door swung shut behind him.

That afternoon he hit on a different tactic. He would write down his ideas about an alternative killer in a note to Inspector Griffin. He thought at first that he would do it in Auntie Ada's name, but then he envisaged the scene when the inspector came round and found out that she didn't really exist. So he wrote everything out as neatly as he could, and signed it himself. He slipped it into his bag when he went on the evening paper round, and as soon as the last newspaper had been put through the last letter box, he made his way to the police station again. He was barely through the door before the desk sergeant was shouting at him.

'Wasting police time is a crime, you know.'

'I just want to drop off a letter for Inspector Griffin.'

'A letter about what, exactly?'

'It's about the murder. To help him find the person who did it.'

'And why should he listen to you? He already has the murderer in custody, as you know only too well.'

'But she didn't do it!'

'So who did?'

'I don't know exactly. But all my ideas are in this letter.' Johnny put it down on the counter.

'And why should Inspector Griffin take any notice of that? Why should he believe a small boy trying to save his mother, and ignore witnesses who've given sworn evidence against her in court?'

'Because I know something they don't know.'

'And it's all in here?' said the sergeant, picking up the envelope.

'Yes. Please take it.'

'Oh, I'll take it, son. I'll take it and I'll file it in the appropriate place.'

'Thank you,' said Johnny. But his momentary relief turned to anguish again as the sergeant tore the envelope in two and dropped it behind him.

'Now I'm warning you, boy,' he said. 'I've had enough of your time-wasting. Keep away from here.' The sergeant lifted a flap in the counter and walked through to the 'public' side of the room. Through the gap, Johnny could see the torn letter in the waste-paper basket. The policeman grabbed his arm and manhandled him through the door. 'I don't want to see you here again,' he hissed as Johnny tumbled down the steps. 'I've a good mind to come round to your house to tell that aunt of yours that if she can't control you, we'll put you with someone who can.'

As he helped Hutch close up the shop Johnny worried that the police were ransacking his home and discovering that there was no Auntie Ada.

Hutch noticed his agitation. 'Are you all right, son?' he asked. 'You don't seem yourself today.'

Johnny wanted to tell him everything, but he didn't think he should betray the Langfords' secret to anyone except the police, and he feared that if he told Hutch that he'd lied about his auntie he might lose the only person he had on his side.

'No. Well. I'm just worried about . . . Well, you know,' he said.

'I understand,' said Hutch, awkwardly restraining himself from giving Johnny a hug. He took a jar of strawberry jam from a shelf. 'Here. Take this home to your auntie. She must be worried too, poor thing.'

Johnny took the jar and ran home. The door was still locked, and there was no sign that anyone had been inside. He got a pillow and some of his mother's clothes, and pulled round the big armchair so that it had its back to the door. He pulled the curtains almost shut, leaving just enough of a gap to satisfy anyone who was determined to look inside. Everything was arranged so that they would think they saw an old woman asleep by the fireplace. He hoped they'd be too polite to try to wake her up.

Chapter 26

THE FARMER

Even with the pretend Auntie Ada in place, Johnny was lonely – perhaps even more lonely than before. Sitting by himself, eating jam straight from the jar with a spoon, he desperately wanted to talk to someone, to tell them what was happening to his mother, and how no one except Hutch believed that she was innocent.

He decided to try again to find Olwen. Although he had met her only once, she'd been on his mind ever since. She'd been kind when everyone else was bullying him, and she hadn't heard any of the nasty rumours about Winnie. He felt that she would understand. He wanted to write to her, but all he knew was that she was with relatives somewhere in Wales. He remembered that she had lived on a farm outside Stambleton, so next morning he set off to walk there, hoping the farmer would know her new address. It was a harder, colder walk than he had expected, and even when he reached a sign saying NEWGATE FARM (which was nailed to a very old-looking gate), a long track wound its way towards the farmhouse. Johnny was trudging round a corner when a battered van came the other way. He jumped aside, expecting it to pass, but the driver, a weather-beaten man wearing an ill-fitting suit, stopped and spoke to him.

'Where are you going?'

'To the farmhouse. I want to talk to the farmer,' Johnny said.

'I'm the farmer. What can I do for you? There's no work here – if you're looking for work, that is. You seem a bit young for that.'

'No, I don't want a job. I'm looking for information. I'm trying to find someone who used to live here.'

'Well, there's no one at home. And I'm on my way to a funeral. That's why I'm all dressed up like this,' the farmer said, running his finger inside the stiff collar of his shirt. 'I can't stop for long, but you can get in if you want, and we can talk in the warm.'

Johnny climbed in and sat beside the farmer. He'd hardly ever been in a car before, let alone a big van like this. It was a real treat. 'Thank you,' he said. 'It's nice to get out of the wind. Do you mind if I ask you questions?'

'Not at all,' said the farmer. 'But you'll have to

speak up. I need to leave the engine running, otherwise it could conk out and I might never get it started again. Now, who are you trying to find?'

'It's a girl called Olwen. She came to my school in September. But she had to leave again. I think her baby sister died.'

The farmer gripped the steering wheel. 'I wish I could help you. I've been trying to find her myself, poor love. It's her father's funeral I'm off to now. He's being buried near that big sanatorium up at Emberley. Her mother's only been gone a couple of weeks. Olwen's all alone now – though she probably doesn't know it. Her folks packed her off to try to keep her safe, and now it's too late to ask them where she is.'

'Olwen told me you knew her dad in the army.'

'He saved my life – dragged me from a shell-hole at the battle of Ypres. He carried me on his back all the way to the dressing station. We lost touch after the war, but I couldn't refuse him when he wrote saying he was in trouble. I'd promised I'd do anything for him. He was desperate. I thought I could give him a roof over his head and a job.'

Johnny had read stories like that in the *Boy's Own Paper*. It was thrilling to hear that such heroism and gratitude happened in real life. He'd often wished that someone would appear on his doorstep with a tale about his own father's war exploits, but this was the next best thing. He was proud on Olwen's behalf, and glad that the farmer had done the decent thing.

'It was kind of you to help them,' said Johnny. 'I know Olwen was grateful. It was one of the first things she told me when I met her. Hasn't she written to you since she went away?'

'Not a word. I think that's odd, don't you? You'd think her people would be in touch. I wish I'd taken more notice when they sent her away, but it was all such a rush, and it wasn't my business, was it?'

The farmer sounded as if he wanted Johnny's forgiveness. Johnny tried to make him feel better. 'Oh, I'm sure you did everything you could. They were lucky you helped them in the first place.'

'To be honest, there have been moments when I've regretted it. People don't trust my milk since they brought the TB here. And burials don't come cheap, even without fancy carriages and flowers.'

'So there won't be anyone else at the funeral?'

'Probably not, unless the hospital's found somebody. But it's not fitting for anyone to be buried without a friend at the graveside, so I'm going: as a last thank-you for what he did for me, and on behalf of the relatives, you might say. It doesn't seem right for young Olwen to miss her chance to say goodbye, but what can I do?'

'Dr Langford said she'd gone back to relatives in Wales.'

'Ah, but Wales is a big place. I know they were from Swansea, but who's to say where their relations live? I couldn't even track down their old home. I must have had their address once, when her dad first wrote to me, but I'm darned if I can find the letter anywhere. If I'd known all this was going to happen, I'd have taken more care. I never expected them all to drop dead before I had the chance to ask where Olwen was.'

'Do you think I could come to the funeral too?' asked Johnny. He remembered a phrase he'd heard his mother use. 'I'd like to pay my respects.'

'Well, that's fine talk from one so young. You're not really dressed for it, but I don't see why not. There won't be anyone there to take offence.'

Johnny looked down at his tatty clothes. In his mother's absence he hadn't paid any attention to washing or ironing, and he knew he must be even more grubby than usual after his long walk. 'I really would like to come, if you don't mind, sir.'

'It will be a pleasure to take you. And good company for me,' said the farmer, releasing the brake.

The van rolled forward, let out a couple of loud bangs, and moved off, bumping so much on the uneven road that Johnny's bottom kept bouncing off the seat. They both started to laugh. That didn't seem right on the way to a funeral, so they decided to sing hymns instead. After 'All People That on Earth Do Dwell', 'He Who Would Valiant Be', 'Praise My Soul the King of Heaven' and 'The Lord's My Shepherd' they arrived at the graveyard at Emberley.

A young vicar was waiting for them. He supervised the burial with minimal ceremony. The gravediggers started filling in the hole, and Johnny and the farmer returned to the van. Johnny was trying not to cry. He was sad about Olwen's father, even though he had never met him, and about Olwen's sister and mother in two fresh graves nearby; but really he was thinking about his own mother, and how she might be buried soon unless he could do something to save her. He wanted to tell the farmer about it. But he couldn't find the words.

In the end, it was the farmer who brought the subject up as they drove back towards Stambleton. He wasn't meaning to, but he recalled that Johnny had mentioned Dr Langford.

'So you knew the old doctor?' he said. 'I couldn't believe it when I heard he'd been murdered.'

'Oh yes, said Johnny. 'I've known him all my life. He was a really nice man.'

'A terrible business. Dr Langford was a real gentleman. And so good with children. He took good care of a fair few at that sanatorium. They were his two specialities, see: children and TB. You should have seen him when we had the epidemic in 1916. I don't think they'd ever have built that sanatorium without Dr Langford raising money and making speeches everywhere. It was thanks to him that Olwen's family were taken in there as charity cases. We've been robbed of a good man. I can't imagine why anyone would want to kill him. That evil barmaid had better swing for it.'

Johnny didn't know what to say. Should he risk letting on who he was? Should he try to explain that Winnie wasn't guilty? Best to say nothing, he thought. He'd be out of the van in a few minutes. He might never see the farmer again. He stayed quiet. But the farmer filled the silence: 'Do you know her? You're from Stambleton. She has a kiddie about your age. You must have seen him at school. You must have come across his mother?'

Johnny started to stutter a reply. He could hardly get any words out. He didn't want to sound as if he was disowning Winnie, but he didn't know how to explain why he hadn't mentioned her before. He wanted to tell the farmer all about her, and how she couldn't possibly have committed the crime. All he managed to do was make himself sound shifty.

The farmer was suddenly suspicious. 'Hang on a minute,' he said, glancing across at his small passenger, 'why aren't you at school today?'

'I don't go any more,' said Johnny. 'I can't because—'

'What's your name?' said the farmer, driving faster and faster as it dawned on him who his passenger might be.

'Johnny . . .'

'Johnny what?'

'Johnny Swans—'

'You're that boy, aren't you?' gasped the farmer, slamming on the brakes so hard that Johnny was thrown forward against the dashboard. 'You're that woman's brat. Get out. Get out! You've got a nerve. I can't believe you tricked your way into my van.'

'But you asked me in. I was only—'

'I should have known. A boy of your age wanting

to go to a funeral? You're sick. Go on. Get out. Now!'

Johnny fumbled with the door handle. At last he was able to climb down onto the road. They were still a couple of miles from Stambleton. The farmer tried to move off, but the engine had stopped, and he had to get out and crank it with a handle. He stood in front of the bonnet, cursing.

'She didn't do it,' Johnny shouted, with tears in his eyes. 'She's innocent.'

The farmer didn't look up. Swearing under his breath, he kept cranking the engine until it spluttered and started running again. Then he pulled out the heavy iron handle and waved it at Johnny. 'Get out of my sight!' he yelled; and, terrified that the man was going to beat him or fling the handle at his head, Johnny turned and started running towards town. A few seconds later the van swept past.

Johnny was shocked by the speed with which the kind man had turned on him. His words had revealed more about local gossip than Johnny had dared to imagine. People really hated Winnie. And there was no hope now of finding Olwen, the one person who might not know what had happened; who might listen to Johnny's version of the story, take pity on him and understand his grief.

Chapter 27

OUTCASTS

At least Johnny had Hutch. He went straight to the shop. It was quiet. A few people came in to buy stamps or cash their pensions at the post office. Some had Christmas parcels to send. One or two used the phone booth just inside the door. But several people cancelled their papers, and even more followed Miss Dangerfield's example and decided to shop elsewhere for their food.

'It's because of me, isn't it?' said Johnny as he and Hutch tidied the stockroom to make space for goods that wouldn't sell. 'It's my fault.'

'No, it's because of me,' Hutch said. 'Because I'm standing by you. And it's the fault of no one except the small-minded people of Stambleton. I'll take over the paper deliveries for a while. I don't want you to have to face abuse every day. You can do extra jobs for me here instead.' He brought down some cardboard and paint from a high shelf. 'And you can start right now. I want you to make some notices. We're going to have to have our post-Christmas sale a little early. This year, it's a pre-Christmas sale. If cut prices don't lure people back in here, nothing will.'

Hutch had a large stock of aluminium teapots filled with Christmas biscuits. He'd ordered them as a seasonal novelty before his customers had deserted him. Other shops were selling them for five shillings. Hutch was marking them down to 3/6. Cheese, ham and bacon were all reduced to a shilling per pound. But the real crowd-puller was to be Keiller's Assorted Chocolates at only tenpence for a half-pound box, with boxes twice the size going for only sixpence more.

So Johnny set to work. Hutch gave him a list of discounts, and Johnny translated them into posters, using bright colours, with lots of red, to make them look Christmassy. He got a ladder and climbed into the window to put up the posters and to build towers of chocolate boxes to attract passers-by. He painted CHRISTMAS SALE in huge letters at the top of the display, and set about arranging tins of crab meat in the shape of a crab, and iced cakes in the shape of a snowflake. Johnny was concentrating hard, determined to produce a show that would bring back the customers Hutch had lost because of him. He didn't notice the growing crowd that was watching him work until they started a rumbling chant. Maybe it was the sign saying KEILLER'S CHOCOLATES that set them off. Soon they were all shouting: 'Killer's son! Killer's son! Killer's son! Killer's son!' Johnny looked up. It was already dark outside, but in the light from the window he could see a few faces he recognized. Some of them were people he knew from his paper round: folk who only a few weeks ago had given him a cheery wave every morning. Albert Taylor and Ernest Roberts were both there on their way home from school, and in the thick of it all was an elderly woman. She looked strong and feisty – you might even say 'in robust health'. It was Mrs Slack, who had apparently recovered from her ailments now that Winnie was no longer available to care for her.

As the abuse grew louder, Johnny went to the front of the window and put his face close to the glass so that she could hear him. 'Mrs Slack,' he cried. 'Please! You know my mother is a good woman. Please tell everyone. Please tell them everything she has done for you!'

'Done for me!' shrieked Mrs Slack. 'Done for me! I'm lucky she hasn't done for me! Every day she came round my house – looking for things to steal, I shouldn't wonder. Or trying to poison me. Strange that I've been better since she's gone, isn't it? String her up, that's what I say!' And she joined in the chant, which was growing louder and more vicious: 'Killer's son! Killer's son!'

A brick flew in, showering Johnny with glass. Hutch rushed to the window, drawing jeers from the crowd, to pull Johnny back into the shop. His weak leg trailed behind him, bringing down the ladder, and with it the paint pot. Red liquid spilled everywhere, and the crowd screamed, 'Blood! Blood! Killer's son! Killer's son!'

The mob was frightening, but its members were not brave. The sound of a police whistle quickly dispersed them; but not before some had reached through the broken glass for chocolate boxes and teapots.

When the crowd had gone, Johnny started shivering uncontrollably. 'It's shock,' said Hutch. 'Come and sit down.' He took Johnny into the stockroom, sat him on a crate and wrapped a sack around his shoulders. 'You'd better keep warm,' he said. 'They say sugar's good for shock, you know. I'll see what I can find.' He was back in no time with a chocolate bar and a fizzy drink. 'Perhaps you'd better go home.'

'No, Hutch,' said Johnny. 'I'll be all right in a minute. Let me stay here. I'd rather be with you.'

Hutch was touched to have Johnny's confidence. 'You sit here for a while then,' he said tenderly, 'and I'll start straightening out the shop. You can join me when you're feeling better.'

So Hutch and Johnny spent the rest of the day clearing the mess and boarding up the window.

'Shouldn't the police arrest those people?' said Johnny. 'We know most of them. We could tell the police their names.'

'No point,' said Hutch. 'I don't think that would win us many friends, do you?'

'But what about the stuff they stole? Aren't you going to report them for that?'

'Who?'

'Well, Albert Taylor for one. And Ernest Roberts. I saw them there.'

'You saw them?'

'Yes, I did. And I don't see why they should get away with it. They've been horrible to me for ages. We should tell the police.'

'You saw them steal the chocolates?'

'Well, no. Not exactly. I didn't see them actually do it. But I know it was them. I just know it.'

'Oh, Johnny,' sighed Hutch. 'Listen to yourself. Can't you hear who you sound like?'

'Who?'

'Like someone who saw your mother at the Langfords' house? Like someone who saw her sitting in a pub? Do you actually know that Taylor and Roberts plundered the window display?'

Johnny was ashamed of himself. 'No,' he whispered.

'Then I think it's best if we say no more about it, don't you?'

'All right. But you'd better close down the shop, Hutch,' said Johnny. 'It isn't safe for you here.'

Hutch disagreed. 'We'll see off those bullies,' he said. 'And we'll beat them by carrying on. I won't close. In fact, I can't close. I have to stay open, because of the post office. It's my duty. It's as simple as that.'

When Johnny arrived home that night, he found a pudding basin on the doorstep. He recognized it as the one Winnie had used to make Mrs Slack a treacle sponge on a cold day at the beginning of December. It was half full of a golden liquid. Johnny didn't stop to investigate what that might be. He could guess. He tipped it away, and dashed the basin against the wall.

Alone inside, he barricaded the door in case anyone tried to break in. He tore up some old newspapers to try to get a fire going in the grate. There was something in one of them about the effort the police were making to find Marie Langford in France, so they could tell her about her husband's tragic death. They didn't seem to be having any luck with their search. Johnny wondered whether they were trying hard enough. Perhaps, if he could find her first, before the police had a chance to poison her mind against Winnie, Johnny might persuade Mrs Langford to help clear his mother's name. At the very least she could tell everyone how honest and reliable Winnie had been in the past. She might even be able to suggest another suspect for the murder. If only he could make contact with Marie Langford, wherever in France she might be.

Someone rapped on the door. Johnny jumped up and turned down the lamp, so that whoever was outside would think the house was empty. But the knocking came again. Then a half-familiar voice. Johnny worked out who it was just before the man said his name. It was the reporter.

Johnny went over to the door. 'Go away,' he

shouted. 'I'm not allowed to talk to you. The police said so.'

'And why should you do what the police say?' asked the man. 'They've put your mother in prison. They don't believe she's innocent. Why should you listen to them?'

'I don't want to get her into any more trouble,' said Johnny.

The reporter pushed open the letter box. Johnny could see his lips moving. 'Pardon me for saying this, Johnny, but when you're on trial for murder, you can't really get into any more trouble. What are they going to do? Hang her twice?' His lips and teeth settled into a sneer.

Johnny felt sick at the thought that his mother might die. 'Go away,' he said, trying to push down the flap of the letter box. 'Leave me alone.'

The reporter pushed back. His voice softened. 'All I want to do is talk to you about your mother. I'm not going to write anything about her in the paper. I'm not allowed to until the trial. But when it's over, everyone is going to want to know about her – what she was really like. Only you can tell me that, Johnny. If you don't tell me the nice things about her, I won't be able to write them down. I'll have to rely on people like Miss Dangerfield. Do you want me to go and talk to her again?'

'No, I don't. And stop talking as if Mum is going to be found guilty. She didn't do it. I know she didn't. Why aren't you and the police trying to find out who did?'

Now the reporter's eyes filled the slot in the door. 'That's a good point, Johnny,' he said. 'Do you have any ideas about who might have done it? I'd love to hear them. Let me in, and we can talk in the warm.'

'It's not very warm in here,' said Johnny.

'Well, maybe I could give you the price of the coal you'll burn while you're talking to me. Perhaps a little more than that. And remember, I can't help your mother if I don't know enough about her to make her case. Let me in, Johnny. Please.'

Johnny was on the point of giving way when he heard footsteps coming down the lane. There were at least two men, and they were getting closer. He could hear their voices. They sounded drunk, but he couldn't make out what they were saying. Then he heard the reporter again. He was shouting now.

'Get out of it!' he yelled.

Johnny peered through the letter box. He could see the reporter grappling with the men. He held one of them by the hair while he punched the other, bringing up his knee to hit him in the groin. Then, while that man rolled on the floor in agony, he jabbed his fingers into the other's eyes and wrenched his arm behind his back. Johnny winced with pain just watching.

The reporter kicked the man on the ground. 'I said clear off. Keep away or I'll get you again. And I'll tell the police too. Do you hear?'

The men swore at him, but they slunk away, back up the narrow alley. The reporter knocked on the door again, and this time Johnny let him in. His lips were swollen and his knuckles were bleeding.

'Why were those men after you?' asked Johnny.

'They weren't after me, son. They were after you. But you won't be troubled by them again. Not if they think I'm protecting you. If there's one thing the war did for the likes of me, it taught us how to fight. Those youngsters didn't have a chance. But you'd better be careful. Watch where you go. Especially after dark.'

The reporter blotted the blood with his handkerchief. Johnny dragged over the armchair, casually dismantling the pretend Auntie Ada. He climbed up to get the ointment down from beside the Peace Mug on the high shelf. 'Thank you,' he said, with his back to the reporter. He felt he owed the man a smear of antiseptic, even if he wasn't supposed to talk to him.

The reporter took the opportunity to get a conversation going. 'Are you getting enough to eat?' he asked, looking around the bare room for signs of food.

Johnny opened a cupboard and showed off the things Hutch had given him since Winnie's arrest. Everything was in tins: ham, peas, some sweet evaporated milk. 'I've got a bit of cheese, too,' said Johnny. He reached across to the windowsill and took down a little parcel wrapped in greaseproof paper. 'Do you want some? I'm afraid I haven't got any bread.'

'That's very kind of you, Johnny,' said the reporter. He put his hand in his coat pocket. 'I've got a couple of apples here. Why don't we share them?'

So Johnny got a knife and two plates from the side of the sink. At first he was going to give the reporter his mother's plate – the chipped one with blue roses round the edge – but then he thought he'd keep that one for himself. He didn't want a stranger to have it. The reporter had Johnny's: plain white, with a red rim.

The apples and cheese went well together, and the reporter started asking casual questions about Winnie while he crunched his way through the fruit. At first Johnny kept his answers short and factual. Then he found himself talking more and more about his mother: how she had been left completely alone when his father was killed, because neither she nor Harry had had any family left by 1918. He described how she looked after the neighbours, how hard she worked, and how worried she was about the rent going up. The reporter listened, and sympathized, and gave Johnny a handful of coins when he left.

'Be careful, Johnny,' he said. 'Lock the door behind me when I go. And if you think of anything else you want to tell me, just get in touch.' He wrote his office telephone number on a piece of paper and handed it over.

As he bolted the door, Johnny felt glad to have met someone who really cared about him. He thought he might ask Hutch if he could use the phone tomorrow. Maybe he could persuade the reporter to help him track down Marie Langford in the hope that she might prove that Winnie wasn't a killer. Perhaps it would be all right to break his promise and tell the reporter about the BCG so that he could help to find the real murderer.

But then Johnny noticed that something was

missing from the mantelpiece. The reporter had taken the photograph of his father. It was the only picture of Harry Swanson that Johnny had ever seen. As far as he knew it was the only image of him anywhere. And that man had taken it. Taken it without asking. Johnny decided to have nothing more to do with him. He would search for Mrs Langford by himself.

Chapter 28

TAKING CHARGE

Johnny realized that his best bet for finding Marie Langford was to use the two tools he knew so well: the post and the newspapers. He put a new personal message in the *London Times*, quoting Auntie Ada's box number, and he helped Hutch sort letters that came into the post office, looking out for anything addressed to the doctor's house. He reckoned that since Mrs Langford was abroad, and didn't know that her husband was dead, she was bound to write him a letter sometime – especially with Christmas coming. The police had the same idea, and an officer came in every day to check for letters from France, but nothing turned up. The policeman wasn't at all interested in doing anything about the broken shop window. He seemed to think that bad feeling against Hutch and Johnny was only natural.

Hutch tried asking the policeman about the investigation. 'Is there anything new? Have you found out any more about the murder?'

The officer's response was steely: 'We've got all the evidence we need. And even if there was a development, why should I tell you, in view of your relationship with the accused?'

Over the weekend, Johnny filled the long evening hours devising new money-making schemes. The rent rise was now only days away, and the savings inside his rabbit wouldn't last long. He couldn't afford to be high-minded about advertising. He roughed out a couple of offers: *Give Your Home a Country Feel.* People who sent him sixpence would be told: *Walk around in muddy boots.*

He even thought of putting a little free sample of dirt into the envelopes. Perhaps he'd add a few seeds, too. He could easily get some from the plants in the graveyard. Maybe he could say they were magic seeds. He got that idea from the posters outside the Playhouse. They were doing *Jack and the Beanstalk* as the Christmas pantomime.

Johnny's most frequent correspondent, the aspiring poet, had sent ten poems at once, asking what the Poetry Police thought of them. Johnny spent two whole evenings writing his replies, glad of the one-pound postal order that had arrived with them, and determined to give value for money so that the man

234

would write again. He put the poems in a stack by the fire, ready to use them as fuel; but then he had another idea. He cut them up into strips, each containing one line of verse, and shuffled them up. A quick advert in the *Stambleton Echo* offered:

The Poetry Kit:
I send the verbiage, you make the verse.
3d. per line.

He ran to the advertising office first thing the next day, and managed to get the advertisement into that evening's edition. The lady behind the counter thought it was one of his auntie's better ideas. The kit would, she said, make an excellent Christmas present. She was right. The response was immediate and enthusiastic.

By Christmas Eve Johnny was confident that he would be able to pay the rent for the whole of January, right up to the date of his mother's trial. He was glad about that, but he was tormented by the thought of how Hutch would react if he found out how he had got hold of so much money.

'I see your auntie is still sewing,' said Hutch when Johnny presented a pile of postal orders for cashing before the post office closed down for Christmas. 'That's good.'

Johnny was on the point of telling him the truth about Ada when a customer came in. Trade was so slow that Hutch could not afford to ignore her, even for a second, and Johnny didn't want to risk reminding her of 'the Bloody Barmaid of Stambleton', so he dived into the stockroom. Yet another chance to own up had come and gone.

Chapter 29

THE PRISON VISIT

In the stockroom, Johnny re-read the letter he had written for Hutch to take to his mother. In it, he apologized for making her so angry on the night they'd last been together, and insisted that the whole terrible mess was his fault. He swore he would do everything he could to get Winnie out of prison. Somehow it didn't seem right to sign off without wishing her a happy Christmas, even though he knew there was no chance of that for either of them. It was nearly noon. Before long, Hutch would be setting off for the prison. Johnny imagined his mother alone in her cell, wondering whether anyone was doing anything to get her released.

In fact, Winnie was worrying about Johnny. She had no idea what had happened to him after her arrest, and no one would tell her. A lawyer, appointed by the court, had been to see her, but had offered little hope. It was clear that he, like the police, saw her conviction as inevitable. Winnie wondered whether she would ever see Johnny again. She was devastated that their last words to each other had been so harsh, and felt that she had let her son down, even though she was innocent of any crime. She was lonely in her cell, but terrified whenever she was let out to exercise with the other prisoners – even though they kept their distance, assuming that she was capable of killing. Winnie had hardly eaten for nearly a fortnight, and was even skinnier than before. There was no mirror, but she knew that now, more than ever, she matched the description Mr Murray had given the court of the dazed and desperate creature he had seen in the pub on that awful night. Her hair was lank and greasy, and she badly needed a proper wash.

When the prison guard took her into the visiting room, Winnie was surprised to see Hutch, large and embarrassed in his best suit, sitting at a tiny table with his bad leg stretched out to one side; but she was thrilled that at last she would have news of her son.

'How's Johnny?' she blurted out, before correcting herself and adding, politely, 'It's so kind of you to come, Mr Hutchinson.'

'Oh, it's a pleasure,' said Hutch, automatically.

'Well, not a pleasure, of course, but you know what I mean.' There was an awkward pause before he continued. 'I brought you some food from the shop: a little pork pie and some chocolates. But they were confiscated on the way in.'

'What a shame. But thank you, anyway. Let's hope the warders enjoy them.'

Hutch was impressed that she had enough spirit to muster a little joke. He took Johnny's letter from his pocket. 'They did let me bring this in. They read it first, of course. They said he's got lovely handwriting.'

'Yes, he has, hasn't he?' said Winnie. 'I'm so proud of him.' She held the envelope against her cheek and cried.

Johnny sat alone in the kitchen, wondering how Hutch was getting on, and wishing he could have gone to the jail. As it got dark outside, he could hear carol singers in the street. He didn't light the lamp. He wanted them to think the house was empty. He couldn't face Christmas cheer, or the prospect of another visit from the thugs the reporter had seen off the week before. But he opened the door when he heard Hutch coming. He recognized his rhythmical limp in the lane. Johnny hoped that Hutch had stopped off at the shop on his way back. He was hungry, and it would be nice to have something special for Christmas. But Hutch arrived empty-handed, looking grave.

'Oh, my boy. What are you doing alone here in the dark?'

'Nothing. I was just thinking about Mum. How is she?'

Hutch sighed. 'As well as can be expected, I suppose. She's worried about you though.'

'She doesn't need to be, Hutch. I hope you told her that. I can look after myself.'

'I told her you were in fine form. But she told me something too – something I should probably have guessed for myself.' Hutch paused, and looked away. Johnny wondered for a moment if he was about to hear a horrible revelation about the court case. But it was a different thing entirely. Hutch took a breath and announced: 'Johnny, I know about your Auntie Ada. Your mother has told me all.'

Johnny was caught between relief that the pretence was over and fear that he was in deep trouble. He couldn't bear the idea of losing Hutch as well as everyone else. 'I'm sorry,' he said. 'I wanted to tell you, but I didn't know how.'

Hutch felt sympathy for the boy, but also outrage at how he had behaved. He tried to stay calm. 'I have to say, Johnny, that I'm shocked. Shocked and disappointed that you have lied to me for so long. In any other situation, I might look for a way to punish you, and I won't put up with being deceived again.' Johnny bowed his head, and Hutch continued in a more friendly tone. 'But what matters now is that you shouldn't be here on your own – especially at Christmas. I'd never have let you come back here every night if I'd known. I've agreed with your mother that you will come and live with me until this business is over.'

'Until after the trial you mean,' said Johnny. 'They'll let her out then, won't they?'

'Yes,' said Hutch, trying to sound convinced. 'It will all be finished then. Now, you run along and get some things together.'

Johnny was back in a trice with a few underclothes tied up in a shirt. Hutch was touched to see that he clung to a toy rabbit as if he would never allow himself to be parted from it. 'If there's anything valuable in the house, you'd better bring that, too,' he said. 'Just in case anyone breaks in while you're away.'

Johnny put down his things and climbed up to get

the Peace Mug. He went up to Winnie's room, lifted a loose floorboard, and took out the box in which his mother kept his father's medals and important family papers. There was nothing else he wanted to take. Except his father's photograph, of course. But that had already gone.

Chapter 30

AT HOME WITH HUTCH

Johnny had never been in the flat above the shop. Compared with his own home it was luxurious, with electric light, lino on the floor, and an indoor bathroom with hot and cold water on tap. At Hutch's suggestion, Johnny had a bath as soon as he arrived, using expensive soap he had stacked in displays but never seen out of its box. Hutch went downstairs to the shop and got Johnny a toothbrush and some of the newest tooth cleaner, which came as a paste in a tube, and bubbled into a sweet minty foam in his mouth.

Afterwards, Johnny found his way to the kitchen. Hutch was mashing potatoes. The room was quite bare, with lots of empty shelves. 'I use the shop as my larder,' Hutch explained. 'I only bring things up here when I need them.' Like the bathroom, the kitchen was full of steam. Hutch had speared two holes in the top of a tin of stewed steak and was heating it up in a pan of boiling water on a trim little gas stove. He had pudding ready alongside: a can of pineapple chunks and a tin of condensed milk. Johnny had seen it advertised in the paper. *Doctors tell other doctors what wonderful results they have had with Nestles Milk*, said the advertisement. He'd thought of stealing that line for one of his own enterprises. But he supposed there wouldn't be any more of them now.

Johnny watched, hungry and amazed, as Hutch stirred large knobs of butter into the potatoes. He kept Hutch talking about the visit to his mother; but he knew the question that was bound to come, and eventually Hutch found the words:

'Now then, Johnny,' he said gravely. 'If there never was an Auntie Ada, where did all those postal orders come from?'

Haltingly at first, but then with relief, excitement and even a hint of pride, Johnny told Hutch everything, from the Secret of Instant Height through to the Poetry Police and Confidentially Yours.

Hutch tried to be kind, well aware of the torment Johnny was enduring, but he couldn't disguise his disapproval of what the boy had done.

'This can't go on. Good heavens, Johnny! Can't you see why it's wrong? Can't you imagine how those people you tricked are feeling?'

'I don't need to imagine. I know. They did it to me first, remember?'

'But that doesn't mean you can do it to other people! It doesn't excuse making total strangers send you money for nothing!'

'They always got something. Even if it wasn't exactly what they were expecting.'

'And what's all this about you selling stamps?'

'I haven't been selling them.'

'You said they were portraits of the King. People paid for them. That's selling stamps.'

'Oh.'

'And selling unused stamps is against the law. If you're not a properly qualified postmaster, that is. I should know. I can show you a copy of the regulations if you want.'

'I didn't realize—'

'And it's worse than that. Presumably, to make any money, you must have been selling stamps at more than their face value?'

'How do you mean?'

'Well, when you sent someone one of these "official portraits", how much did you charge?'

'A shilling.'

'And you sent them one-shilling stamps?'

'Of course not. Penny stamps; threepenny stamps; sixpenny stamps. It depended on what I had at the time.'

'So you were making a profit.'

'That was the point.'

Hutch thumped the table. 'But that makes it even worse. It's a crime, Johnny. You have committed a crime! Here we are with your mother unjustly imprisoned and you really *are* a criminal. I should turn you in, Johnny. I might even lose my job if I don't.'

Johnny was blinking hard, trying not to cry. 'I'm sorry,' he said weakly. 'I was only trying to help.'

Hutch was still angry. 'Well, you haven't helped, have you?'

'I've got enough money to pay the rent.'

Hutch couldn't stop himself. His next words spilled out before he could think. 'But your mother might die!'

The silence that followed wrenched at them both. Eventually Hutch had to break it. He could see that Johnny was on the verge of tears. Hutch was calmer, but still stern. 'Well, Johnny, it's all got to stop now, hasn't it? I'm not going to tell the police: for your mother's sake, if nothing else. But if any more letters come to that private box, we'll just return them unopened to the main sorting office.'

'No, you can't do that!' cried Johnny, thinking of the advert in the personal column of *The Times*. He explained how he was looking for Mrs Langford in the hope that she would be able to help prove Winnie's innocence. 'You see, Hutch, it's not just that Mrs Langford can tell everyone what a good woman my mother is. She can give new evidence.'

'Like what, exactly?'

'For a start, she knows my mother didn't have any keys to her house. The police don't believe Mum, but they'd believe Mrs Langford.' Johnny wondered whether he should break his promise and tell Hutch about the BCG. He started cautiously: 'And there's another thing. *Someone* killed Dr Langford, and if it wasn't Mum, it must have been somebody with a reason. Mrs Langford might know who it was, and why.'

Johnny was surprised by Hutch's response. 'Your mother was talking about that too,' he said. 'She's been running over in her mind everything she knows about the Langfords, looking for a motive for the murder. And she thinks it might have been something to do with the doctor's work. I thought he'd retired completely, but apparently he was still keeping his hand in. He'd hinted to your mother that he was involved with some sort of new medicine. Something to do with TB.'

'Phthisis,' said Johnny.

Hutch jolted with shock. 'I beg your pardon?' he said, thinking Johnny had used a dirty word.

'Phthisis. It's another word for TB.' Johnny felt his way cautiously, wondering how much Winnie knew, and what she had told Hutch. 'Dr Langford told me about it. He was hoping they'd find a cure.'

'Well, your mother thinks he might have done that, or that he knew a way to stop people getting it in the first place. He told her about some vaccine they've developed in France. It's called BBC or something.'

Johnny realized that Dr Langford had been incapable of keeping his mouth shut. It bolstered his theory that the killer was a medical rival or a blackmailer who had found out what the doctor was doing. He felt relief wash over him. He wasn't really breaking a confidence by talking about the BCG. The doctor had told Winnie; and now she'd told Hutch. Surely it didn't count as a secret any more?

'Mum's right,' he said. 'Has she told the police?'

'She's tried to. But they won't take any notice. They don't want to hear about anything that spoils their case against her. And anyway, she doesn't know for certain that it's true.'

'But it is. Dr Langford told me himself. He was involved with someone who's making the vaccine.'

'Who? Where?'

'All I know is that they're working in a laboratory "in the wilds" – somewhere they won't be found. I heard Dr Langford say that.'

Hutch was despondent. 'So it could be anyone, anywhere. What good is that?'

'If we could find Mrs Langford in France, we could ask her where the laboratory is. And we could warn her. She might be in danger too.'

'But how can we track her down when the police can't?'

'Do you think they're really trying? I went to the police station to tell them all this, and they wouldn't even listen. If they've decided Mum did the murder, why would they want to look for someone else? Why should they spend a fortune trying to find Mrs Langford abroad?'

Hutch shook his head. 'It looks as if it's all down to us now, Johnny.'

'I've tried to trace her. I've done that advert.'

'But if Mrs Langford's in France, she's hardly likely to see it, is she?' said Hutch. 'I think we need to do another advertisement, Johnny – something bigger that stands a better chance of being noticed. We can ask anyone who knows Mrs Langford's whereabouts to get in touch.' He paused for thought. 'And we need to put it in all the major national and regional papers so that whoever was working with Dr Langford might see it.'

'But that will cost a fortune.'

'Don't worry, son, I'll pay. But I think we'd better keep our identities secret, don't you, just in case the murderer gets the idea we're on his trail?'

'You mean . . . ?'

'Yes,' Hutch sighed. 'Auntie Ada can have one more outing. And we'll use her private box as the address for the reply.'

Chapter 31

LOOKING FOR MRS LANGFORD

Hutch made up a bed in the spare room at the back of the flat. Johnny lay down surrounded by boxes of official Post Office forms which Hutch felt were too important to be kept in the stockroom downstairs alongside the custard powder and fish paste. He clutched his old rabbit, just as he had at the beginning of this business, on the night when he'd wet himself after the revelation that the Secret of Instant Height was a trick. He was exhausted, but unable to get to sleep in the unfamiliar surroundings; and he was excited by the idea of having Hutch to help him search for Mrs Langford and the real murderer. He wondered who it was. It had to be someone who knew about the BCG. Another doctor perhaps? Maybe someone from France? It could even be the man with that useless drug from Africa. After all, he'd be out of business if someone found a way to stop people getting TB. Johnny tried to remember the name at the top of the advert Mrs Langford had thrown onto the fire after Dr Langford's joke about the Wimbledon racket. Umba . . . Umca . . . Umcka . . . Umckaloabo. He drifted off at last to the exotic rhythm of the word. He had completely forgotten that tomorrow would be Christmas Day.

Hutch hadn't, and Johnny woke to find presents at the end of his bed. He knew where they had come from. He recognized the chocolates, jellies and candied fruit he had unpacked when they'd been delivered to the shop weeks before, and which had so spectacularly failed to sell since his mother's arrest. Of course he knew that Hutch must have crept downstairs to fetch them in the middle of the night, but somehow he almost believed in Santa Claus for the first time in years. The Christmas lunch he and Hutch enjoyed together was the most lavish meal he had ever eaten, but he couldn't really enjoy it because the person he loved most in the world wasn't there.

After the meal, he and Hutch sat down together and composed their advertisement. After a lot of deliberation they came up with:

Langford
Anyone knowing the whereabouts of
Mrs Marie Langford,

widow of the late Dr Giles Langford,
believed to be staying with relatives in France,
is kindly invited to contact
PO Box 9, Stambleton, Warwickshire.
This is a matter of the utmost importance.

They got it into the first post after Christmas, and it was in papers across the country before New Year.

Over the next week, a number of letters arrived addressed to PO Box 9, but they all turned out to be replies to Johnny's last spurt of adverts before he had confessed all to Hutch. With Hutch watching over his shoulder, Johnny sent all the money straight back.

Then a letter came that didn't contain a postal order. It was just a small sheet of paper saying:

I do not know where Marie Langford is, but if you value your safety, you will stop asking questions.

It was unsigned.

Hutch looked at the postmark. 'It was posted in Brecon,' he said.

'Should we go to the police now?' asked Johnny.

'I'm not sure,' said Hutch. 'Maybe we should try to find out more first.'

'Where is Brecon, anyway?'

'It's near Swansea, I think. In Wales.'

'I know someone who comes from Swansea,' said Johnny, excitedly. 'Olwen. That girl from school I told you about. If we could find her, maybe she could help.'

'Don't be silly. That way we end up searching for two people, not just one. And anyway, what use can a child be?'

Johnny had to admit that Hutch was right. 'I know,' he said, calming down. 'I didn't really mean it. We'll have to do something else.'

Hutch was thinking. 'We could put in another advertisement – in the paper that covers the Brecon area. How about: *Langford. Any news? PO Box 9, Stambleton.*'

'No,' said Johnny. 'Don't mention Stambleton. That's put the wind up someone already. Let's get a box number at the paper this time, and ask them to send any replies on to us.'

Hutch found out the phone number of the local paper, and called to ask about their advertising rates. He was allocated Box 102. He sold himself a postal order to cover the fee, and asked Johnny to write the message out neatly, and to put everything into an envelope.

Johnny went upstairs and did as he was told. But sitting there with pen and paper, he couldn't resist working out the wording for another advert that had come into his mind in an idle moment. He thought quite a few people might fall for it, and though he knew Hutch wouldn't approve, he felt uncomfortable without any cash coming in. After all, he couldn't live off Hutch's kindness for ever, especially with business so bad, and he wanted to keep paying the rent on the house in Dagmouth Lane, ready for his mother's return.

He still had some postal orders he'd received just before Christmas, from people who had been so desperate about the behaviour of their pets that they had written in to find out how to *Solve the Problem of a Barking Dog*. They had each paid a shilling, only to be told to *Swap it for a cat*.

Johnny wasn't particularly proud of that one. But as so often, a simple idea had turned out to be very lucrative. He knew Hutch would never cash the postal orders now, and he thought he should probably return them to his 'customers', but he had lost their addresses when he had sent back their stamped addressed envelopes. So he thought it wouldn't do any harm to use them to pay his next advertising fee. There was enough for a few more words than usual. He wrote out the advert:

Change Your Appearance Permanently.
Unhappy with the way you look?
Transform yourself Instantly and For Ever.
Send 1/– to Box 102.

With only a moment's hesitation, he popped it in the envelope alongside Hutch's personal ad about Mrs Langford. He sealed the letter and took it downstairs just in time to catch the postman, who was collecting the outgoing mail.

The response to both advertisements was quick and surprising. A week later, Hutch answered the phone in the kiosk by the shop door. People who had no phone at home occasionally arranged to take calls there, but at that moment (as was so often the case since Hutch had taken Johnny in) there were no customers in the shop.

'Hello,' said Hutch.

There was a pause while the person at the other end spoke.

Hutch replied in his 'post office' voice. 'I'm sorry, that's quite impossible. The identity of a box holder is a confidential matter . . .'

Johnny was weighing flour from a huge sack into three-pound bags, and it took a little while for him to notice that Hutch's tone had changed, and that he was leaning out of the phone booth, clicking his fingers to attract Johnny's attention.

'. . . but as it happens,' Hutch was saying, 'the lady is in the shop at the moment. I'll put her on.' He called across to Johnny, hoping he'd take the hint that the person on the phone was calling in response to the advertisement about Mrs Langford. 'Ada!' he shouted. 'Ada. You have a telephone call.'

Hutch handed Johnny the phone, but stayed close, listening in.

'Hello?' said Johnny, hoping that his voice sounded more like a woman's than a boy's. 'Can I help you?'

'You can help yourself, darling,' said a man's voice at the other end. 'You must be mad if you thought I wouldn't spot that new advert in the local paper. *Langford. Any news?* Well there's no news, and there won't be any. I told you before. Keep your nose out if you want to stay safe. Do you hear? And remember. I know where you are.'

The line went dead. Johnny was scared. It was true. The caller knew where Ada lived, even if he was unaware that she didn't exist. And if he came to Stambleton, he wouldn't have any trouble finding the post office. He might use force to get Hutch to say who Ada really was. Things could turn nasty. But the man on the phone had given Johnny and Hutch some important information, too. He was the author of the threatening letter; he was involved in the Langford case; and, most importantly of all, he had a Welsh accent.

Almost as soon as he had posted the Change Your Appearance Permanently advert, Johnny had regretted it. He had made a solemn promise to Hutch to stop the advertising scams, and he had broken his word the first time he was tempted. He prayed that no one would reply, and dreaded the arrival of a package from the Welsh newspaper, even though it might contain information about Marie Langford. He could picture Hutch's rage if he found that the contents of Box 102 was a haul of postal orders and stamped addressed envelopes. So he was relieved that Hutch was out on the paper round when a fat letter arrived from Wales.

Johnny took the packet upstairs to open it, sensing that Change Your Appearance Permanently had been one of his greatest successes. He was right, but the old feeling of excitement was mixed with a sense of shame as he split the seal. No one had answered the personal ad, but there were thirteen replies to the other one. Despite his promise to Hutch, Johnny knew he would secretly write out the answer thirteen times and stash the postal orders inside his rabbit. He shuffled through the stamped addressed envelopes. Most of them were cheap little things, the kind Hutch sold for 4d. a dozen. One was thicker, with scalloped edges to the flap. Another was pink and scented. Halfway through the pile, he found a buff-coloured envelope that looked as if it had come from an office. It was made out to an address in Wales, and the distinctive, curly handwriting seemed familiar. The address read:

Mrs J. W. Morgan
Craig-y-Nos Castle
Near Brecon
Wales

He couldn't remember where he had seen the writing before. He was pretty sure that it was different from the earlier, menacing, note from Brecon, but he thought he'd better make sure. He'd put that one aside in his mother's box, safe with the medals and birth certificates in case he ever needed to show it to the police. He compared the two. He was right. There was no similarity at all. And yet he was sure he had seen the writing on the new envelope recently. Was it an old customer? One of his lonely hearts, perhaps? If it was someone unlucky in love, they might well want to change their appearance. But how could he ever check? He had burned all their desperate letters, to keep himself warm when he had been alone at home.

He went to put the threatening letter back in the box. And that was when he saw it. There, alongside the telegram announcing his father's death, was the testimonial that Mrs Langford had written for his mother on Remembrance Day. The envelope said simply:

To whom it may concern

The similarity to the writing on the new envelope was unmistakable. The 'w' of 'whom' began with a swirl on top of the first downstroke, almost like a child's drawing of a snail's shell. 'Wales' in the new address began in the same way, and so did the 'w' in J. W. Morgan. The 'con' in 'concern' matched the end of 'Brecon'. Johnny unfolded the letter of recommendation. The 'w's in the heading 'Mrs Winifred May Swanson' both had snail-shell swirls. There was also a flourish on the last leg of the 'm's, just like the 'm' in Morgan on today's envelope. Johnny knew what that meant: Marie Langford and J. W. Morgan were the same person; Marie Langford was not in France – she was living in a castle in Wales; and for some reason she wanted to transform herself instantly, and for ever.

Chapter 32

THE DARK ROCK

Johnny put the stack of new letters under his mattress and ran down to show Hutch the new envelope from Brecon.

'Hutch! Hutch! We've got a reply,' he shouted as he bounded into the shop.

Hutch had only just returned from delivering the papers, and he was preoccupied with opening up for the day.

'Look, Hutch! Look! It's in Mrs Langford's hand-writing.' Johnny thrust the envelope in front of Hutch, who took it and examined it carefully.

'And what does she say?' he asked.

Johnny was silent.

'We said, *Langford. Any News?* What's the reply?' Hutch looked inside the envelope. It was empty. He was puzzled for a moment, and then furious. And Johnny knew at once that he should have covered his tracks more carefully.

'Johnny,' said Hutch, sternly. 'Johnny, tell me, and

tell me honestly. Why has this woman sent us an envelope addressed to herself?'

It was a sorry scene, which might have had terrible consequences for Johnny had it not been pensions day, with a stream of customers coming in to use the post office. In whispered conversations between transactions, Johnny admitted that he had run one final scam in the Welsh paper, and Hutch left him in no doubt that he was even angrier than before. But his rage was tempered by the need to be polite to the customers, and the dawning realization that at last they had a lead on Mrs Langford's whereabouts. Hutch was intrigued by the address:

'Craig-y-Nos Castle. It sounds like an imposing place.'

'How can we find out more about it?' said Johnny. 'Shall I go to the library?'

'No. I doubt you'd find much about Wales in there.' Hutch pushed back his shoulders and straightened his tie. 'I think this is a sufficiently important matter for me to use my Post Office contacts.'

So Hutch put in a long-distance call to his opposite number in Brecon, more than 150 miles away. Johnny listened in to them sharing Post Office chit-chat (both of them had received a circular from Head Office saying that they must empty the coin boxes on their telephones at least once a month; both of them thought that an unnecessary imposition). Then Hutch asked his question. His bad leg was twitching. Johnny could tell that he didn't like lying.

'I've got a letter. It's somehow ended up here, and I'm thinking that it might be important. It has that sort of "urgent" look you get a feel for, if you see what I mean. But the handwriting is very bad. Let me tell you what I think it says.' He read out the Craig-y-Nos address, spelling it out with all the hyphens, and pretending to have trouble reading it, though it was, in fact, perfectly legible – if a little unusual.

Johnny could hear the voice of the man at the other end, but he couldn't work out what he was saying in the long pauses between Hutch's questions. Eventually Hutch ended the call. 'Right you are, then. Many thanks. I'll forward it on.'

Johnny couldn't wait to hear what Hutch had found out.

'Well,' said Hutch, as he put down the receiver. 'That was very interesting indeed. This Craig-y-Nos place. The name means Dark Rock, or Rock of the Night.'

'Never mind that,' said Johnny, impatiently. 'Where is it? What's it like?'

'It really is a castle, apparently – but a modern one.

And it used to belong to a famous opera singer: Adelina Patti. She spent a fortune on it. It's got its own theatre, massive grounds, even its own station. Oh, she was a big star before the war.' Hutch seemed to have become infected with the Welsh postmaster's long-windedness.

Johnny interrupted again. 'What would Mrs Langford be doing staying with an opera singer?'

'Ah, but that's the thing, see. Madame Patti's long dead. And Craig-y-Nos Castle isn't a private residence any more. It's been turned into a hospital.'

Johnny gasped, and Hutch delivered his next fact with a flourish of triumph. 'And guess what kind of hospital it is?'

Johnny was bursting with anticipation, desperate for Hutch to get on with it.

Hutch puffed out his chest, and announced: 'Craig-y-Nos Castle, Johnny, is now a sanatorium.'

'That's it!' yelled Johnny. 'Mum was right. That's what this whole business is all about. Everything's linked to phthisis.'

'It seems so, Johnny. But please call it TB like everyone else.'

'Shall we tell the police?' said Johnny. 'Surely they'll listen to us now?'

'Yes, I'll phone them straight away.'

Hutch went back into the booth. Johnny hovered outside trying to listen in, but Hutch dropped his voice very low when he heard the bell on the shop door announce the arrival of a customer. Johnny served her. She was curt with him, like most people nowadays, and made it clear that she had only come in because she had unexpectedly run out of matches, and it wasn't worth her while to walk to another shop to buy some more. She left just as Hutch slammed down the phone. Johnny opened the door to the kiosk, hoping for good news. Instead he found Hutch punching the wall with rage. He had never heard him curse before.

'It's no good,' said Hutch. 'Johnny, there's nothing we can do to get through to those people. They've made their decision. As far as they're concerned, your mother's guilty, and anything you or I say is just made up to try to get her off. He wouldn't even give me time to tell him that we'd found Mrs Langford.'

'So what can we do now?' said Johnny. 'Do you think we should go to Craig-y-Nos ourselves and find out what's going on?'

'I'd like to, Johnny. Believe me, I would. But I can't leave the shop.'

'Surely it wouldn't matter if you closed – just for a day or so?'

'The shop would be all right,' said Hutch. 'To be honest, it's costing me money to open since all this fuss. It's the post office I'm worried about. I have a legal duty to run it. People need the service. I can't just shut it down.'

'But what would happen if you were ill?'

'I'd have to contact Head Office, and they would send a substitute postmaster. But they wouldn't like it. And if they found out afterwards that I hadn't been ill at all, I'd probably lose my job. I'd never be able to be a public servant again.'

'But they needn't find out.'

'Not if we fail, Johnny. But what if we succeed? If we can solve the murder, your mother will be let out, and there will be lots of publicity. Questions will be asked. My lie would be exposed.'

Johnny was fired up by the thought that they might succeed, and that with Mrs Langford's help Winnie might be freed. But he could see Hutch's point.

'I'll go by myself,' he said.

'Are you serious?' said Hutch.

'Of course I am. My mother and Mrs Langford are

both in danger. It looks as if I'm the only one who can help them. I really have to go.'

Hutch was thoughtful. 'I'm not sure I should let you. I promised your mother I would keep you safe.'

'Hutch, I'm sorry,' said Johnny defiantly. 'I know I should do what you say, but if you don't let me, I'll just go anyway. There's no way you can stop me. I've got enough money to buy a ticket. If you help me, I might at least get on the right train.'

Hutch gave in eventually, and looked up the route and train times in a large book he kept under the counter in the post office. He worked out that if Johnny started early enough, it was just about possible to get to Craig-y-Nos and back in one day. He made Johnny a packed lunch for the journey, and wrote a list of the stations where he would have to change trains.

'If you have any problems, ask a lady,' he said, 'or the guard or the ticket collector. Don't stick your head out of the window – you might get it knocked off. And don't use the lavatory while the train is in a station – it's not allowed.' He asked for the list back and scribbled something new on the bottom. 'It's the phone number here, in case you hit trouble.

You'll have to ask the operator to put you through.'

'I know how to work the phone,' said Johnny wearily. 'I sometimes went to the telephone box by the Town Hall to send in adverts. It meant I could use papers all over the country.'

'But how did you pay them?'

'Oh, I sent postal orders. Sometimes I could put two or three adverts on one bill. The *Yorkshire Post* even gave Auntie Ada an account.'

Hutch shook his head. 'So much knowledge for one so young,' he said.

Johnny didn't dare tell him that he'd never been on a train in his life.

Chapter 33

JOHNNY'S JOURNEY

Johnny loved the railway. He often watched from the footbridge over Stambleton station as snorting steam engines powered through on their way from places like Birmingham, Rugby and Crewe to all parts of the country. Even the little local trains that puffed to a stop at Stambleton were exciting.

On board for the first time, Johnny rocked with the rhythm as the wheels bumped over the joints in the track. He stared out at the unfamiliar perspective on the town he knew so well, and then, only minutes later, on a rural landscape he had never seen before. He adored the smell of the sooty steam that blew in through the little sliding window at the top of the compartment. It mingled with the aroma of cigarettes and pipe-smoke clinging to the itchy upholstery, which left patterns on the backs of his legs. Hutch had put some comics in his bag, but Johnny didn't want to read. There was too much to see. And anyway, he was worried in case he missed the two connections he would have to make before arriving at Penwyllt, where a station had been built at Adelina Patti's own expense especially to serve Craig-y-Nos. Johnny thought how much Dr Langford would have loved those place names, heavy with consonants and mystery.

His last change involved a cold wait for the local service to Penwyllt. There was a refreshment room at the other end of the platform. Johnny wondered whether they would let him sit inside to keep warm. He had a shilling in his pocket, but Hutch had given it to him for use in emergencies only, and he didn't want to be forced to spend some of it on a cup of tea. He decided to go in, sit down, and see if he got thrown out. It would be worth the embarrassment to have the chance to get the feeling back in his feet and fingers again. But as he pushed open the door, letting out a blast of steamy brightness, he caught sight of a group of women surrounded by baskets and parcels, chatting and laughing together. They were wearing uniforms with broad aprons and large white hats. Johnny guessed they must be nurses from the Craig-y-Nos sanatorium, returning after a day out at the shops.

Johnny had brought the 'J. W. Morgan' envelope with him so that if he were stopped by anyone at the sanatorium he could say that he had come to visit her, and at the very least buy himself some time. But what if the nurses talked to him now? What if they asked him who he was and where he was going? What if they made a fuss of him so that he didn't get a chance to look round the sanatorium secretly, to try to find out what was going on there? Or, worse still, what if they didn't believe him, and sent him back to Stambleton when he was so close to Craig-y-Nos. He decided to stay out of the nurses' way for as long as he could. Reluctantly he gently let the door close again, and walked up and down the platform, trying to keep warm.

A porter cleared his throat and spat onto the rails. *Haemoptysis*, thought Johnny, remembering Dr Langford again. In the cold, his excitement was waning, and the sight of the nurses and the porter's sputum had reminded him why the sanatorium existed. It wasn't just Mrs Langford's prison. Craig-y-Nos Castle must be full of people with a deadly disease. For the first time on this adventure Johnny was frightened. Until now he hadn't let himself admit that if he went to Craig-y-Nos he might catch TB. He might die. It was stupid to put himself in contact with all those germs.

Now he wanted to go home. After all the bravado and exhilaration that had buoyed him up through the journey so far, Johnny was at last struck by the madness of this whole adventure. He was only a boy. He was in unfamiliar territory, and he didn't really know what he was looking for. He might meet a murderer: that Welshman on the phone had already threatened him. Why had he ever come up with the idea of trying to investigate Craig-y-Nos on his own? Hutch should never have allowed him to set off in the first place. You could tell that he wasn't used to looking after children. His mother would never have let him go.

His mother. That was why he was doing it. Johnny might be afraid; he might long to go back to Stambleton; but he knew that if he did, someone else could die. Winnie was in real danger. He was facing a risk – but her fate looked certain. Johnny imagined what would happen if he failed to find Mrs Langford. Although he was staring at columns of figures on the railway timetable, all he could see was the hangman putting a noose round his mother's neck. He couldn't get the image out of his mind. He knew he had to carry on.

When the little train came in, Johnny watched to see which carriage the nurses chose and then got into the other one. He was all alone. As the train rattled along, the scenery grew ever greener and more dramatic, with waterfalls gushing down rocky hills. Occasionally Johnny caught a glimpse of a mighty building nestling halfway up the valley. Part of it was made of sparkling glass, the rest of solid brown-grey stone. It had two towers: one tall and pointed with big white clock-faces on every side, and a stout square one with battlements on top, like a castle in a history book. Although it was early afternoon, the winter light was already fading, and the building looked sinister in the gloom. It must be Craig-y-Nos.

Chapter 34

AT CRAIG-Y-NOS

Penwyllt station was high on a windswept hill. There was no sign of the castle now, nor of any people apart from the station master and the group of nurses who had just got off the train. A cart was waiting to take them to Craig-y-Nos. Johnny buttoned up his coat, pulled down the big woolly hat that Hutch had insisted on lending him to keep warm, and followed the cart down the hill. The road twisted in huge loops, and Johnny managed to keep up by running in a straight line, taking short cuts through the bushes, ducking down so that he wouldn't be seen. He stayed outside the gates of the castle, watching as the cart turned into a courtyard and drew to a halt alongside a fountain in the shape of a golden bird. The driver helped the nurses climb down, and they ran inside, too busy with their bags and their gossip to notice a little boy in the shadows.

Close up, the castle looked friendlier than it had from a distance. As well as the two big towers there were smaller turrets, sloping roofs, and all sorts of out-buildings joined together with walls and arches. The windows were wide, not at all like the arrow-slits Johnny had expected (and even hoped for). They made the place look more like a country house than a fortress. Through the glass, Johnny could see that the rooms had electric lights, and warm fires in the grates. He walked round the outside and looked out across the valley. At the back of the castle the ground fell away steeply, and Johnny could hear rushing water down below. There must be a river at the bottom. It was almost dark now. Nurses were wheeling beds and chairs inside from the gardens. Even in early January they believed in exposing their patients to fresh air whenever they could. The beds seemed rather short. The chairs were small. All at once Johnny realized that Craig-y-Nos was a children's hospital. He was going to find it easier to blend in than he had expected.

Nevertheless, he was careful. He crouched in a corner of the courtyard, waiting for the nurses' chatter to die away before risking going inside. He saw a child shuffling along in the shadow of the wall. Like him, she was trying not to be seen, but his eyes were drawn towards her at once because of her shoes. They were far too big for her and the laces were undone, so she couldn't help making a clattering, dragging noise as she crossed the stone path to a back door. She wore a heavy coat over her pyjamas. That was the wrong size too. Its sleeves hung down past her hands, and the pockets were bulging. Johnny guessed that she'd been up to no good – that she'd borrowed someone else's clothes to sneak outside from one of the wards, and wouldn't want to be caught as she found her way back in. He followed several paces behind her, hoping that she would lead the way through parts of the building where no one would spot him either.

He tracked her from one corridor to another, past dormitories and treatment rooms, a laboratory, work-shops and a kitchen. Through half-open doors he caught glimpses of nurses busying about their work, and he knew that sooner or later he was bound to be discovered, but he wanted to see as much of the hospital as he could before then, if only so that he could plan his route to make a quick getaway if he had to.

A sudden cry and a crash behind him made him instinctively spin round. Someone had dropped some plates. There was uproar in the kitchen, but the corridor was empty. He was safe. He hadn't been seen.

He turned back again. The girl had been startled by the smash as well, and she too had looked in the direction of the noise. Now she was staring at Johnny through her round glasses.

'Who are you?' she asked.

Johnny reached into his pocket for the J. W. Morgan envelope, ready with his explanation.

The girl interrupted: 'I've seen you before somewhere . . .'

As she spoke, Johnny recognized her too. 'Olwen?' he asked. 'What are you doing here? I'm Johnny. Johnny Swanson. You came to my school in Stambleton. I tried to find you . . .'

Olwen's words came out in a rush of excited surprise. 'You were nice to me there. You were the only one. Have you seen my family? Are they here too? I've been so worried. They don't tell us anything in this place, you know. We might as well be in prison. We're not allowed letters or anything like that. I've been hoping for so long that Mam and Dad would come to get me. Oh, what a relief that you're here now. There's nothing wrong with me, you know. My uncle should never have put me in here.'

Johnny was panicking. It was clear that Olwen didn't know that her parents and sister were dead;

even if she'd imagined the worst, she was frantically clinging to the idea that all was well. He knew he would have to tell her what had happened, but he couldn't find a way to begin. He tried first to explain that he hadn't come to Craig-y-Nos for her.

'I didn't even know you were here,' he said. 'I'm looking for someone else. But, Olwen, I have got some news.'

'About my family? You know how they are?'

'Yes,' he said, realizing instantly that he had accidentally given her hope.

'Are they coming for me? Have they sent you with a message?'

He stuttered something unintelligible, and was saved by the sound of footsteps. Olwen grabbed his arm and tugged him down some stone stairs. 'In here,' she whispered urgently, opening the door to a dark windowless room that smelled of antiseptic and damp. It was full of boxes, like Hutch's stockroom. Dismantled beds and bits and pieces of medical equipment were propped against the walls.

'No one will find us,' she said. 'They're all too scared to come in. Even some of the nurses think there's a ghost down here.' Olwen was giggling. 'They say it's where Madame Patti was laid to rest after she died.' She put on a dramatic voice: 'They embalmed the body on this very table.'

There was just enough light for Johnny to see Olwen hoisting herself up onto a marble slab in the middle of the room. She sat there with her feet swinging in mid air. 'Close the door,' she said. Johnny did, and they were suddenly in total darkness. One of Olwen's shoes fell off. Johnny gasped in fright.

Olwen laughed. 'Don't be silly. There's nothing to be scared of. I don't believe in ghosts – and even if they do exist, I think I'd like to meet one. I'd ask what it's like being dead. Wouldn't you?'

Johnny was glad Olwen couldn't see his face in the darkness. He hated hearing her talk so casually about death when he had such bad news for her.

She was badgering him for information. 'Come on, then. Tell me what's going on. But be quick, mind. I've got to get back to the ward before the nurses notice I'm missing.'

'Were you running away?'

'No, though I'd love to if I had anywhere to go. It was my turn to go down to the bins to see if there was any left-over food. I've got some stale cake here, and a bit of cheese rind if you want it.'

Johnny could hear her digging into her coat

pocket. 'Stop it, Olwen,' he said. 'Be quiet for a minute. This is no time for messing about with cake. I've got something serious to say.'

Olwen's tone changed. 'Is it the baby? They took her to the sanatorium, you know. Mam promised they would make her better.'

Johnny took a deep breath. Even in the darkness he could tell that Olwen had guessed part of the truth and didn't dare ask the question that was really on her mind. He forced himself to answer.

'I'm sorry, Olwen. Your sister died. I know that the doctors did everything in their power, but she was desperately ill. They couldn't save her.'

He waited for Olwen to ask more. He wanted her to prompt him to talk about her parents, but there was silence. 'I'm sorry. I'm really sorry,' he said. He was trying to speak normally, but his voice came out in breathy croaks. Olwen still didn't say anything, and Johnny knew he had to carry on. He swallowed hard. 'It's not just the baby,' he said. 'It's your mother and father.'

'Have they come to collect me? If the baby's dead, they don't need to spend all their time looking after her any more, do they? They can take me home now, can't they?'

'No, Olwen. They can't come.'

'Are they ill too? Is Dad still bad?'

'No, it's not that . . .' Johnny could tell he was making a mess of it, taking far too long to break the news, and dangling another moment of false hope. In the end he had to accept that there was no easy way to say it. 'Oh, Olwen, I'm so sorry. They died too.'

If he'd expected anything, he'd been prepared for tears; but Olwen was suddenly angry. 'No they're not. Don't lie. They're not,' she shouted. 'Someone would have told me.'

Johnny fumbled in the darkness for her hand. 'Please, Olwen, believe me. It *is* true. I've seen their graves. They both had TB, and they both died in the sanatorium at Emberley. I'm sure someone would have told you if they could, but I don't think anyone knew where to find you.'

'But you did.'

'No I didn't, Olwen. I tried to tell you before. I came here for another reason. Something really important.' He knew at once that it was the wrong thing to say.

Olwen snatched her hand away. 'Really important? How? My family are dead. What could be more important than that?' She was sniffing now. She must be crying.

'Important to me, I meant. And to my mother.' It seemed wrong to be changing the subject, but he wanted to explain. His words started tumbling out. 'There's someone here who might be able to save my mother's life. It's Mrs Langford. The old doctor's wife from Stambleton. Do you know her? Is she here? She might be calling herself Mrs Morgan.'

He could tell that Olwen wasn't really listening. She was sobbing quite loudly now. He wanted to comfort her, but didn't know how. He fumbled in the dark, trying to put his arm round her, but they both pulled away, startled at the sound of brisk footsteps on the stairs.

'We've been here too long! They're looking for me,' Olwen gasped through her tears as she slipped down from the table.

'Please, don't say that I'm here,' Johnny whispered back, fearing Olwen might tell on him in revenge for his bad news. He stumbled into a pile of boxes and curled up behind them, hoping that nothing would show if someone came looking.

The door swung open and the light from the stairway flung a huge silhouette of a nurse across the back wall. The points of her starched headdress looked like horns on an angry bull in the contorted image.

A fierce voice boomed out. 'Here you are! I might have known. You come out from there, young lady! This time you've gone too far!' Johnny heard Olwen sobbing as the furious nurse dragged her from under the table. 'I've had enough of you and your disobedience. Now stand up and stop that stupid crying!'

Through a gap in the boxes Johnny saw the nurse shaking Olwen, tearing off her overcoat and rummaging through its pockets.

'What's this? Cake! Cheese! Have you been thieving again?'

'No, not stealing. It doesn't belong to anyone. It's rubbish.'

'As if you don't get enough for nothing! You'd better watch your step, my girl, or you'll get thrown out. And then where will you be? That uncle of yours doesn't want you back, you know. If you ask me he's dumped you here, living off charity. Can't say that I blame him. Nobody would want you, you nasty, deceitful little madam!'

Johnny wished he could defend Olwen. He wanted to jump out and tell the nurse about Olwen's parents, and how she'd only just found out that she was all alone in the world. But he had to stay quiet. The nurse wasn't looking for him, and with luck she wouldn't spot his hiding place. But it hurt to hear Olwen under attack.

'I said stop that stupid grizzling!' The arm of the giant shadow rose and swung. There was the unmistakable sound of flesh striking flesh. 'Now, what have you got to say for yourself?'

Olwen sobbed and started to speak. 'It's my mam and dad. And my sister—' she began, but the nurse was in no mood to listen.

'I don't want excuses. You've been here long enough to get over homesickness. Stop that snivelling and tell me where you got this food.'

Olwen was shaking with tears as the nurse slapped at the thin fabric of her pyjamas.

'You've been rooting through the dustbins, haven't you? You're just a greedy, stinking animal. No better than a pig.'

Olwen's next breath, caught up in tears and snot, came out as a noisy snort.

The nurse held the coat in the air. 'And what about this? It looks like Dr Howell's. Did you take it from the staff cloakroom? You know you're not allowed to go in there.'

Olwen sniffed. The nurse picked one shoe up off the floor and wrenched the other from Olwen's foot.

'You're coming with me to take these things back straight away. And since you like delving in dirt so much, you can spend the rest of the day scrubbing the outside toilets. You can start with the boys'. You'll miss all the fun and games tonight, you nasty, scheming, ungrateful child!'

Olwen tried to speak, then bowed her head and left the room. The nurse followed her and slammed the door behind them, shutting Johnny in the dark again.

Chapter 35

THE THEATRE

Johnny was furious with himself for saying nothing while Olwen was being attacked by the nurse. He made a silent promise that he would try to sort out Olwen's predicament as soon as he'd completed his own mission. Then he waited until there was no sound from the other side of the door, and crept out into the corridor to search for Mrs Langford.

He could hear the angry nurse again, shouting somewhere in the distance. There were other noises too. He knew that only luck had stopped him being discovered already. After seeing how the nurse had treated Olwen, he doubted whether anyone would give him a chance to explain why he was there. Every time he turned a corner he dreaded walking into a potential captor. Each creak and footfall was amplified in the part of his mind where terror lived.

Then, all at once, he found himself in a corridor with a dead end. He could hear footsteps: brisk, feminine footsteps, closing in behind him. Someone was coming, and there was no way out. Panicking, he rehearsed his cover story: how he was there to find a Mrs J. W. Morgan – how he had brought her an important message that he had promised to deliver in private and in person. As the clicking of high-heeled shoes grew nearer, he flattened his body against the wall.

Except it wasn't a wall. He was leaning on a pair of double doors that slowly began to give way under the pressure of his back. The footsteps were getting nearer, so he allowed himself to slip through into the dark unknown on the other side.

His eyes started adjusting. He could tell that this was a huge space, like the assembly hall at school. Then the doors opened again, swiftly and deliberately this time, and he squashed himself behind one of them as somebody came in. With the clunk of a heavy switch, there was a blast of light that blinded him for an instant. He blinked, then sneaked a look round the side of the door, trying to keep himself out of sight. With the lights on, the hall was transformed into a glorious theatre. Its blue walls and ivory ceiling were heavy with golden images of angels and harps. The flat curtain across the wide stage was decorated with a gigantic painting of a warrior queen in a chariot pulled through the clouds by two white horses. At first Johnny was stunned; then he remembered what Hutch had told him: a famous opera singer had built a theatre as part of this grand house before it became a sanatorium.

A woman was shuffling between rows and rows of chairs, setting down a sheet of paper on each seat. Johnny recognized her straight away. He had known that upswept hair, the long graceful neck and those elegant movements all his life. It was Marie Langford. He couldn't believe his luck and ran towards her. 'Mrs Langford!' he cried. 'I've found you.'

She looked at him with horror and disbelief. 'Johnny?' she gasped. 'What on earth are you doing here?'

'I had to find you, Mrs Langford. You must help me. Mrs Langford, it's awful. They think my mother killed your husband. She's in prison, Mrs Langford. She might die!' He hugged her tightly, burying his face in the rough tweed of her suit.

She pulled his arms away and sat down on one of the chairs. 'Be quiet, Johnny,' she said, looking anxiously around to make sure that no one else was in earshot. 'And don't call me Mrs Langford. No one here calls me that. If you let them know who I really am, we could both be in a lot of trouble.'

'So you are J. W. Morgan, then?'

'What? How do you know that?'

Johnny took the crumpled envelope out of his pocket and handed it to her. 'Change Your Appearance Permanently,' he said. 'You answered that advert. Mrs Langford, I know you want a disguise.'

Mrs Langford sat in silence, turning over the envelope while Johnny burbled on. 'I knew it was you. And I've worked it all out. Someone is holding you prisoner here, aren't they, Mrs Langford? That's why you need the disguise, isn't it? You want to escape.'

Mrs Langford was still for a few more seconds, then nodded, gazing down at the letter. 'Tell me more, Johnny,' she said quietly. 'Tell me everything you know.'

'Well, I know that my mother didn't kill Dr Langford for a start—' He stopped suddenly, remembering Olwen's reaction to unexpected news. 'Oh, Mrs Langford. I'm sorry. Forgive me. Did you know? Your husband is dead.'

She didn't raise her head, but nodded, and whispered, 'Yes, Johnny. I know.'

'He was murdered, Mrs Langford. While you were in France—'

'In France?' She paused and mumbled, 'Oh yes . . .'

Johnny was getting excited and talking more quickly. 'And the police think my mother did it. But she didn't, and you can tell them she didn't. The police won't take any notice of me. But they'll listen to you. You know she'd never do a thing like that, don't you?'

Mrs Langford said nothing.

'Help me, Mrs Langford. Tell the police it was nothing to do with my mother. You must know it wasn't. And you must have some idea who it was. I've worked that out too. It must have been somebody who knew about the BCG. Was it the Umckaloabo man? Was it somebody here? There was a Welshman who warned me to stop looking for you. Is it him, Mrs Langford? Did he kill your husband? Is that why he's hiding you here? To keep you quiet?'

Mrs Langford pulled Johnny close to her and whispered urgently, 'Johnny, you're the one who had better keep quiet, or you are going to make things very difficult for both of us.' She split her pile of papers in two and handed him half. 'Come on. Help me put these out on the seats, and I'll try to explain.'

Johnny took a look at the heading on the top sheet. It read:

THE STAFF OF CRAIG-Y-NOS PRESENT

CINDERELLA

He understood now why the nurse had told Olwen she'd be missing 'fun and games'. 'A pantomime? Is there going to be a pantomime?' he asked.

'Yes, Johnny. Tonight everyone at Craig-y-Nos will be in this hall. It's a special treat. Now, come on. I haven't got long to finish getting things ready.'

They walked between the rows putting out the programmes, and Mrs Langford began. 'As you know, my husband was doing some important work to do with TB. One of his old students, Dr Howell, was producing the BCG vaccine for him – here, in the laboratory.'

Dr Howell. Johnny had heard that name just a few minutes earlier. Olwen had been wearing his coat and shoes.

Mrs Langford continued: 'My husband got him some of the original culture, and told him how to do it.'

Johnny's mind ran on. 'And then Dr Howell got jealous, and killed your husband so he could pretend the vaccine was all his own work.'

'Oh Johnny, what a clever boy you are,' said Mrs Langford. 'But it was worse than that. You see, Dr Howell wanted to sell the vaccine.'

'Like the Umckaloabo man? The man who put that advert in the paper!'

'Yes, Johnny. Just like him. But of course Dr Howell couldn't advertise BCG openly because it was against the law for him to have it. So he planned to frighten people into thinking their children might die if they weren't immunized, and then to charge them a fortune to buy the BCG secretly. He was going to target rich people. He knew they'd pay him a lot of money if he promised not to tell anyone that they'd used an illegal vaccine.'

'So it was a kind of blackmail too?' said Johnny. 'Dr Langford wouldn't have liked that.'

'No indeed,' said Mrs Langford. 'My husband wanted the vaccine given free to all children, just as it is in France. He was terribly shocked when he found out about Dr Howell's plans. He protested, and he paid with his life.'

Johnny interrupted her. 'So Dr Howell was waiting

for your husband when he got back from France. Waiting to kill him, so he couldn't spoil his plans. I guessed ages ago that it must be something like that,' he said, triumphantly. 'I tried to tell the police, but they just wouldn't listen. But surely you could have told them?'

'No, Johnny. I haven't been at liberty for a moment since my husband died. This man, this Dr Howell . . . he watches over me all the time. I have to stay in his cottage overnight, and in the daytime I work here as a secretary. He got me the job so he could guard me round the clock. He's told them I'm his aunt—'

'Mrs J. W. Morgan!' said Johnny, understanding instantly how a fictitious aunt could be useful. 'I see it all now.'

'Exactly,' said Mrs Langford. 'So that's it. I'm trapped.'

Johnny jumped in, thrilled that his theory was proving to be correct, and Mrs Langford nodded in agreement as he babbled through the story. 'He knew where to find you in France, he brought you here so you couldn't tell anyone about him, and he's been keeping you prisoner ever since. Which is why you wanted the disguise. You wanted to get away . . .'

'Yes. About that, Johnny. I don't really understand. How are you connected to that advertisement?'

Before Johnny could reply, a man in a white coat strode in through the double doors. He shuffled from foot to foot anxiously, nibbling at his fingernails.

'Get a move on,' he said roughly. 'We haven't got much time.' Johnny listened hard. Was this the same man who had threatened him on the phone at the post office? He wasn't sure. The accent was the same, but no doubt lots of people in Wales spoke like that. The man continued, getting more agitated: 'One of the nurses held me up. Some nonsense about a girl stealing my coat. I could have done without that, today of all days. Anyway, it's up to you to make sure this panto starts on time. Are you absolutely sure that everyone is coming?'

'Yes, of course, Dr Howell,' said Mrs Langford, and Johnny froze beside her. Now that he'd heard the name, he was certain that he was in the presence of a murderer.

Mrs Langford kept her composure. She took the remaining programmes out of Johnny's arms. 'Thank you for your help, son,' she said, as if he were one of the patients and had simply been lending her a hand. 'I'll finish off here. You run along, now.' She bent down and added in a whisper, 'Come and find me in the office after the show has started.'

Johnny turned to leave. 'Of course, Mrs Morgan,' he said at the top of his voice, trying to give Dr Howell the impression that he was just another inmate. He was grateful to Mrs Langford for giving him a chance to get away from the menacing man; and he was determined to make good use of the time before he saw her again. He set off to find the outside toilets, and Olwen, who would by now be scrubbing them out as her punishment.

Chapter 36

IN THE TOILETS

It wasn't hard to find the boys' toilets. Johnny needed only to follow his nose. This might be a hospital, but boys in a hurry could lower the tone of a lavatory anywhere. The smell was familiar from school, and the chilly brick block was very similar to the grim outdoor shack in the playground back in Stambleton. At least here there were electric lights, though all they did was show up the chipped surface of the long porcelain trough that served as a urinal, the rude words and pictures scraped into the peeling paint of the cubicle doors, and the muddy footmarks swirling in the stinking liquid on the grey stone floor. There were even footprints on the ceiling. Johnny worked out how they'd got there. A thick pipe crossed the room high up above the doorway. If you swung on it and kicked really hard, you could hit the roof. He was tempted to have a go, but this was not the time.

Olwen, still in her pyjamas, was in the far corner,

on her knees with a bucket, sniffing in time to the rhythm of her scrubbing brush. She didn't respond to Johnny at first.

'Olwen?' he said. 'It's me. Johnny. Olwen! I need your help.'

Gradually her scrubbing slowed and she looked up, pushing a stray strand of hair out of her eyes with the back of her wrist. 'Why should I want to help you? Why should I want to help anyone? All my people are dead, and no one here cares. They don't even want to know anything about it.'

'I care, Olwen,' said Johnny. 'I really do. And there's someone else too. She's bound to want to help you. I tried to tell you before. It's Mrs Langford, the doctor's wife from Stambleton. Or widow, I should say.'

'I don't know what you're talking about.'

'Do you remember the doctor who came to take your sister off to the sanatorium?'

'Of course I do. He's the one who sent me back to Wales. He said it was for my own good. But my uncle didn't want a child in the house, and he was scared that I was bringing germs with me. So as soon as I caught a cold, he put me in here and then he moved away. Do I remember that doctor? If it wasn't for him

I'd never have been dumped here. I wish he was dead.'

'He *is* dead, Olwen,' said Johnny. 'I've been trying to tell you about it ever since I got here. Dr Langford was murdered.'

'Serves him right.'

'Olwen! How can you say that? He was a nice man. He was good to me, and I know he must have thought he was doing the best for you.' Johnny told Olwen about the murder. 'Anyway,' he said, drawing his explanation to a close, 'Dr Langford's wife is here. She's calling herself Mrs Morgan, and she's the person I've been looking for.'

'So?' Olwen was still dazed by her own news.

'Mrs Langford's in trouble, Olwen. We have to help her. There's a man called Dr Howell. He's the real murderer, and he's holding her prisoner.'

'Dr Howell?' Olwen was shocked. 'But he's really kind. He didn't make a fuss at all when the nurse told him I'd taken his coat. I think she was really disappointed. She says she's going to report me to Professor Campbell instead.'

'Who?'

'Professor Campbell. He's in charge of the whole hospital. The nurse said she'll recommend a very severe punishment.'

'I'm sorry about that, Olwen, but if you ask me, Dr Howell's only pretending to be pleasant. Mrs Langford seemed really scared of him. Your problem with Professor Campbell isn't nearly as serious as what he might do to her.'

'But what's that got to do with me? Or you, for that matter?'

'I told you. Everyone thinks my mother killed Dr Langford. She's in prison, and only Mrs Langford can put her in the clear. If she doesn't, do you know what will happen to my mother?'

'Just think yourself lucky you've got a mother,' snarled Olwen. 'I haven't. Not any more!' She started crying, and Johnny knelt down on the wet floor to try to comfort her.

'I know,' he said, 'and I'm truly sorry. But if I don't do something to stop it, my mother will be found guilty. Do you know what that means? It means that they'll hang her. They'll make her stand with a noose round her neck and then they'll open a trapdoor so that she falls through and is strangled by the rope. Her body will be left swinging there, dead, and afterwards she'll be buried in an unmarked grave. And then I won't have a mother either. Is that what you want? I'm sorry you've lost your family, but why should I lose my mother too? You must be able to imagine how that will make me feel.'

Olwen's voice softened. 'I dare say I can.'

'Then help me.'

'How? What on earth can I do? I'm stuck here scrubbing the floor.'

'We've got to call the police. And we must go to that man – that Professor Campbell you talked about. We can tell him the truth about Dr Howell. But the police first. We need a telephone. Do you know if they have one here?'

'There must be one in the office, I suppose. I don't know. I've never been in there.'

'But you know where the office is, don't you?'

'Of course I do.'

'Well, show me, please. I've got to meet Mrs Langford there after the pantomime's started. If I get there first I can use the phone before she comes. And while I'm doing that, you can find Professor Campbell and tell him that Mrs Langford – Mrs Morgan – is in danger. Say that he's got to protect her from Dr Howell.'

Olwen tried to protest: 'He won't take any notice of me. If that nurse has already told him about the coat, he'll think I'm just trying to get out of trouble.'

Johnny was desperate. 'But he might believe you. Olwen, you're my only hope. There may not be time for me to phone the police *and* find Professor Campbell. I don't even know what he looks like. Please. Do this for me, and when we've dealt with Dr Howell – or even if it all goes wrong and I get caught – I'll tell the professor everything that's happened to you. I promise. I'll make sure he does something about it. Now come on. I've got to make that phone call.'

'All right,' Olwen sighed. 'I'll show you the way to the office. Then I'll try to find Professor Campbell. But we haven't got long for that, either. He's in the pantomime, you know. He's one of the Ugly Sisters. He's probably getting into his costume now.' She dropped her scrubbing brush into the bucket and Johnny helped her to her feet. 'Follow me,' she said. 'It's dark enough for us to take a short cut across the courtyard. But keep your head down. We don't want anyone to see that we're there.'

Chapter 37

THE OFFICE

Johnny and Olwen cut across the yard. Olwen pulled him into the bushes beneath the office window. 'Lift me up,' she said. 'I'll look in and see if there's anybody there.'

'Climb on my back,' said Johnny, crouching down in the mud; and Olwen stepped on him and pulled her chin up to the level of the windowsill.

'The lights are off,' she whispered. 'There's nobody inside. But there is a telephone. I can see it on the desk by the typewriter.'

'Right. Tell me which door it is and I'll go in,' said Johnny.

'What if it's locked?' said Olwen. 'And what if someone sees you in the corridor?'

'I could go in through the window. Can you get it open if I raise you a bit higher?'

Olwen pushed at the window, and it started to lift up.

'Swap over,' said Johnny. 'I'll stand on you and climb in.'

Neither of them was very big, but somehow they managed to launch Johnny over the sill. He dropped down onto the floor inside the room. As soon as he landed he knew it would be hard to climb back out. But he'd deal with that later. The important thing now was to phone the police. He picked up the receiver and dialled the operator. It seemed to take ages for the mechanism to click and whir its way to a connection, but at least that gave him time for a brainwave. He breathed deeply, and when a response came from the other end he spoke calmly, in his most adult high-pitched voice:

'Hello. My name is Mrs Ada Fortune. I'm calling on behalf of Professor Campbell at the Craig-y-Nos sanatorium. We need the police here on a matter of the greatest urgency and importance.'

The operator wanted more details.

'I'm afraid I am not at liberty to go into the particulars. Suffice it to say that this is a matter of life and death. Hurry, please.'

Johnny slammed down the receiver, hoping that would help convince the operator that something serious had happened, and rushed to the door. Olwen was right. It was locked. He dragged the chair from the desk to the window, but it swivelled beneath him

304

when he tried to jump up, and without Olwen to give him a push he couldn't manoeuvre his body over the sill. He looked around for something higher and more stable to climb on. There was only the desk; but it was at least three times the size of his kitchen table at home and, with rows of drawers on both sides, far too heavy for Johnny to pull across the room.

He was stuck there. He turned on the desk lamp and looked around, hopelessly searching for another way out. It was a drab, functional place. There was a bookcase full of files, an etching of the King on the wall, and a notice board covered with lists of staff and their rotas. Johnny saw that Dr Howell was on duty that night. Alongside was a newspaper cutting about a huge donation raised for the hospital in a local collection at Christmas. Johnny's eye was naturally pulled to the small ads at the side of the page. A sheepdog needed a new home. Someone else was selling an unused wedding dress. And then he saw it: his own advert, *Change Your Appearance Permanently*. That must be where Mrs Langford had seen it. It explained why she hadn't answered the personal message in the same edition appealing for news of her whereabouts. That must have been printed on a different page.

There was nothing Johnny could do except wait for

Mrs Langford to come. He pulled the chair back to the desk and sat down, wondering whether to phone Hutch, if only to let him know that he was safe (so far), but that would mean talking to the operator again, and he didn't want her to get suspicious. The desk was littered with piles of paper. There were brown envelopes, just like the one Mrs Langford had sent to Johnny, and leaflets everywhere, some in English, some in French. All of them seemed to be about TB. Many were annotated in Mrs Langford's snail-shell handwriting. It reassured him that he was in the right place. This definitely was her office. What a relief! With luck, it wouldn't be long before the police arrived and she could tell them the truth about the murder. Dr Howell would be arrested, and Mrs Langford and his mother would both be safe. Johnny leaned over to read the sheet of paper that was sticking out of the typewriter. It was headed *The War Against Tuberculosis*. On the next line it said:

Future Mothers! Young Housewives! Did you know that Tuberculosis kills 25 per cent of infants born to parents with the disease, or growing up in infected surroundings?

Johnny turned the wheel at the side of the machine so that more of the writing would show.

It also kills, sooner or later, many children born of healthy parents, and brought up in healthy households.

But did you know that there is something you can do to protect your children?

You can VACCINATE them.

He recognized the style. He had read claims like that about everything from tonic wine to disinfectant. He guessed that Mrs Langford was typing an advertisement. Dr Howell must be making her do it as part of his plan to sell the BCG vaccine. Johnny wanted to read more.

Then he heard a voice outside. It was Mrs Langford. She had come, as she had promised, to meet him there. He'd just have to explain that he'd climbed through the window because the door was locked. She would understand. But as she turned the key he heard someone else; and he recognized that voice too. Dr Howell was with her. There was no way he would forgive Johnny for breaking in. There was only one place to hide. Johnny turned off the lamp and slid down from the chair. As Mrs Langford switched on the main light, he crawled into the arched footwell under her desk. It smelled of furniture polish, perfume and shoes.

'What's that window doing open?' said Mrs Langford, striding across the room. 'I could have sworn I closed it earlier.'

Dr Howell laughed. 'Maybe Professor Campbell's been in. You know what a demon he is for the healing power of fresh air.'

Johnny was surprised at how friendly they sounded. Mrs Langford chatted happily as she shut the window, 'Well, I'm not ill,' she said, 'and I don't like a draught.'

'I see you've got the leaflets done,' said Dr Howell.

Mrs Langford sat at the typewriter. Johnny had to squash himself even deeper into the tight space to make sure she couldn't feel him with her feet. He hoped she'd have the presence of mind to say nothing if she realized he was there. He listened hard. He couldn't see anything now. Mrs Langford's legs blocked off what little light had come through the arch, and the footwell had no opening on the side facing the door. But at least that meant no one could see Johnny.

'Here you are,' said Mrs Langford. 'I've just finished

the last translation.' The typewriter gave a mechanical ripping noise as she pulled out the page. 'You see. There's nothing to worry about. Everything's ready to go.'

'Just as well,' said Dr Howell, sounding anxious. 'Time's running out. Are you certain that absolutely everyone will be in the theatre?'

'Of course. That's the whole point, isn't it? It took me ages to talk Professor Campbell into including the entire staff. Mind you, I convinced *myself* in the end. It's silly to have a beautiful theatre and not to make use of it. And it's true: nothing will make the children laugh louder than the sight of all the doctors and nurses dressed up in silly costumes. Old Campbell thinks you've made a real sacrifice, offering to be the only doctor on call. You've done yourself some good there.'

Johnny was confused. Why was Mrs Langford being so nice to Dr Howell? Why did she seem so relaxed, and he so nervous? It sounded as if they were planning to do something while the pantomime was on; but what?

The corridor outside started to fill with childish chatter and the rattle of beds being wheeled into the theatre. Johnny could hear Dr Howell pacing the room and muttering.

'I wish they'd hurry up,' said the doctor. 'We need everyone out of the way.'

'Calm down,' said Mrs Langford. 'And for goodness' sake stop biting your nails. Now listen. Don't be alarmed, but there's something else we've got to deal with first.'

'What?' said Howell, clearly annoyed. 'There's little enough time as it is.'

'Remember that boy you saw me with in the theatre?'

'The one who was helping you with the programmes? Not really. I wasn't taking much notice.'

'Well, he's coming here in a minute.'

'What! Why?'

Johnny couldn't understand. Why was Mrs Langford talking about him?

'He's not one of the patients. He's from Stambleton—'

'What! Have you lost your senses?' Dr Howell thumped his fist on the desk somewhere near Johnny's head.

'I said calm down. We can deal with him. He's come here looking for me.'

'But how did he find you?'

'Never mind that. He doesn't know anything, I'm

pretty sure of that. He's got it into his head that you are holding me here against my will.' She giggled. 'He wants to rescue me!'

'Why on earth . . . ?'

'He's the son of that cleaner. The one they've arrested. He wants me to go to the police, to prove that she didn't do it.'

Under the desk, Johnny was beginning to panic. Why was Mrs Langford telling Dr Howell so much? How could she be so stupid? Even though he couldn't see Howell, Johnny could tell that he was jumpy. Maybe he'd strike out if things didn't go his way. Couldn't Mrs Langford imagine what he might do to them both; especially with everyone else out of the way?

Dr Howell's next words started the awful explanation forming in his mind. 'So he doesn't know the truth?'

'Absolutely not, it seems. It's rather sweet really, little Johnny coming all this way to ask me, of all people, to help his mother. He has no idea how important it is for us that the police think she did it.'

'But where is he?' asked Dr Howell. 'What have you done with the boy?'

'Nothing, yet,' said Mrs Langford, 'but I've asked

him to meet me here once the pantomime has started. He should come any time now.'

'Have you gone mad? We don't want anyone around—'

'He won't be here for long. Or he needn't be, if you've got the courage to do something about him.' Her next words terrified Johnny. 'A little injection perhaps? It would only take a jiffy.'

Chapter 38

DEATHWATCH

Dr Howell sounded shocked. 'Now look – I can't just—'

Mrs Langford's voice grew cold and stern. 'But you have to. There's no alternative. We can't risk him surviving. He's determined to save his mother. He might start asking questions.'

Johnny was frozen with fright. All he could see was Mrs Langford's legs, casually crossed at the ankles, with one foot twirling in circles as she calmly plotted his death.

'But we can't. It's not that simple. For one thing, we'll have to deal with the body.' Howell sounded horrified.

'And can you think of a better place in the world to do that? We've got sheets and blankets, wheelchairs, trolleys, miles of parkland and a rushing river. Even a drip like you could make someone disappear here!'

Howell lurched round the desk and grabbed Mrs Langford, pulling her up out of her chair. Johnny could tell by the way her feet twisted and rose onto tiptoe that Howell was using all his might against her; but her voice stayed strong as she took control, saying icily, 'The boy might walk in at any moment. Is this what you want him to see? It's no more than he'd expect, you know. He thinks you're out to hurt me. He'd run straight off to get help.'

Howell slackened his grip, and Mrs Langford's feet steadied again.

'Look, we haven't got much time,' she said. 'Have you got a key to the dispensary?'

'Of course.'

Mrs Langford walked over to the door and listened. 'It's all quiet out there. Everyone's in the theatre now.' She spoke with great authority. 'Go quickly and get something that will do the trick straight away. I'll keep him here if he arrives before you get back. Don't worry. He trusts me. He thinks he's protecting me. He has no idea that he's the one who's in danger.'

But of course Johnny now knew only too well, and under the table he was quaking.

Dr Howell opened the door to leave, and the sound of the pantomime overture burst into the room, followed by joyous laughter as the Ugly Sisters took to the stage. For a moment, Johnny contemplated the idea of coming out from his hiding place while Mrs Langford was alone. He might be able to reason with her, or to overpower her and run away. But he couldn't be sure. She might grab him and hold him till Dr Howell got back with whatever he was collecting from the dispensary. He couldn't take the risk. Shivering and sweating with fear, he curled up even tighter as Mrs Langford returned to her chair and stretched out her legs. The toe of her shoe was a hair's-breadth from his face. He dared not breathe too deeply in case she felt the warm damp air against her skin.

Then the door handle rattled, and she was on her feet again as a burst of hisses from the theatre accompanied Dr Howell's return.

'OK,' he said. 'But this boy of yours had better come soon. We haven't got long, remember.'

Johnny heard clinking glass, and things being put down on the desk, just above his head. He pictured jars of poison and hypodermic needles waiting for his arrival in the room.

Mrs Langford was calmly planning out how the ambush would work. 'You stand behind the door,' she said to Howell, 'then I'll coax him over here. You can grab him from behind. It will all be over in an instant.'

Dr Howell and Mrs Langford stopped talking. They

waited for Johnny with only the faint sounds of *Oohs* and *Aahs* from the pantomime to break their silence. All Johnny could do was try to stay still, and hope that somehow something would happen to make him safe.

Eventually Dr Howell spoke. 'I thought you said the boy was on his way,' he snapped, from his position beside the door.

'He'll come,' said Mrs Langford. 'He's probably just making sure the coast is clear.'

Under the table, Johnny's terror was mixed with curiosity. He still wanted to know what it was that Mrs Langford and Dr Howell had originally been planning to do while the pantomime was on. It was obvious that Mrs Langford had organized the play simply to make sure that the two of them could be alone together. They kept saying that there wasn't much time, and that they had to get Johnny out of the way first. But before what? What were they talking about?

After a few minutes, as a song struck up in the theatre, Dr Howell started pacing again. 'Come on! Come on, boy!' he muttered impatiently. He started rearranging the paraphernalia of death on the desk. Every shuffle and clink made Johnny's heart thump harder. Then Dr Howell rushed back over to the door. 'He's here!' he cried.

'Oh my goodness!' said Mrs Langford, flustered for the first time that night.

Under the desk Johnny wondered what they meant. Suppose it was Olwen, come to report back to Johnny and Mrs Langford on her mission to Professor Campbell? There was no way Johnny could warn her – nothing he could do to stop her entering the room. *Please, Olwen*, he prayed. *Please don't come in!* He heard the squeak of the handle, and a chorus of 'Look behind you!' from the children at the pantomime as the door opened. He felt sick, expecting a scream as Dr Howell grabbed Olwen and administered the poison.

Instead, a man spoke. *The police! Of course! It's the police. They've come!* thought Johnny as a wave of relief swept over him. But no. It didn't sound like a policeman.

'Hello, you two.'

Johnny knew that voice. He'd heard it on Remembrance Day and again the day after Dr Langford's body was discovered.

'That was a hell of a drive! Got anything to drink?'

It was the voice of Johnny's landlord, Frederick Bennett. But what on earth was Mr Bennett doing at Craig-y-Nos?

Chapter 39

A MATTER OF PRINCIPLE

Back in Stambleton, Hutch had closed up the shop for the night. He was on his way upstairs to the flat when the doorbell rang. Hutch limped back down and pulled on the string of the brown roller-blind that covered the glass in the front door. It snapped up to reveal a policeman. Hutch's thoughts went straight to Johnny. He unlocked the door and let the officer in. He was relieved that the policeman hadn't brought bad news – or at least not bad news of that type.

The officer took off his helmet and addressed Hutch in a portentous tone. 'Mr Hutchinson, I regret to say that I have been sent to investigate a very serious matter.'

'I'll be delighted to assist you, Officer, if I can. I have been trying to help for some time, but have received only rebuffs.'

'This is not about the murder, sir. We have received a complaint.'

'A complaint? About me?'

'Not about you, sir. About one of your customers.'

'Which one? Who? What have they done?'

'I can tell you, sir, that this is an allegation of fraud. Of obtaining money by deception. But I'm afraid I cannot tell you the name of the culprit.'

'I quite understand if it is a matter of confidentiality. But how can I help?'

'It's not a question of propriety, sir. I'm not telling you the name because I do not know it myself. That is why I have come to you.'

'I don't understand. I have hundreds of customers,' said Hutch, adding, under his breath, *Or I did have until recently*. 'I'm afraid I know little of what they do outside this shop. I certainly am not aware of anyone trying to defraud me.'

'As far as I know, you have not been defrauded, sir. But I think you will sympathize with the victim if I tell you the nature of the evidence. The complainant asserts that he has twice sent money to someone using a private postal box at this post office – and both times he has been the victim of a trick.' The policeman consulted his notebook. 'The complainant paid sixpence to find out how to save money on tea. Fair enough, you might think. In this day and age we're all looking for ways to make economies, and the gentleman was hoping to be put in touch with a supplier charging reasonable prices. All he got was advice that he should "stop using sugar and milk". He might have overlooked that, had he not received another note, in the same handwriting, when he paid a shilling for an appliance to take the backache out of cutting his toenails. That note said, "Get someone else to do it for you."'

Of course, Hutch knew immediately what the policeman was talking about, but he wasn't going to let on. He waited for the officer to say more.

'Now, I have been given the number of this private box,' said the policeman. 'It is the link between the two advertisements, and I am asking you to tell me the identity of the person who has rented it. Then I will be able to proceed with my enquiries.'

Hutch paused. He was in no doubt what his reply should be, and it would be the same whether the matter involved Johnny or not. 'I'm sorry. I can't help you,' he said.

'But surely you know who holds this box? No doubt they come in here to collect their mail?'

'I dare say they do. And I dare say I know the name. But I have to tell you that his, or her, identity is a matter between that person and the Post Office.'

'But this is a serious allegation.'

'That's as may be. And if it is serious enough, no doubt you can persuade a judge to issue you with a warrant permitting you to acquire the information you seek. But until then, I'm afraid my duty is to protect it.'

The policeman was beginning to get cross. 'But, Mr Hutchinson, you are already co-operating with us over Dr Langford's mail. You've let me and my colleagues examine that every morning.'

'May I remind you, Officer, that Dr Langford was murdered? Now, that *is* a serious matter. And of course, Dr Langford is dead. His relationship with the Post Office is now profoundly altered.'

'But be reasonable, man. The chances are that we'll get to the bottom of this fiddle, if fiddle it be, in the end anyway. We'll just find out sooner if we don't have to go through the rigmarole of getting the courts involved. Come on, Mr Hutchinson. It's PO Box number nine. Now, you know whose box it is, don't you?'

Hutch tried not to let his face show a thing.

The policeman tried again. 'Is it somebody local, or someone passing through?'

Again, Hutch stood silent.

'Am I going to have to take this higher?'

'It seems so. Officer, if you had paid for me to protect your privacy, I expect you would want me to keep my word?'

The policeman was exasperated now. He turned to go. 'I will be consulting my superiors. I'd rather you didn't leave the premises, Mr Hutchinson. I may be back before too long.'

'Certainly, Officer,' said Hutch. 'I was not planning to go out, anyway, and that is why I will be here. I think that if you ask your superiors you will find that you have no more right to restrict my movements than you have to demand the information you desire. We will talk again when you have satisfied yourself as to the legal position.'

The policeman left, muttering under his breath. He was fed up with Hutch and his pomposity. What right had he to be so proud, when he'd taken in that kid – the son of a killer?

Chapter 40

CONSPIRATORS

'What do you mean, a complication?' shouted Mr Bennett.

Mrs Langford tried to explain. 'There's a boy,' she said calmly. 'He's come here from Stambleton. He's Winnie Swanson's son. He's been looking for me.'

'What! How on earth did he find you?'

'I don't know. But he's coming to this room at any moment, and we're ready for him.'

Johnny could imagine her motioning towards the deadly drug waiting on the desk.

'Look, I don't need to be part of anything like that,' said Bennett. 'You deal with the boy. Give me the next batch of vaccine and you can have your share of the money for the last lot. Get a move on. I don't want to hang around.'

'Here's the box,' said Howell.

There were two thuds on the desk. Bennett had thrown down a couple of packets of money. 'There you are. Not a bad piece of work, eh? The whole batch gone. You were right, Marie. We can hook in customers every way. We can play on them as rebels who want something illegal; or as social climbers after something no one else has got; or as anxious parents worried that their babies might get sick. I tell you, by the time I've finished with them, they're scared *not* to buy it. I could do with those leaflets you promised me, though. I need to make the medical details more convincing. Some people prefer things in black and white.'

'Here they are,' said Mrs Langford. 'It's word-for-word what they say in France. She declaimed the first sentence grandly: '*Faites préserver vos enfants contre la tuberculose par le vaccin BCG* . . . Save your children from TB with the BCG vaccine. I've copied out the whole thing – except for this bit here of course.'

Bennett read out a sentence in a schoolboy French accent. '*Délivré gratuitement par l'institut Pasteur sur demande du médecin ou de la sage-femme.*'

Mrs Langford translated it for him: 'Delivered for free by the Pasteur Institute at the request of a doctor or midwife.'

Bennett laughed, but Howell was serious.

'It should be free,' he said. 'I never wanted to charge for it.' Bennett groaned as Howell continued, 'This doesn't feel right. I only helped Dr Langford because he wanted to save lives, and now we're exploiting people.'

Johnny was beginning to work out what was going on. Perhaps he'd been wrong about Howell. Maybe he had never meant to get involved. It was *Bennett* who was at the heart of the sales scheme, and Bennett was so clever that he was even giving Howell and Mrs Langford some of the takings so they would share his guilt.

But Johnny shuddered when Mrs Langford's voice broke in, with a sarcastic ring. 'Forgive me, Doctor, but I don't see you turning down your share of the proceeds. And why are you so high-minded about human life all of a sudden?' Johnny heard her pick up a glass jar from the desk. 'Look at this, Bennett,' she hissed. 'When you came in, our saintly friend, the doctor, was preparing to kill somebody!'

'I told you. I don't want to know about that,' said Bennett. 'I'm off.'

Johnny heard Howell step aside, blocking Bennett's path to the door.

'Don't go yet,' said Howell. 'I want to know what to do about the boy.'

'I've told you what to do,' said Mrs Langford. 'We haven't any choice.'

'But won't someone come looking for him?' said Howell. 'Maybe he told someone he was coming here.'

'Will you stop worrying!' said Mrs Langford. 'He's alone, I'm sure of it. And better still, he's told me that the police won't listen to him. Even the boy himself is convinced that I was in France at the time of the murder. That letter you made me write seems to have done a good job, Bennett.'

Johnny was trembling in his hiding place, sure now that he and his mother were both doomed. He was still trying to make sense of what Mrs Langford was saying.

Dr Howell was bemused too. 'What letter?' he said. 'What have you two been up to behind my back?'

'Don't be so dramatic,' sneered Bennett. 'We haven't been keeping anything from you. We had to do something to fill in a few gaps. It was our own fault. We didn't think things through properly at the beginning, when you made the Langfords come here in such a rush . . .'

'I had to,' said Howell. 'The culture wasn't growing properly. I needed Dr Langford's help, or we'd never have got the vaccine going.' He sounded close to tears. 'But neither of us wanted to sell it. It was just you two!'

'But you're in on it now, Howell,' said Bennett. 'You've already supplied the stuff, and now you've given me more.' He tapped his parcel. 'How will you explain this to the police?'

'They're not going to worry about that when I tell them how Dr Langford died!'

'You—'

Johnny heard the sound of a punch, a groan and a scuffle as the two men fought.

'Let me go!' screamed Howell, whose arm had been bent behind his back by Bennett.

Mrs Langford leaped up from her chair. 'You're not going to tell anyone anything, Howell!' she cried. There was a demonic chuckle behind the menace in her voice as she asked Bennett, 'What do you say, Frederick? Shall we do away with him, too?'

Howell was struggling against Bennett's grip. 'No! Don't! I'm not going to talk. Anyway, what could I say? I wasn't even there, was I?' His voice became muffled. Bennett had a hand over his mouth now. Johnny could hear Howell trying to shout. He was kicking too, trying to break away. Great blows from his feet thundered against the desk, and into Johnny's backbone.

Johnny could see Mrs Langford's feet pacing round

the desk. She tormented Howell as he squirmed against Bennett's grip. 'You know, you'll be much more useful to us dead than you've ever been alive,' she said. 'It's true, there'll be no more vaccine, but we'll be able to split the money we've already got two ways instead of three.'

Bennett picked up her drift. 'You're right, Marie. And if we're ever caught, we could say it was Howell's idea to sell the vaccine, and not yours at all.'

Johnny was stunned. So Mrs Langford was the mastermind. He had been completely taken in by her pretence of friendliness. He didn't want to believe it, but somehow it made sense. He knew that the Langfords had been hard up. Mrs Langford had even sent off for *Make Your Money Go Further*. And then Johnny felt a new twist of panic. To his undercurrent of terror was added a sickening wallop of guilt and regret. He was having another clong. He remembered showing Mrs Langford the Umckaloabo advert. He recalled asking why Dr Langford couldn't sell the BCG vaccine in the same way, and how the doctor had criticized Chas. H. Stevens, of Worple Road, Wimbledon, for making money by playing on the anxieties of the unwell. Had Johnny unwittingly given Mrs Langford the idea which had led to her husband's death and Winnie's arrest? Could she have thought up the whole scheme, and chosen Bennett to be her salesman? After all, as she herself had told Johnny when they'd talked in the theatre, the best customers were rich people: people who would keep quiet because they had a lot to lose if they were discovered. Bennett moved in those circles, and Mrs Langford had known him since he was a child. And Johnny knew that Bennett needed cash, too. He'd said as much when he'd joked with Inspector Griffin about the pile of bills on his desk. Johnny thought back to Remembrance Day, and Bennett's earnest conversation with Mrs Langford at the service. Then there'd been the sudden news that Bennett was invited to the Langfords' for supper. If the plot had been hatched that day, it would explain how unprepared they were when Howell had phoned during the meal to say that he needed Dr Langford's help.

Mrs Langford carried on taunting Dr Howell, whose shouts were still muffled by Bennett's grip. 'I really can't think of any reason to keep you alive, you know,' she said, with an air of exaggerated calm. 'It must be worrying for you. What a pity you can't move your arms. You could nibble those nails of yours even shorter. Maybe even make them bleed.'

'Come on then, woman, let's get it over with,' said Bennett, as Howell squealed and grunted. 'I can't hold him for ever.'

Johnny pictured Mrs Langford advancing on Howell with the loaded syringe.

Suddenly Bennett swore. Howell had bitten his hand and twisted out of his grip. Johnny heard more bumps and thrashing as the two men jostled with each other, lashing out and cursing. Howell threw Mrs Langford across the room, and Johnny stifled a gasp as one of her high-heeled shoes rolled under the desk, only inches away from him. He heard her pulling herself up again, panting. Then she let out a bizarre shriek and Dr Howell gave a desperate cry of resistance that was strangled into an agonized gargle, a wheeze and a cough. His rigid body thumped against the desk and onto the floor next to Johnny. Everything was still.

In the theatre, twelve chimes rang out as Cinderella ran away from the ball.

Chapter 41

COVER-UP

Johnny could sense frozen panic in the room.

Bennett spoke first. 'It's all right. It's all right,' he repeated as if trying to reassure himself. Then his tone shifted from distraction to resolution. 'I'm going,' he said.

'Take me with you,' said Mrs Langford, with a breathy coolness. 'Let's leave now, while there's no one around.'

'No. Someone would come looking for you. I couldn't risk having you in the car. The panto's nearly over. We wouldn't have time to get far before the body was discovered. We might even meet the police coming the other way.'

'Then stay. Stay and help me talk my way out of this. I can say that Howell attacked me, and you fought him off. We could make it look like self-defence.'

'No, I'm getting out of it. No one knows I've been here. There's no reason for me to be mixed up in this at all.'

Mrs Langford barred the door. Her tone had turned from pleading to menace. 'Unless I say something. After all, Howell's not around now to keep an eye on me. There's nothing to stop me telling everyone that you killed my husband.'

'Is that a threat?' Bennett sounded panicky.

Mrs Langford kept her spiteful calm. 'Take it how you like. I'm simply being practical. We're in this together, that's all. Keep your head, and we can come up with a story that puts us both in the clear.'

'How are you going to explain the poison? Isn't it a bit fishy that it just happened to be to hand?'

'I'll say Howell brought it with him. To kill me. To shut me up because I knew he killed Giles.'

There was a pause. When Bennett spoke, it sounded as if he was happy to go along with the plan. 'You should look a bit more roughed up,' he said. 'You'll have to play the victim a bit. A sweet little lady in the power of a homicidal brute.'

'Don't worry. Being a quiet, kind old woman is my speciality.'

Exactly, thought Johnny. *I was certainly taken in.*

Bennett and Mrs Langford stood in silence. Johnny was terrified that they would hear him breathing, and felt a rush of relief when the band in the theatre started playing 'Happy Days Are Here Again' and all the children in the audience joined in, filling the room with song.

'Maybe we should raise the alarm,' said Bennett. 'That's what you'd do, isn't it? If you'd really been attacked?'

'Yes, I'll call the police,' said Mrs Langford, limping round the desk to reach the phone.

Johnny's heart sank. If she got through to the operator, Mrs Langford might find out that the police were already on their way. She might panic. She might run. She might dive under the desk to find her shoe. She might see him. There might be some poison left in the jar, and Johnny knew now that she was not afraid to use it.

Mrs Langford lifted the receiver and dialled the operator. A second later she had dropped the phone. It swung to and fro across the mouth of the footwell. Johnny could hear the woman through the earpiece, shouting out, 'Hello . . . Hello . . . Hello?'

They were the same words used by one of two policemen who had just entered the room.

Johnny was flooded with joy. His earlier call to the operator hadn't been ignored.

Mrs Langford kept her creepy calm. 'Oh, Sergeant . . . and Constable . . . Thank goodness you are here,' she said, trying to conceal her bewilderment at their arrival.

Bennett took charge. 'This poor lady has been the victim of a savage assault,' he said. 'She was lucky I arrived.'

Then the door opened again and Johnny heard Olwen's voice: 'Johnny, are you in here? Mrs Langford? I've brought Professor Campbell.'

'What the devil . . . ?' said the policeman as everyone else in the room gasped in unison.

Johnny was feeling exactly as he had back in Mr Bennett's grand house, hidden under the big fur cloak. He could stay hidden and wait for a chance to run away, or he could show himself and intervene in the action. At Bennett's, fear had got the better of him. Now he took courage. He uncurled himself and shuffled out from under the desk. Everyone was paralysed – looking the other way, towards the door. And Johnny found himself just as aghast as they were. For there, holding Olwen's hand, was a six-foot-tall man with grotesquely rouged cheeks, wearing a multi-layered crinoline dress, hooped earrings and a fluffy blonde wig.

The senior policeman, with a deep Welsh voice, spoke for everyone. 'Will somebody please tell me what on earth is going on?'

Chapter 42

ARRESTS

'**I** can explain!' said Johnny, and everybody turned to face him.

'Johnny!' gasped Mrs Langford. 'Where did you come from?'

'I've been under the desk,' said Johnny. 'I heard everything. Officer, you must arrest that woman, and Mr Bennett, too. They haven't been telling you the truth.'

'But Johnny,' said Olwen, 'you told me Mrs Langford was in danger. It looks as if you were right.'

'No. I was wrong,' he gabbled. 'She killed Dr Howell. And Mr Bennett here, he killed Dr Langford.'

Bennett made a move for the door, but Professor Campbell opened his giant pantomime fan and blocked his path. 'This is preposterous,' said Bennett. 'I don't have to stay here and listen to the incoherent ramblings of a deranged child!'

'I think you'd better stop where you are, sir,' said

the sergeant, calmly. 'I'm sure we can get this cleared up.' He turned to Mrs Langford. 'Madam, perhaps you can enlighten us?'

Mrs Langford took a handkerchief from her sleeve and dabbed her eyes. 'It's as I said just now. Dr Howell attacked me, and Mr Bennett came to my rescue.'

'No!' cried Johnny. 'It wasn't like that. She killed Dr Howell, and she was going to kill me!' He pointed at Bennett. 'And he killed Dr Langford.'

'No he didn't,' came a voice. 'That's not quite right.' Everybody froze as Dr Howell's body began to stir. He sat up and spoke. 'It's all right. I haven't come back from the dead. I was only pretending. It seemed safer than letting myself be knocked about by those two thugs.' Howell pulled himself to his feet and seized the jar of liquid from the desk, hurling its contents into Mrs Langford's eyes. 'Did you really think I would murder a child? Did you really believe this was poison? You sick, depraved woman. Officer, she's your murderess!'

'But you're not dead,' said the sergeant in confusion. 'There is no victim.'

'Yes there is,' said Howell. 'Not me, Officer, but Dr Giles Langford, this woman's husband. She killed him. She's admitted it to me a hundred times, threatening to do the same to me unless I went along with her plans. And this man' – he pointed at Bennett – 'this man has forced me to hide her from the law.'

Johnny was stunned. Mrs Langford, a murderess? 'But she's an old lady,' he cried. 'Old ladies don't kill people! She loved her husband. He loved her. She can't have killed him.'

The sergeant interrupted. 'And where is the body – this Dr Langford?' he asked.

'Buried. In Stambleton, before Christmas,' said Howell.

'And my mother is in prison, charged with the murder,' said Johnny. 'And she didn't do it!'

'I don't understand,' said Professor Campbell. 'What has all this got to do with Craig-y-Nos?'

Dr Howell tried to explain. 'It all started when I took on some . . . some unconventional work for Dr Langford . . .' As the constable struggled to take notes, Howell told the story of how Langford had hoped to develop the BCG to do good, and how, in a panic on Remembrance Day, he himself had asked Langford to come to Wales to help him. 'I wasn't expecting Mrs Langford to come too,' he explained. 'I didn't know that she and Bennett had a very different plan for the vaccine.'

Mrs Langford interrupted. 'I had to come. I knew that if my husband was near a sanatorium he wouldn't be able to stop himself wandering around, chatting to people and hinting at what he was doing. I had to make sure he stayed in Howell's cottage. I knew he couldn't keep a secret. He'd even told that boy!'

Professor Campbell was struggling to keep up. 'You mean to say you've been cultivating a vaccine here? In our laboratory?'

'That's right,' said Howell. 'But at first my involvement was purely scientific. I was never happy about the idea of selling it.'

'So why didn't you tell someone what Bennett and Mrs Langford were planning?' asked the professor.

'I was scared,' said Howell, hanging his head. 'I'm ashamed to admit it, sir, but I was frightened. At first it was bad enough that I might ruin my career, but by the time I found out they wanted to sell the vaccine I knew that Mrs Langford had already killed once, and that Bennett had looked on while she did it. And I was right to be careful. Look what they tried to do to me when I finally crossed them!'

The sergeant, overwhelmed by the welter of information, opened his mouth to ask a question, but Johnny got in first.

'But why was Dr Langford murdered?' he said. 'You said he knew nothing of what his wife was up to.'

'Nothing until that final night,' said Howell, 'when I thought he was safely back in Stambleton. We'd finished here. The first batch of vaccine was a success, and I was sure I could carry on without Dr Langford's help. When Bennett came to collect him and his wife from my cottage to drive them home, I thought he was acting as a generous friend, not as a conspirator. They all left in good spirits.'

The policeman tried to intervene again, but Mrs Langford turned on Bennett. 'And you couldn't resist it, could you, you fool? Everything would have been all right. We were safely home. Giles would never have suspected a thing. But you had to boast about the money. You had to go and break his heart.'

'But you're the one who broke his head!'

The two policemen held Bennett and Mrs Langford back as they flew at each other.

'You know how angry he was,' Mrs Langford yelled at Bennett. 'You saw the fury in his eyes when you told him what we'd planned.'

Bennett sneered, 'Don't try to make it sound as if you were defending yourself.' He turned to the sergeant. 'She was frantic. First she flung an ashtray at him, and when that missed and went through the window, she bashed his head against the mantelpiece.'

'Don't you understand?' said Mrs Langford. 'He had to die. I couldn't live with him knowing that I was selling his dream.'

Howell spoke up. 'Listen to her. She's speaking as if she were doing her victim a favour – killing him to protect him from the knowledge of how she was funding their old age. Don't you see? She's lost her mind. She'd rather her husband died than that he knew she'd let him down. She killed the person she loved most in the world to shield herself from his disapproval.'

All eyes were on Mrs Langford. She was shaking and staring ahead blankly, as if re-playing the murder scene in her mind. 'There was so much blood,' she said, rubbing her hands on her skirt.

Bennett shouted at her again. 'But you didn't do anything to save him, did you? You were more interested in saving yourself. What's it going to sound like in court when I tell them you were on your knees mopping the floor before your husband was even dead?'

'My mother's apron!' said Johnny as the constable closed his notebook, defeated by the rush of revelations. 'You used my mother's apron, didn't you? That's why the police suspected her in the first place.'

Mrs Langford snapped into defiance. 'What about you, Bennett? You can't pin it all on me. You made me write that letter, remember? And you showed it to the police, to make out that I was in France. How are you going to explain that? Or why you drove me back down here and forced Howell to give me shelter? I'm not a fool. I know you didn't do that for my sake. You wanted me here to make sure Howell kept producing the vaccine. And you hid me from the police because I might have told them you were involved – not just in selling illegal medicine, but in the murder, too. Well, you can't get out of it now. I'm going to tell them everything. You're up to your neck in all this, and if I swing for it, so will you.'

'My crimes are going to look pretty pathetic alongside yours,' sniffed Bennett. 'You've killed your husband, you tried to kill Howell, and you wanted to kill the boy . . .'

Johnny joined in: 'And you would have killed my mother! She still might be hanged because of your lies. Oh, Mrs Langford! Mum and I thought you were our friend. We've never done anything to harm you. I even wanted to rescue you when I thought you were imprisoned here by Dr Howell. But you're the jailer. You knew they'd arrested my mother. You knew she was innocent and you did nothing to help her.'

The sergeant unfastened the handcuffs from his belt and nodded to his constable to do the same.

'I'm not sure I'm following all this, Officer,' said Professor Campbell, flapping his fan. 'It seems I have been sorely deceived by Dr Howell and Mrs Morgan – or should I call her Mrs Langford? I thought they were among the most diligent members of my staff! No doubt there are some arrests to be made here.'

Howell sat down on the edge of the desk, put his hands, with their well-bitten fingernails, over his face, and cried. 'I'm sorry,' he sobbed. 'I don't know how I got caught up in all this.' Johnny wondered how he could ever have believed that Howell was the murderer, and that Mrs Langford had been scared of him.

The sergeant at last got a chance to speak. 'I think I had better call Stambleton and see what they want me to do with the prisoners.'

Johnny picked up the dangling receiver. He heard a high-pitched 'Hello?' The operator was still on the line. She had been listening in to everything. Her garbled version of events would be all round the district by morning.

Chapter 43

ANOTHER PLACE, ANOTHER FIGHT

Far away from the mayhem at Craig-y-Nos, Hutch was sitting in an armchair reading (or rather dozing with a book on his lap and his glasses sliding down his nose) when he heard the doorbell. It was ringing hard and repeatedly. It must be the policeman, back with his warrant. Hutch had been in the chair for so long that his bad leg was stiff, and it took him a while to get down the stairs and into the shop. He turned on the light, hoping it would signal that he was on his way, but the bell kept going, nagging him to answer the door.

Hutch opened up. It wasn't the policeman. It was the reporter, as impatient as ever. 'I thought you were out,' he said.

'I was asleep,' Hutch said crossly. 'I'd nodded off. I'm allowed to do that in my own home, aren't I?'

'What about the boy? Couldn't he answer the door?'

Hutch said nothing.

The reporter continued: 'The boy. Johnny Swanson. He is here, isn't he? Very brave of you to take him in. And just as well, as it's turned out. I've had a look at his house. Every window smashed now. And rude words on the door.'

Hutch was still not fully awake, but he was uneasy. The boy. He hadn't heard anything from Johnny. Did that mean he was all right, or in trouble? Could the phone have been ringing while he was sleeping upstairs? All the fuss about the policeman's attack on Post Office protocol had distracted Hutch from thinking about Johnny. And now he realized that he had no idea exactly where the child was. It was nearly ten o'clock. There was only one more train due in to Stambleton. He hoped Johnny would be on it.

The reporter asked again, interrupting Hutch's thoughts, 'Mr Hutchinson? The boy, Mr Hutchinson? Is he well?'

'Well? Yes . . . he's well. Just not here tonight. I'm all alone. Is that all you wanted to know?' Hutch tried to usher the reporter back towards the door.

'Oh no,' said the reporter. 'I didn't come about Johnny at all. Like you, I don't like being up so late, especially for work, but they've sent me to check on a story. Trouble is, this one involves the paper itself, and we never like that sort of news to go public. The police have been round at the office, asking about bogus adverts that we've printed in our paper, tricking people into parting with money. Apparently it involves a post office box here. Have the police been to see you too?'

'Yes, they have. But I couldn't help them. I can't go giving out people's personal details just because some policeman decides he wants them. I told him to go off and get a warrant.'

'And did he?'

'I don't know. He hasn't come back yet.'

'Well, we'd better wait for him together. Then maybe we can clear all this up tonight.'

Hutch didn't want to take the reporter up to his flat. He hated the idea of the man mooching about among his things and looking for signs of Johnny. So he gave him the chair he kept for old ladies to sit on while they were doing their shopping, and dragged out the high stool from behind the post office counter for himself. He perched on it uncomfortably, but he preferred to be higher up than his unexpected guest. Their conversation was fitful. Both of them were getting more and more annoyed.

The reporter turned to the subject of the trial. 'So whatever happens, you will accept the verdict?' he asked.

'I don't think I'll face a problem there. Mrs Swanson will be found not guilty, I'm sure.'

'And that's the reason you've taken her son under your roof?'

'That, and the fact that the poor boy has no one else in the world.'

'You don't see it as a conflict with your responsibilities as a postmaster?'

Hutch corrected him: 'Sub-postmaster.'

'Oh, *sub*-postmaster. Of course. No doubt standards are somewhat lower for a *sub*-postmaster.'

Had he been less tired, Hutch would not have risen to the bait. But he was worried about Johnny, and about the possible return of the policeman, and the one thing he could not stand was cynicism about his duties as an employee of the Post Office.

'Standards are the same for everyone involved in public life,' he said.

'Public life! That's raising your status rather high, isn't it, Mr Hutchinson? Selling stamps, fruitcakes and carrots counts as "public life" now, does it? I'll try to remember that I'm in the presence of an eminent public official when I next pop in for some toilet paper!'

Before he had finished the last word, Hutch was off his stool and had the reporter by the lapels. They were both ex-army men. They both knew how to fight. The reporter had the advantage of height; Hutch had bulk, and familiarity with the terrain. He knew just when he could reach out and grab a jug or a wooden butter-pat to use as a weapon. The two of them wrestled and rolled, bringing jars of sweets down from the shelves. Soon the floor was covered in bulls'-eyes, pear drops and cough-candy twists. The reporter lurched towards Hutch and slipped on some humbugs. He grasped for something to steady him, but only found one of the bags of flour Johnny had filled the day before. The packet exploded under the force of his grasp, showering both men with white powder. The reporter picked up the high stool and swung it round, hoping to knock Hutch off balance. Hutch caught the other end of it, and tried to change its trajectory. The reporter pushed back, and the two of them lurched and skidded towards the front of the shop. Then, at the last minute, the reporter let go of his end, and Hutch was pulled by his own weight right through the front door, splintering the wood and breaking the glass.

It was not his lucky night. He landed right on top of the policeman, who had come to report that an angry judge, called away from a delightful dinner party, had refused to issue a warrant for the information about PO Box 9.

The equally angry constable took great pleasure in escorting the sub-postmaster and the reporter to the police station.

Chapter 44

TRANSPORT

In Wales, the sergeant was on the phone, making arrangements for a special van to take his prisoners to Stambleton.

'What about me?' asked Johnny, rummaging in his pocket. 'I've got a return ticket, but it's getting late. I might not be able to catch a train tonight.'

Professor Campbell broke in while the sergeant continued his phone call in the background. 'I'm sure I could make arrangements for you to stay here.'

'Thank you,' said Johnny, trying not to sound as unenthusiastic as he felt. 'And, Professor, if you don't mind, there's something I want to talk to you about.' He was remembering his promise. 'It's Olwen, sir.' Johnny told Professor Campbell how Olwen had been orphaned, and how badly the nurse had treated her.

Olwen gave way to tears again. The professor enfolded her into a hug. Her slight body sank into the soft folds of his Ugly Sister dress.

'Don't cry, my dear, we will sort this out too,' the professor said, kindly.

'Is Olwen very ill?' asked Johnny. 'Does she really need to stay here?'

'No, the symptoms she came in with have cleared up. It wasn't TB after all. In fact, she shows all the signs of immunity. I've thought for some time that she could be discharged. We've been having trouble contacting her relatives.'

'My uncle's dumped me,' sniffed Olwen. 'And now I'll be here for ever.'

'Can't she come home with me?' asked Johnny.

'Does she have relatives in Stambleton who could look after her?'

'Well, no,' said Johnny. 'Not family exactly. But there's a farmer who knew her parents. I don't know his name. Or better still, the postmaster. He looks after me. He's called Mr Hutchinson . . .'

'I can't let Olwen go to just anyone. We must get permission from her legal guardian. She will have to stay here for now. But we will look into the matter. Perhaps you could ask this Mr Hutchinson to get in touch with me?'

'I should phone him anyway,' said Johnny. 'He must be wondering what's happened to me. I need to tell him I won't be coming home tonight. He might be worried.'

The sergeant finished his conversation and put down the receiver. 'No need for that,' he said. 'We're going to take you. Inspector Griffin's given us permission to commandeer Mr Bennett's car. He wants it back in Stambleton so they can search it for evidence. I'll be driving you myself.'

Johnny could hear angry shouts from Bennett in the police van as the sergeant opened the door of his precious limousine.

'Why don't you go in the back, son,' said the policeman. 'It's a long way, and you'll be able to lie down and get some sleep. Look. There's a blanket here.' Johnny slid across the shiny leather seat. The sergeant shook out the soft woollen travelling rug and tucked it around Johnny's legs.

'I'm not tired,' said Johnny. His excitement at being in a car at all was immense, but to be in this car, a Rolls-Royce Phantom II, made his blood fizz. On his only other rides he'd been hidden on the floor of the reporter's battered Morris Oxford, and bounced around in the farmer's ageing van. He didn't want to miss a moment of this journey.

Settling into the driver's seat, the sergeant fumbled

around until the headlights came on and the engine purred into life; then he pulled out of the courtyard, followed by the police van. Olwen stood on the steps of the building waving, and the professor flapped his fan in a final farewell.

Chapter 45

COMING HOME

Hours later, Hutch and the reporter were still sitting on an uncomfortable bench in a corridor at Stambleton police station. Hutch was worrying about Johnny. What if he got back to discover the door bashed down and the shop ransacked? He wanted to tell a policeman about Johnny, but he didn't want the reporter to hear, even though they had long since patched up their quarrel. In any case, the desk sergeant was busy with something else. The phone was ringing well after midnight. A couple of drunks were taken out of the cells and allowed to go home. Plain-clothes detectives arrived, including Inspector Griffin. Hutch recognized him from Winnie's court hearing. He knew Griffin was a very important police-man. He hoped he hadn't been called in to deal with the fight in the shop. A criminal conviction could mean the end of Hutch's Post Office career.

At one a.m. there was a shout of 'They're here!' and all the staff who were on duty gathered by the door.

'They made good time,' said a constable.

'Well they had a fast car,' said another. 'Kindly supplied by one of the prisoners.' Everybody laughed.

The reporter sensed that he might be missing a story, and tried to join the crowd of policemen. He was manhandled back to his place. A few minutes later, a strange procession of tired, deflated people passed by the bench he shared with Hutch. First came Mrs Langford, handcuffed to a stocky policeman wearing an unfamiliar uniform. She was stooping, and looked ten years older than she had before her husband was killed. Behind her was a young man in a white lab coat with his hands chained together. Even so, he managed to raise them to his mouth to nibble his nails. He was followed by another officer, manacled to a well-dressed man who was trying to shield his face with his hat. The reporter had to be forced back to his seat again when he saw that it was Frederick Bennett. At the end of the line – the only one who was smiling – was Johnny Swanson. The grumpy desk officer had shown no reservations about letting him into the building this time.

Johnny ran over to Hutch, babbling on about Mrs Langford being the murderer, and how his mother would have to be freed.

'Thank you so much for coming, Hutch. I'm sorry they've kept you up so late. It was a long drive.' Johnny couldn't disguise how much he had enjoyed his trip in Mr Bennett's grand car, even if the policeman who'd driven it had sometimes shown a dizzying unfamiliarity with the controls.

Hutch was embarrassed. He came clean. 'The fact is, Johnny old chap, I didn't know you were on your way. I got here under my own steam, you might say.'

Johnny didn't understand. But he did notice that Hutch and the reporter were both covered in a dusting of flour, with patches of unidentified foodstuffs sprayed across their dishevelled clothes.

Hutch began an explanation. 'This gentleman and I had a bit of a . . .'

'A bit of an altercation, you might say,' said the reporter.

'About what?' asked Johnny.

Neither of them wanted to admit that it had been, at least in part, about Johnny and his mother.

'Good question,' said the reporter. 'I really can't remember.'

Inspector Griffin approached them. 'Mr Hutchinson, I believe,' he said, holding out his hand.

'I must apologize for my behaviour,' said Hutch,

assuming that Griffin had come to question him about the fight at the shop.

'Never mind that,' said Griffin. 'It was your own property you damaged, and if this gentleman is prepared to let the matter drop, I think we can forget the whole episode. The person I'm most eager to talk to is this young chap.' He tousled Johnny's bouncy curls. 'Mr Hutchinson, would you care to sit in? I understand that you've been looking after Johnny while his mother's been . . . away.'

'Of course,' said Hutch, and he accompanied Johnny into the interview room, where the three of them sat down at a small bare table. Inspector Griffin took notes as Johnny explained what had happened in Wales, summed up the vaccine plot, and described how Dr Langford had died.

Inspector Griffin scratched his head. 'Thank you, Johnny,' he said. 'I think I understand. You've been very helpful.'

'It's really Mum I wanted to help,' said Johnny. 'She can come home now, can't she?'

'Yes, indeed. There'll be some formalities, but we'll get her back to you as soon as we can.'

'What will happen to Mrs Langford and the others?' asked Johnny. 'Will they all be hanged?'

'I can't say. Dr Howell should get away with a prison stretch. It sounds as if he's guilty of contravening the Therapeutic Medicines Act, and of obstructing the police; but things look bad for Mrs Langford, despite her age – and Bennett certainly seems to be implicated in covering up the murder, even if he didn't strike the fatal blow. Don't worry, Johnny. You're safe. We'll be keeping them under lock and key until we can confirm what you've told us.'

'It's all true, I promise.'

'Yes, Johnny,' the inspector said kindly, 'I believe you, but there's no way a court would accept your word as evidence on its own. With a bit of luck the three of them will speak out against each other, but the trouble is, a jury might think they're each trying to save their own skin. We really need someone else, too. If only there were another, adult, witness to all this.'

'I was thinking on the way home,' said Johnny. 'There is somebody else – someone who might have heard Bennett and Mrs Langford plan the BCG scam, at least, and may even know the truth about the murder.'

'Really? Who?'

'Mr Bennett's girlfriend,' said Johnny. 'She was

there on Remembrance Day. She went to supper at the Langfords' that night. I've been wondering what happened to her.'

'Bennett said they had parted,' the inspector said.

'I know,' said Johnny. 'I was there when he told you.'

Inspector Griffin raised an eyebrow.

'I didn't mean to listen in, but I was hiding. I'd gone to see Mr Bennett myself, but you asked him everything I wanted to know,' Johnny confessed.

'I'm glad to hear that you approve of my methods,' laughed Griffin. 'I recall him saying that the young lady was now performing at the Gaiety Theatre in London. I will make contact with her in the morning.'

'But the thing is,' Johnny continued excitedly, 'what if she's not there?'

'Why shouldn't she be?'

'Because her cloak was still in Mr Bennett's house the morning after Dr Langford's body was found. I know. I was hiding behind it.'

Hutch let out an exasperated sigh, and Griffin shook his head. 'It sounded to me as if she went away after a disagreement,' he said. 'Maybe she flounced off without it.'

'But suppose . . .' said Johnny. Then he saw the

look on Hutch's face, and was reminded of all his warnings about jumping to conclusions.

The policeman wanted to hear more. 'What are you suggesting?' he asked.

'Only that there might, possibly, be something suspicious about her disappearance, too,' said Johnny, stopping himself from making wild allegations.

Inspector Griffin was lost in thought for a moment. 'Have you mentioned this to anyone else?' he asked.

'No. Just you,' said Johnny. 'And Hutch knows now, of course.'

Hutch put his finger to his lips. 'I won't tell a soul,' he said.

Inspector Griffin's tone was serious. 'I'd appreciate your silence, sir. We will follow up this lead first thing in the morning. This could be an even more convoluted case than I thought.'

Hutch stretched out his bad leg and stifled a yawn. 'Is that all for tonight, Inspector? I'm sure you'll agree that Johnny should really be in bed.'

'Yes. We can talk again tomorrow.' Griffin closed his notebook. 'But before you go,' he said casually, 'tell me, Johnny, how did you know that Howell, Bennett and Mrs Langford were going to meet at Craig-y-Nos last night?'

'I didn't,' said Johnny. 'I'd never even heard of Craig-y-Nos until Mrs Langford replied to one of my advertisements.'

Hutch put his head in his hands.

The inspector was bemused. 'Your what, Johnny?'

'Well, you see, I put in this advert' – he knew it off by heart – 'Change Your Appearance Permanently. Unhappy with the way you look? Transform yourself Instantly and For Ever.'

Hutch could see Inspector Griffin registering that Johnny was probably the culprit in the case of PO Box 9.

Griffin was silent for a moment and then spoke sternly. 'You may not be aware, Johnny, that while you've been in Wales this force has been dealing with an allegation of fraud in relation to advertisements very like the one you've described.'

Johnny had another clong. With a few unguarded words he had landed himself in trouble. He felt sick with shame. He had already faced Hutch's wrath over his adverts. Now the police knew. He had heard of guilty children being tried in the juvenile courts and sent away to special schools. Would that happen to him, just when his mother was coming home? Had he messed things up yet again? Would Winnie's freedom be laced with new worry and grief?

The inspector could see that Johnny was panicking. He was stern but understanding. 'Johnny, I know you've been through a lot in the last few weeks. We may be able to resolve the matter of the advertisements if I give you the name and address of the person who has complained, and you send him back his money.'

Johnny sighed with relief. 'Thank you, sir,' he said gravely. 'I promise I'll do it tomorrow.'

'In that case,' said Inspector Griffin, 'I think it is time you went home.' He stood up and took a step towards the door. Then he stopped abruptly and turned to Johnny, thinking out loud. 'So Mrs Langford wanted a disguise . . .' he mumbled. 'She must have been planning to get away – to hide and leave Bennett and Howell to face the music. Perhaps she was even planning to pin Langford's murder on them.'

'And?' said Hutch, not really following the policeman's train of thought.

'Well, it just might help me when I'm talking to the others. If I can show that Mrs Langford was preparing to double-cross them even before their plot was discovered, it might break down any last vestige of loyalty between them.'

Johnny interrupted. 'There wasn't much sign of loyalty when they were arguing in Wales. If you ask me, it's more likely that she was going to kill the others so they couldn't tell on her, and then change her appearance so she would never be found.'

Inspector Griffin nodded. 'Either way, sending off for that disguise shows how devious she's been. If she tries to defend herself against the murder charge by saying it was self-defence or a single moment of madness, we'll be able to demonstrate how she kept on plotting to save herself.'

'I'd never have thought she could be like that,' said Johnny.

'You'd be surprised,' said Inspector Griffin, 'how people behave after they've killed. I've seen quite a few murderers in my time. Many torture themselves with guilt; but some plot a killing in cold blood, and then seem perfectly normal – even congenial – once they've got rid of the person they despised. Others, who've surprised themselves by killing, entirely lose their grip on what's right and wrong.'

'Is that what's happened to Mrs Langford?' asked Johnny.

'I'd say so. She killed a decent, loving man. No one else matches up to her estimation of him, and no crime she might commit in future can seem as bad to her as what she's already done. So why shouldn't she kill again? That's why she thought nothing of threatening you and Howell. She might eventually have moved on to another stage, enjoying killing and taking a pride in avoiding capture. Some killers even manage to convince themselves that they're not guilty, when all the evidence points the other way.'

'And some suspects really are innocent, despite appearances,' said Hutch severely.

Inspector Griffin knew he was thinking of Winnie. He gave an embarrassed cough. It was the nearest he came to an apology. 'Anyway, Johnny,' he said, trying to lighten the mood, 'that advert of yours may have done the trick in solving this crime. I think we'll be able to turn a blind eye to how it got in the paper – just as long as there are no more.'

'Oh, I promise,' said Johnny, meaning it. 'I'll never, ever do it again.'

Hutch interrupted. 'There's something I would like to ask Johnny, if I may,' he said to the detective.

'Go ahead,' said Inspector Griffin, hoping for another revelation that might advance the case.

'Well, Johnny,' said Hutch, 'I was just wondering . . .'

'Yes?' said Johnny. 'You know you can ask me anything, Hutch.'

'I was wondering. How *do* you transform yourself instantly and for ever? What's the answer to that one?'

Johnny was abashed. He looked at his feet and muttered, 'Cut your head off.'

Hutch shrugged his shoulders. 'Not one of your best, son,' he sighed. 'Maybe it is time to call it a day.'

Chapter 46

RELEASE

The next day, the phone in the wooden booth at Hutch's shop kept ringing. There were calls from newspapers, well-wishers, and Inspector Griffin, who was over at the prison organizing all the paperwork so that Winnie could come home. Johnny told Hutch about his meeting with Olwen, and persuaded him to phone Professor Campbell at Craig-y-Nos to find out how she was. It was hard to get through. The Welsh sanatorium was also besieged by the press, but eventually Hutch had some news for Johnny.

'Well, he wouldn't tell me much over the phone,' he said. 'Quite right, of course, I could be anybody. But it seems that Olwen's going to stay at Craig-y-Nos until her next of kin are found. But the professor promised to pass on a letter, if you want to write to her.'

'Of course I do,' said Johnny.

'If you're quick, we can get something in the post tonight. Then, I hope, we'll be able to go and pick up your mother as soon as I've closed the shop. Inspector Griffin has offered to take us to the prison in his car.'

Johnny and Hutch waited in the police car while Inspector Griffin went into the jail to complete the last of the formalities. He seemed to be gone for ages, though it was really only a quarter of an hour; and Johnny started to worry that something had gone wrong. To avoid crowds gathering outside the prison, Griffin had told the press that Winnie wouldn't be released until the next day.

In the chill of the evening the deserted street was made even gloomier by the shadow of the high prison wall. There was a small door cut into one side of the massive prison gate. Eventually, it opened, throwing a rectangle of light across the street, and Inspector Griffin stepped out. At first Johnny feared he was alone, but then the detective turned and helped a tiny figure through behind him. Winnie was weak, and bewildered by her sudden freedom, but she spread her arms wide as she saw Johnny leap from the car and run towards her.

'Mummy!' Johnny cried, calling her by the name he hadn't let himself use since he was ten. He wanted to tell her everything, but all he could say was: 'Oh, Mummy! Mummy! You're back! You're back!'

Winnie's voice cracked as she hugged him and whispered, 'Yes, darling. And I know I'm free because of you. Oh, Johnny. I couldn't be more proud of you.'

By now they were both in tears, and inside the car Hutch was reaching for his handkerchief.

Winnie's neighbours had been busy all day. Anxious to pretend to themselves that they had never despised or disparaged her, they had mended the windows of her house and cleaned off all the slogans from the walls. The farmer from Newgate had driven to town with some eggs and milk. He left them on the kitchen table with a note humbly apologizing for being so cruel to Johnny, and he laid a fire in the grate. Even Mrs Slack brought something. It was a pan of hot soup. Johnny wouldn't eat it. He was scared it might contain an extra, yellow, liquid ingredient; but he told Winnie he just wasn't hungry. He didn't want her to know all the horrible details of his time alone at home.

'At least with Bennett in jail, the rent won't be going up,' said Johnny, as he sliced the pie Hutch had brought for their supper. 'And you don't need to go out to work for a while, Mum. I managed to save up some cash while you were away.'

Hutch and Winnie, sitting in front of the fire, exchanged a glance that told Johnny she knew about the advertisements. He was relieved not to have to explain it all himself. He started to say sorry.

'We'll talk about that some other time,' said his mother, pouring him another cup of tea.

Johnny and Winnie both slept late the next day. After breakfast they had a visitor. It was the new doctor, who had taken on Dr Langford's patients when he retired. He gave Winnie a thorough check, and examined Johnny to make sure he had not picked up any nasty germs at Craig-y-Nos.

'Everything's fine, Mrs Swanson,' he reassured Winnie, as he put away his stethoscope. 'Keep him off school for a week or two, just to make sure he's not brewing anything. After that I'll do regular tests, but I don't think you have anything to worry about with this splendid young lad.'

The doctor had a copy of the morning paper in his bag. The reporter who had christened Winnie 'the Bloody Barmaid' had written an article based on all the nice things he had learned about her during his conversation with Johnny over the apples and cheese.

THE ANGEL OF STAMBLETON
By Our Special Correspondent

Winifred Swanson, the war widow freed from prison (see page 1), was today hailed by friends and neighbours as a credit to the community, caught in a web of intrigue woven by the real killers of Dr Giles Langford. 'Winnie was always there with a smile and a kind word,'said Mrs Edna Slack (57). She visited me every day Nothing was too much trouble for her. I was lost without her when she was taken away.' Millicent Roberts (34) spoke of Mrs Swanson's devotion to her son, Johnny. 'She worked all hours to keep a roof over that boy's head,' said Mrs Roberts.

WAR HERO

Young Johnny never knew his father, Private Harry Swanson (pictured, right), who was killed in France within days of the end of the war, just a month after his 20th birthday.

BOY DETECTIVE

It was Johnny (11) who rescued his mother from the gallows. Police in charge of the case refused to speak publicly at this stage, but it is believed that they feel great admiration for Johnny's initiative and tenacity in proving his mother's innocence and providing evidence which led to the arrest of three new suspects. Johnny, a pupil at

Continued on page 5

That afternoon, Johnny went round to the shop, where Hutch had begun repairing the damage from the fight. He went upstairs to collect his rabbit, the Peace Mug and Winnie's special box of medals and documents. He remembered the twelve remaining 'transformation' letters under the mattress. Without regret, he put the postal orders into their stamped addressed envelopes, ready to return them to the poor fools who so badly wanted to change their looks.

When he got downstairs, Hutch was taking delivery of the evening papers. He cut the string on the bundle and opened out the top copy.

'Hey, Johnny, take a look at this,' he shouted.

There was a picture of Frederick Bennett on the front page. The headline was in bigger type than usual. Johnny could read it from the other side of the shop: LOCAL SQUIRE ON MURDER CHARGE.

'But that's not right,' said Johnny. 'I told them. Mrs Langford was the killer, not Bennett.'

'It's a different murder,' said Hutch, reading out the strap-line on the lead story. '*Actress's body found in wood*. You were right, Johnny. Bennett got his girl-friend out of the way.'

'What else does it say?'

'Not much. Remember what that reporter said when your mother was arrested? Once they've charged someone, the papers aren't allowed to print everything they know.'

The bell jangled as the battered shop door opened. 'I'm glad you were paying attention,' said a familiar voice. It was the reporter. 'You're right. There's a lot of detail that will have to wait for the trial.'

'Like what?' asked Johnny.

'Like the fact that the link to Bennett was confirmed by the blanket the body was wrapped in. It matches one that's still in the back of his car.'

Johnny remembered slumbering under that blanket on the journey back from Wales. He shuddered.

The reporter continued. 'The body was found in a wood more than twenty miles away. It chills me to think of it, but I may have seen the mud from that journey being washed off Bennett's car.'

Johnny recalled the scene outside Bennett's house too, but he said nothing.

'Apparently the body was in such a state that they had to identify it from the necklace in one of her publicity photos.'

Hutch flinched. 'That's enough,' he said, reminding the man that a child was present.

The reporter cast his eye around the shop and changed the subject. 'I see you're getting straight again,' he said.

Hutch nodded. 'I suppose you want to use the phone.'

'No, I haven't come here to work,' said the reporter. He took out his wallet and put two £5 notes on the table. 'I came to contribute towards the repairs, and to give Johnny this.' He handed over a small parcel, wrapped in brown paper and tied with string. 'Open it carefully,' he said. 'It's made of glass.'

Johnny tore off the wrapping. It was the photograph of his father, in a beautiful new tortoiseshell frame. Hutch came over to have a look. 'He was a grand man, your dad,' he said, holding the picture up alongside Johnny's face. 'I can see the likeness. He would have been proud of you.'

'I should never have taken it,' said the reporter, ashamed. 'I'm sorry. Forgive me.'

'Mum will be pleased to have it back,' said Johnny, curtly. He couldn't really find it in himself to forgive the theft.

'Since I'm here, Johnny,' said the reporter, taking out his notebook, 'I wonder if there's anything you'd like to tell me about Mr Bennett? A contact of mine in the police tells me you've been very helpful, giving them leads.'

'I've nothing to say,' said Johnny. 'I'm not supposed to talk to anyone until after all the trials are over.'

'He's right,' said Hutch, holding the door open. 'I think it would be best if you kept your distance for the time being, don't you?'

'My source had some nice things to say about you, too, Mr Hutchinson.'

'Oh, really?' said Hutch, surprised.

'He didn't go into details, but I gather we have you to thank for that complaint about the advertisements being withdrawn. Reading between the lines, I'd say someone had a word with the man behind PO Box Nine.'

'I couldn't possibly comment,' said Hutch.

'Of course not. I understand. You have a duty of confidentiality as a postmaster.'

'Sub-postmaster,' said Hutch.

'Let's not split hairs. If the adverts are going to stop, I thank you.'

Johnny said nothing as the reporter slapped him on the arm in a friendly gesture of farewell. 'So what's next for you, son?' he asked.

'I'll be going back to school soon.'

'And then what? When you leave school? Has this business given you a taste for detective work? Are you going to join the police? Or go into journalism perhaps?'

'I don't know,' said Johnny. 'I haven't really thought about it. Maybe I'll open a shop.'

As the reporter took his leave, Hutch started marking up the papers for the evening delivery round, feeling a glow of almost paternal pride.

Chapter 47

A NEW WORLD

A fortnight later, the new doctor visited again.

'I think it's time to send you back to school, old chap,' he said breezily. 'You'll be glad to see all your friends again.'

Johnny tried to look pleased, but he was dreading returning to the playground bullies.

On his first day he deliberately took longer than usual over his paper round, and arrived at school just as the bell was ringing. Mr Murray was standing by the gate, waiting to catch latecomers.

'Another lucky escape, eh, Swanson?' he snarled as Johnny ran to his classroom.

Mrs Stiles called the register: 'Morrison, Noble, Parker, Roberts, Swanson . . .'

She shushed the titter that ran round the room at the sound of Johnny's name. 'That's enough. Welcome back, Johnny,' she said, dipping her pen in the inkwell. 'It's good to be able to tick you off again. Taylor, Tompkins, Venables . . .'

At break time, Johnny dawdled into the yard with his head down and waited for the first taunts. To his amazement, he was quickly surrounded by children asking questions about the murder. He had never been so popular.

Albert Taylor broke through the crush and strode towards him. Johnny tried not to flinch, but he expected Taylor to lash out, verbally at least. Taylor reached for his pocket. What would it be? A knuckle-duster? A catapult? A knife?

It was a bar of chocolate. Albert broke off a square and offered it to Johnny. 'Here, Detecko. Take it.'

Detecko. A new nickname – short for detective – a name that played on Johnny's strengths at last. Taylor didn't need to spell it out to the others. From now on, anyone caught calling Johnny 'Quacky' or 'Swingson' would be for it. It was time to let Johnny join in their games.

In the weeks ahead, one of those games got quite nasty, and Johnny was far from proud of his part in it, even though it was exhilarating to be admired by Taylor's gang. The ill-will against Winnie had found a new home. It was redirected towards Miss Dangerfield. The old lady had never been liked, but now she was not even feared. Johnny did nothing to stop the boys who had once taunted him throwing bricks through her windows and painting LIAR across her front door. Her walking stick was found floating in the duckpond.

'Poor woman,' said Winnie, as she and Johnny sat over their tea one night. 'I know what it's like to have the whole town turn against you. I wouldn't wish it on anyone.'

Johnny pretended his mouth was too full to reply.

In the Easter holidays, a FOR SALE sign went up outside Miss Dangerfield's house just as a SOLD notice was taken down by the new owner of the Langfords' across the road. The young doctor had moved in. It was the last straw for Miss Dangerfield. He was unmarried, had a motorbike, and left his bathroom window open. She let the vicar know exactly what she thought of her new neighbour:

'If I stand on the stool in my bedroom, I can see him with his shirt off when he's shaving,' she said. 'It's too bad.'

On the day the removal vans came, Johnny climbed the tree in the doctor's garden to watch – just to make sure that Miss Dangerfield was really going. She was belligerent to the last, haranguing the moving men as they manhandled her furniture across her front garden.

'Mind that radio-gramophone!' she squealed. 'It's a Lissenola New Era.'

But she had lost her power. The men shrugged, and bumped the wooden cabinet against the gate.

Johnny ran down the hill to the shop to collect the papers for his evening delivery round. He was surprised to find his mother sweeping the floor.

'Hutch has offered me a job,' she said. 'He says I can help out here.'

Hutch looped the bag of papers over Johnny's shoulder and steered him out onto the pavement. 'I hope you don't mind, son,' he said. 'You can still do bits and pieces for me too, but I knew your mother needed the work. That doctor asked her if she wanted her old job back at the Langfords' place. I think we should keep her away from there, don't you?'

So through the summer, Winnie spent her days at the shop, and sometimes Hutch came round for supper at Johnny's house. Then, while Johnny did his homework, Winnie and Hutch would go out for walks, or to the pub, where Winnie was now a celebrity, not an outcast. School was better too. Even Mr Murray, seeing that Johnny was growing taller and stronger, included him in teams, and started picking on someone in the year below.

Every now and then Johnny got a new idea for an advert, but he managed to stick to his promise never to place one again. The poet still wrote regularly. For a while Johnny just sent his postal orders straight back, but the man pleaded with him for guidance on his writing, and so Hutch told Johnny that he could reply, so long as he never charged for his advice.

'Think of him as a pen-pal,' said Winnie. And that's what Johnny did.

Olwen wrote to Johnny too. She was still at Craig-y-Nos: stuck there, miserable, living on charity until her uncle was found.

'Can't we do something for her?' asked Johnny over supper one night.

'I've been looking into it,' said Hutch. 'I've had quite a correspondence with that Professor Campbell of yours. I didn't want to talk about it in case it all came to nothing, but I think I can tell you now.'

'What does he say?' Johnny asked.

Hutch took Winnie's hand. Johnny blushed at his tenderness and tried not to look. 'Well,' said Hutch, 'it may be possible for me to give Olwen a new home.'

'That's wonderful. Will she come back to Stambleton to live with you?'

Winnie answered. 'With us, Johnny. With all three of us.'

'You mean . . . ?' said Johnny, guessing the answer but still wanting to ask. 'You mean you are going to get married?' Halfway through the question his voice cracked and swooped into a different register.

'Well, that's the end of Auntie Ada,' laughed Hutch. 'She won't be making any more telephone calls!'

'Do you know, I'm rather sorry to see the back of her,' said Winnie. 'She may have caused a lot of trouble, but in a way she brought us together.'

'Yes,' said Hutch. 'We're going to be a real family, Johnny. You, Winnie and Olwen will come and live with me over the shop.'

Johnny thought for a moment, imagining his new life. 'Does that mean I'll be Johnny Hutchinson?'

Winnie glanced across at the picture in its tortoise-shell frame, and Hutch answered for her. 'No, Johnny. I couldn't do that to your dad. He might never have known you, but he would have been proud of you – of all your funny schemes and scrapes, and of the hard work and bravery that saved your mother's life. I couldn't take away his name from the last, and best, thing he left behind.' He patted Johnny's golden curls. 'Dear boy. I swear that in the years ahead I will love and care for you as if you were my own child. But I promise you, because I think it is the right and proper thing, that whatever happens, you will always be Johnny Swanson.'

A note about money

In 1929 British money worked in a different way:

The smallest coin was a farthing.
Two of those made a halfpenny (pronounced haypny).
Two of those made a penny.
There was a small silver coin worth three pennies, called a threepenny bit.
The sixpence was a slightly bigger silver coin.
Two sixpences made one shilling (worth twelve pennies, or 5p in modern money).
The two-shilling coin was called a florin.
A large coin, called a half-crown, was worth two shillings and sixpence.
A crown was worth five shillings.

After that there were bank notes, worth ten shillings (50p in modern money), one pound, five pounds, ten pounds, and so on.

One pound was worth twenty shillings, or two hundred and forty pennies.

Sums of money were written like this:

One penny	1d.
Sixpence	6d.
One shilling	1s. or 1/-
One shilling and fourpence	1/4
Two pounds, nine shillings and elevenpence	£2 9s. 11d. or 49/11

A daily paper cost 1d. A weekly comic cost 2d. (less than one penny in our 'new' money.)

In an age when very few people had bank accounts or chequebooks, sending even small sums of money through the post was impractical and insecure, not least because the coins were so heavy. For this reason, postal orders were popular. You paid the money in at your local post office, and received an official coupon which the recipient could cash in at their post office, or use again to send to someone else.

Without postal orders, Johnny Swanson would never have been able to run his business.